old friends in
Rosemary Beach

YOUNG AT HEART ~ BOOK TWO

CECELIA SCOTT

Cecelia Scott

Young at Heart Book 2

Old Friends in Rosemary Beach

Copyright © 2024 Cecelia Scott

This novel is a work of fiction. Any references to historical events, real people, or real locales are used fictitiously. Other names, characters, places, and incidents are the product of the author's imagination, and any resemblance to actual events or locales or persons, living or dead, is coincidental. All rights to reproduction of this work are reserved. No part of this publication may be reproduced, stored in or introduced into a retrieval system, or transmitted, in any form, or by any means (electronic, mechanical, photocopying, recording, or otherwise) without prior written permission from the copyright owner. Thank you for respecting the copyright. For permission or information on foreign, audio, or other rights, contact the author, ceceliascottauthor@gmail.com.

The Young at Heart Series

In a heartwarming saga of family, friendship, and forgiveness, Vanessa Young and her long-lost daughter, Emily, reunite after thirty years. Together, they embark on a fresh start against the backdrop of white sand beaches and the colorful, small-town charm of Rosemary Beach, Florida. As they navigate a sea of new challenges and old wounds, the women find themselves surrounded by the loving embrace of close family and dear friends. The extensive cast of characters faces all of life's ups and downs with laughter, joy, and unwavering love.

Chapter One

Gloria

"Are you ready?" Gloria handed her sister a full glass of chardonnay as if she were offering a fellow soldier some ammunition for a tough battle.

A very, very tough battle.

Reading the letters their mother wrote to their father, who'd passed away six weeks earlier, would be emotional under normal circumstances for two grown women. But these circumstances? Nothing, not a single thing, was normal.

One hour earlier, Gloria and Vanessa finally decided to wade through forty or fifty envelopes addressed to their father, uncertain what they'd find. Then the world tilted sideways as they saw the first correspondence was dated *after* their mother "died" in a car accident.

For the next thirty-five years, Violet Young—legally known as Clarinda Smith, news they'd learned when a second will had been located—had secretly written to her husband. And in those letters, she presumably answered the question that now plagued the sisters: Why had they been told their mother was dead?

They were about to find out. Which would, of course, beg the obvious follow-up question: Was she still alive?

With a humorless clink of the wine glasses and a shared look of dread, they settled onto the back porch of Gloria's ground-floor beachfront condo. Sunset turned the normally navy waters of the Gulf of Mexico into glittering gold with streaks of violet while a salty breeze fluttered the first open letter on the coffee table.

"I'm ready," Vanessa said, lifting the single page. "Ready to find out why she pretended to die. She must have had a really good reason."

Gloria took a deep drink. "Lying to two young girls about their mother dying is one unforgivable sin, no matter the reason. Do the honors and read, Ness."

Vanessa cleared her throat. "All righty, here we go. May 16th, 1979."

"Three weeks *after* she died," Gloria muttered darkly.

"Do you want to read, Glo? Then you can skip the editorial comments, or we'll be here until tomorrow."

"Fine." She slipped the paper from Vanessa's fingers, snapping it to the right distance for her fifty-year-old eyes, scanning the slanted cursive ink strokes on peach-toned stationery.

"'Dearest William,

'My heart is so heavy today, and I already miss you, even though it's only been a few days since I left. I hope that one day you can find it in your heart to forgive me. Please understand that I had to do what was best for the girls, for you, and for myself.'"

Gloria dropped her hand to her lap with a thud,

turning to Vanessa. "What was *best*? Pretending to be dead?"

Her sister nodded at the paper, squinting to make out the script. "Keep reading."

"'You know as well as I do that if I don't give myself the chance to achieve the ultimate dream, I will regret it for all the days of my life. As I've said a million times, I'm sorry I'm not cut out to be a wife and a mother. I was destined for something greater, something world-changing. I still don't expect you to understand this now—or ever—but this is the only way I know how to express it to you. You are all too familiar with how this dream haunts me, wakes me in the night and grips me in my soul. If I don't chase it, Bill, I'll be empty and miserable forever.'"

"Dramatic much?" Vanessa cracked.

But the overwrought writing didn't bother Gloria. She was stuck on the words. "Chase...a dream?" Gloria scoffed. "She left her daughters and husband to chase some sort of *dream*?"

Vanessa swallowed, taking a sip of her wine while staring out at the water in thought. "I mean, I left Emily to go pursue my career and not be a mom. She acknowledges she wasn't cut out for the role. Maybe I'm not all that different from her."

"Nessie Young!" Gloria shoved her, giving her sister a stern look. "You were sixteen, alone, and you gave your baby up for adoption to a wonderful woman. That is *not* the same thing as walking out on a marriage, a family, a home, and a life to go pursue some...girlhood fantasy, whatever it might be."

Vanessa chewed her lip. "I guess I can't argue that."

"This is completely different. This is..." Gloria's chest tightened as she remembered all the tough times being raised by a single father. "This is wrong."

"Should we continue?" Vanessa's shoulders sank. "We're only on the first letter."

"Yeah. Sorry. Processing it all." Gloria held the paper back up, grateful she didn't have to do this alone, and that the only other person on the planet who could understand what she was going through was sitting right next to her.

"'I know you made the choice to tell the girls that I passed away suddenly, and I respect and understand that decision. It is for the best that these ties are cut, so they don't spend their lives wondering. I will continue to write you as much as I can, holding out undying hope that one day you might write me back. Yours always, Violet.'"

She set the paper on the coffee table, her mind spinning.

Vanessa pushed her hair back, turning to face Gloria. "So, worst fears realized, I guess. She left us because she didn't want to be a mom."

Gloria nodded, swallowing the horrific truth. "And Dad did us dirty by playing along in one heck of an ugly way. Why not just break the news that we had a lousy mother? Why make us miss her and mourn her?"

"Because that way we'd never go looking for her," Vanessa said.

"Or maybe it really was Dad trying to protect us from

the pain of reality—that she didn't want to be our mom. Either way, she went along with it."

Vanessa squeezed her eyes shut. "Shall we continue?"

Gloria picked up the envelope and pulled out the next letter. "I'm afraid we have no choice, now. Let's find out what her dream was. Cure cancer? Climb Everest? Or maybe she just wanted to write the Great American Novel."

It didn't take too many more letters to figure out that Violet's dream was no different than millions of others—to sing, dance, and act on Broadway.

With every letter and every line, Gloria got sicker in her heart. She'd gone her entire life thinking her mother had died young and far too early when she'd really packed up and headed to the Big Apple in search of *stardom*?

It hurt to even think about it.

Letter after brief one-page letter, Violet detailed her "roadblocks"—each and every one a cliché. No callback, rejected for her looks, not fitting into the tightknit world, getting hit on by producers, and living paycheck to paycheck in service jobs to stay alive.

It wasn't until 1983, and letter number seventeen, that Violet landed her first role in a tiny off-off-Broadway amateur production with an original script.

Gloria held up the paper, reading the last few lines of it.

"'I am so certain that I made the right decision four years ago, despite the massive sacrifices. When I took that stage tonight, Bill, I had no doubts that I did the right thing. It won't be long now until I'm on the Great White Way (that's what they call Broadway)! Everything will be worth it then. I'm certain that you are doing your best, and I wish you peace. Love, Violet.'"

"Let me get this straight." Gloria slapped the paper on the table next to her nearly empty wine glass. "She got some crappy role in an off-off-*off*-Broadway play that probably six people went to, so she's sure she made *the right decision?*"

Vanessa swallowed, shaking her head in frustration. "I guess she had some sort of identity crisis."

"But crises end, Ness. People have a crisis and they do something impulsive and stupid, but then they snap back to reality." She huffed out a sigh as she pulled out the next letter. "She just gets more delusional and selfish as the years go on."

Vanessa held up her glass. "I'm gonna need a refill."

The next group of letters detailed most of the eighties, where their most decidedly *not* dead mother hopped from one amateur play to another, always one flop away from her big break.

Though the content of each letter changed, the tone never did. She was *so* close to making it big on Broadway, she was positive she'd made the right choice to leave and chase her dream, and she never, ever mentioned Gloria or Vanessa.

That part hurt the most.

"It's like when she died to us, we died to her, too." Gloria lowered letter number thirty-one or two—she'd lost count—peering out at the last vestiges of sunset while twilight descended over the Gulf.

Even though it would never, ever make sense.

"Maybe it was a coping thing." Vanessa lifted a shoulder. "She had to basically pretend we didn't exist in order to live with her decisions."

"I wonder if she ever made it onto Broadway."

Vanessa tapped the remaining stack. It was taking a while to get through the letters, mostly because they did have to talk after each one, and they did have to take the time to let this shocking new worldview make sense.

"We'll have to read on to find out."

The answer, the sisters discovered, was no.

In the mid-nineties, their mother finally gave up on the Broadway dream and flew across the country for a new start on the opposite coast. She decided that Broadway was too cutthroat and competitive, but she was sure to make it in TV, so she moved to Hollywood.

"Wow." Vanessa exhaled at this twist in their mother's tale. "She was in Los Angeles in..." She glanced at the date on top of the letter. "In 1998. I was there, too, working as a stylist. Who knows? I could have had her as a client."

Gloria lifted her knees up and hugged them to her chest. "It's creepy and sad," she said. "All these years, these decades, our entire lives! Dad just lied and she just...died."

"She *was* dead, in a sense." Vanessa said. "I still can't believe we lived in the same town—and trust me, it's small—at the same time. I could have met her and never known. She would have had to have recognized my name."

At the break in Vanessa's voice, Gloria put a hand on her arm.

"No, Ness. Don't go there. It doesn't sound like she was ever relevant enough to have a stylist, anyway. She said she couldn't even get a cameo on a sitcom. Trust me, she didn't hire you to dress her for the Emmys. Come on. Let's finish this nightmare."

They trudged through the rest of the letters, which described their mother trying to make it big as an actress and, again, failing. She stayed in Los Angeles, consistently writing to Bill several times a year, and painting a picture of a sad and empty existence. No love, no partner, no breaks, no fame, no fortune.

By the time they reached the last letter, they were reading by the glow of Gloria's vineyard lights.

This one was dated in the end of 2014. In the last few very short notes, Violet seemed to finally realize that the big break was never going to happen. Yet she stayed firm in her belief that leaving her family was the right decision, and in all of her letters to the husband she abandoned, she told him she missed him. Never the girls, though.

"Last one." Gloria exhaled loudly, unfolding the final envelope, and wondering how things were going to close.

"Maybe she gave up."

"On acting or on writing to Dad?" Gloria asked.

"Both." Vanessa shrugged. "I mean, the letters end."

"Let's find out why." Gloria held it up in the light, flattening the page as she began to read.

"'My dearest William,

'Today I met a producer who said I have a "good look" for his next project—a family sitcom—and we exchanged numbers. It was quite promising! Now that I am older, the roles I can accept are limited to mothers and side characters, but perhaps that's what I was destined to be all along!'"

"To play a mother on TV?" Vanessa interjected.

Gloria rolled her eyes. "But not be one in real life."

"Finish reading, Glo."

She nodded, continuing the letter.

"'He said he's going to call me when casting begins, and I have a really good feeling about this one. Things are tough as usual, scraping by to pay rent and frequently skipping meals to save a buck, but hey. That's the life of an aspiring star, I suppose. I do wish you'd write me back one day, but I understand you're hurt. As always, I wish you peace. Love, Violet.'"

"Wait a second." Vanessa sat straight up, her brows knitting together in a confused frown. "That's it? No big ending? No grand farewell? She just..."

"Stopped writing," Gloria leaned back, stymied. "She didn't say goodbye or tell Dad she wouldn't be writing anymore or...anything."

"You're sure that's the last one?" Vanessa asked. "You're positive?"

"Unless there's another stash somewhere," Gloria said. "It would have to be hidden pretty darn well, because every single item in Dad's possession has been organized, filed, and handled."

They sat together in silence for a few moments, the harsh, cruel reality of their mother's abandonment washing over them like waves in the Gulf.

Gloria looked back on her life, her mind replaying flashes of her childhood—all the times when she ached so desperately for her mother she felt like she was going to crack in half.

"I mean, who is this woman?" she asked her sister rhetorically. "This pathetic, desperate wanna-be who would rather spend her life scraping pennies together and getting rejected than being with her own family?"

Vanessa closed her eyes, sinking into the sofa. "There has to be more to the story, doesn't there?"

Gloria arched a dubious brow. "I think we just read the entire story."

"But what about after 2014?" Vanessa asked. "After that last letter when she just randomly went ghost after writing him for over thirty years?"

Gloria leaned her head on Nessie's shoulder, watching the reflection of the full moon roll over the waves in front of them. "I wonder if she's still alive."

"She could be, or she could be dead," Vanessa said, matter-of-factly. "She could be on the streets or maybe she stopped writing because she did get her big break and our mother is…Meryl Streep."

Gloria snorted at that but sighed. "I hate the not knowing," she whispered.

"Me, too," Vanessa said, giving Gloria's arm a loving

rub. "Give it time. At least we have each other, and we can go through this together." As if reading Gloria's mind, she added, "I'll never leave you again. You know, I was gone a long time, too."

"But never out of touch," Gloria said. "Now what do we do?"

"Find out what happened to her," Vanessa said without a second of hesitation.

Gloria pulled back, surprised at that. "Seriously? You want to hunt down this...this pathetic creature who dumped us for fame and fortune and...do what? Let her have it?"

"I don't know, but I think we should find her." Vanessa sucked in a breath, pinching the bridge of her nose and shaking her head. "If she's alive, I do want to talk to her. I want to ask her if now, as a seventy-two-year-old woman, she still thinks this whole charade was worth it."

Gloria pondered the idea, but it was so late, she couldn't think straight. "How would we even do that? We don't have anything about her life past 2014. That was almost eleven years ago."

Vanessa shrugged. "We could hire a private investigator. There has to be records of her, and now we know her real name."

Gloria considered, looking out at the darkness of the Gulf. "I could be talked into that, I guess. But Nessie, don't you think she probably doesn't want to be found?"

"Too bad," Vanessa said on an eye-roll, kicking her feet up onto the coffee table and leaning back in her rocker. "We didn't want to be raised by a single dad believing that our mother was dead our entire lives, and yet here we are."

Gloria couldn't argue that. "Fair enough."

"I mean, aren't you curious? Don't you want some, I don't know, closure?"

Would she ever get that? And what would she say if she were to come face to face with the woman who'd abandoned her daughters? Gloria Bennett wasn't generally a grudge-holder by any means, but this was different.

She was going to hold this grudge forever. And if Violet was alive? Well, she sure as heck wouldn't be nice to her.

But the idea of seeing her and showing her how she'd grown and blossomed and raised a family of her own despite the woman's cruel absence...well, there was a bit of poetic justice and retribution in that. Violet had missed a lot more than just her daughters growing up—she had grandchildren now, and Rosemary Beach had gone from a glimmer in a developer's brain to one of the crown jewels of the Gulf Coast.

Yeah, there might be a great big satisfying moment to revel in.

"Looking into a private investigator wouldn't hurt," she said after some time. "But no one else can know."

"Not Emily or Daisy?" Vanessa asked.

"Okay, we can tell our daughters," Gloria agreed. "I can't keep that from Daisy and Emily should know, too. But can you imagine if Cricket got ahold of this information? That woman would tell every client in her salon, and it would be all over Rosemary Beach in a week."

"True," Vanessa added. "We tell no one but our girls."

"I'm just glad I have you, Nessie." Gloria looked at her sister and gave a weary smile. "I couldn't handle this on my own."

"Not true. You can handle anything. Although, I'm glad I'm here, too. There was a reason I came back when Dad was on his deathbed. I may have missed a reconciliation with him, but now we have an all-new goal to find Violet…er, Clarinda."

Gloria nodded, in full agreement. "And so we shall."

"What does this mean about the will? You know, if she's still alive. Dad put her in the will as the recipient of the property where I'm only a couple weeks away from opening a business."

Gloria put her hand on Vanessa's leg. "You're not going to lose your shop, Nessie. We will fight tooth and nail to make sure it stays yours. Besides, she hasn't exactly come forward to claim it. She's off the grid."

"True." Vanessa sighed. "I guess we'll cross that bridge when we get to it. For now, let's find out if she's even still alive."

Chapter Two
Vanessa

"Are you seriously telling me that your mother who died when you were six months old might *still be alive*? My grandmother?" Emily's jaw dropped as she processed the shortened version of Violet Young's sad biography and the news that her letters stopped with no explanation of why or a snapshot of where she was now, dead or alive.

"She might be, but don't worry," Vanessa said quickly. "I know there was a second will giving her this store"—she gestured to the soon-to-open Young at Heart boutique they'd spent the last six weeks creating in the space where Dad's sporting goods store once stood—"but she'll have to fight me for it, and I'll fight to the death. We don't even know for sure if she's alive or wants the store or...anything."

"I'm not worried about the store, I'm just..." Emily shook her head, then gave a disbelieving laugh. "It's a wild story. She took off and left her daughters and husband and never mentioned you in all those letters?"

Yes, it was painful and preposterous, but true.

Vanessa shrugged. "We're going to hire a PI to see if we can find her," she said. "But in the meantime, no one can know. You, me, your Aunt Gloria, and Daisy. But not Cricket or...anyone."

"And by anyone, you mean Noah Ellison," Emily said.

Vanessa and Emily might have been separated for almost thirty years after Vanessa gave her baby up for adoption, but in the less than two months they'd been reunited, reading each other's thoughts had become remarkably easy.

"Yes," she said simply. "Last night was hard enough."

It had been the first time Vanessa had seen Noah since she'd been pregnant with Emily. She didn't want the second time to be about her super-weird disappearing mother.

She didn't want the second time to be...anything at all.

Emily swallowed, pressing her lips together. "I'm beyond stunned. I can't even begin to imagine what you're feeling. And on top of everything with reuniting with Noah..."

"We didn't reunite. Just said hello."

And that had been a lot.

The past six weeks or so of Vanessa Young's life had been a whirlwind to begin with—she did reunite with Emily and, together, they'd come back to Vanessa's hometown, both in search of a fresh start.

If those emotions weren't overwhelming enough, Vanessa missed the passing of her father by mere hours, solidifying the fact that she'd never make amends with the man who cut her off when she was sixteen and pregnant.

Dad had left Vanessa this store, though, and she and Emily had worked tirelessly to create an inviting, upscale, beach-friendly women's clothing boutique that would appeal to locals and tourists.

No wonder she was reeling.

Emily pushed her hair back, still in visible shock from Vanessa's latest atomic bomb of a discovery. "I know things are tense for you and him," Emily said. "But don't forget the man came and did me a solid. I would never have been able to find an attorney to effectively plow through a divorce for me. Now I'm rid of the worst weight of my life, and it's thanks to Noah."

That was true, and Vanessa was grateful Emily could be done with her abusive ex. And the fact that her biological father made it happen? It was sweet and kind and a little wonderful.

"How long has Aunt Gloria had these letters?" Emily asked, bringing them back to the subject of Violet.

"She found them cleaning out Dad's house but barely looked at them, expecting them to be sad. Some love letters from before they were married or something. So, after we found out that Clarinda Smith—the person named in that weird will—was also Violet Young, we decided to read them." She choked. "Imagine our surprise when we realized they were written *after* she died."

Emily arched a brow. "But she didn't."

Vanessa swallowed, the shock of last night's discovery still reverberating through her ribcage. "No, she didn't. These letters had dates, every single one of them, and they spanned from 1979 to 2014—and never once did she mention the daughters she abandoned."

"That had to hurt."

Vanessa lifted a shoulder. "I gave a daughter up for adoption, as you know. But Glo insists this was different."

"She's right," Emily assured her. "You gave me to a wonderful mother and my darling Grandma Gigi. Nothing about that hurts."

Vanessa took a step closer, putting an arm around Emily, who proved every day she had incredible strength. "Thank you for being so understanding. I'm so happy to have you in all this craziness."

Emily smiled and dropped her head toward Vanessa's shoulder, the loving gesture saying so much.

"Strange that your dad kept the secret all those years, isn't it?"

"Well, you didn't know William Young, but he was a bit of an odd duck, which was why I took off when I was pregnant with you. He did say he couldn't handle the memories and moved us here—which wasn't even Rosemary Beach back then, just Inlet Beach. But yeah, the man could keep a secret."

Emily frowned. "You guys never asked any more questions about her? About Violet...or Clarinda, I guess?"

"No, we...we sort of learned not to." She walked over to a rack of newly displayed summer maxi dresses and absentmindedly smoothed out the soft linen fabric. "He'd get so weird about it. He'd just...shut down. We always assumed it was grief."

"Grief over a woman who wasn't dead."

Vanessa glanced at her daughter, chills dancing up her spine. "And maybe still isn't."

"Oh, you could reunite with your long-lost mother just like I did!" She gestured between the two of them, enthusiasm dancing in her blue-gray eyes before it faded. "But I guess you'd have to forgive her."

"I would," Vanessa agreed, studying her beautiful, grown daughter, which was a bit like looking in the mirror at her twenty-nine-year-old self, with just enough Noah Ellison mixed in there to make her heart tug.

Visibly sensing her mother's internal struggle, Emily sweetly backpedaled. "You know, you and Aunt Glo could pretend you never saw those letters. Just let Violet stay dead."

She shook her head. "I don't want to do that," she said. "We found a PI in Destin and if she's alive, I want to meet her. I'd like to know why she didn't want us, for one thing. Glo wants her to wallow in regret for all she's missed."

"I can't even fathom it." Emily closed her eyes, shuddering softly.

"I'm still struggling," Vanessa admitted, glancing around. "And I don't want this new wrinkle to put a damper on this fabulous boutique we're about to open."

Emily followed her gaze, a smile spreading across her face as she crossed her arms and nodded with satisfaction. "We kinda crushed it, didn't we?"

From the soft peach walls to the white shiplap accents and blond wood chandeliers, the store was luxurious and fun. Vanessa could hardly believe that just a month ago, this corner property in downtown Rosemary Beach had been the empty remnants of a sporting goods shop.

"Completely." Vanessa took in the sophisticated and chic design of their clothing store, which she had filled with stunning pieces of clothing that ranged from relaxed beachwear to upscale resort dresses, specifically catered to women of all ages.

After she'd basically gotten aged out of her job as a Hollywood stylist, Vanessa thought she'd never do anything in the fashion world again. But Young at Heart, perfectly named for co-owners Emily and Vanessa Young, was her pride and joy. Sharing that with Emily—the business brains behind the whole operation—was her greatest gift yet.

"So..." Emily said as they folded some blouses and shorts on the front table display. "We haven't talked about the fact that I met my birth father."

Because her birth father was a hard subject for Vanessa. "I was a tad preoccupied with my mother possibly coming back to life."

Emily smiled. "Fair enough."

"Well?" Vanessa looked over the display at her daughter. "What did you think of...him?"

She still had a hard time saying Noah's name out loud. After their awkward and tense interaction—their first in thirty years—Vanessa was left with a bitter taste and a heavy heart.

Noah made it clear he'd never forgiven her for taking off when she was sixteen and pregnant with their baby, abandoning their lifelong friendship and youthful but quite real romance.

She had to remember, however, that Noah may be her ex, but he was also Emily's father, and that was bigger and more important.

"It was...really cool." Emily gently laid down a perfectly folded button-down, running her finger along the lace detail of the collar. "He was a bit quiet, for sure. Maybe he just has to warm up to me." She sighed, her eyes bright. "I just can't believe what he did for me."

"An expedited divorce in the Dominican Republic." Vanessa laughed softly, shaking her head. "That was quite the power move."

"I mean, I knew he was a lawyer, of course, because Cricket had told me," Emily prattled on, perfecting the clothes. "But I never thought in a million years that he could help me get divorced. He works on massive mergers and antitrust stuff, according to his mom. Also, I didn't think he'd want to help me but...he did."

Vanessa studied Emily, her expression hopeful. "Yes, he did." She thought carefully about what to say next, not wanting to burst Emily's bubble, but also knowing that Noah had no intention of having any kind of relationship with his biological daughter.

Not because he didn't want one, necessarily, but because he'd made it pretty clear that he intended to stay far, far away from Vanessa and keep himself out of her life forever.

"It's crazy, because I've never had a dad." Emily pressed her lips together. "Even when I was little, before

Joanna died, she adopted me as a single mom. Then it was just Grandma Gigi and me. And I know I only met Noah once, and it was brief, but...what he did for me? That was seriously amazing. I'm really hoping I can get to know him."

Vanessa sucked in a breath, truly not knowing what to say.

Noah Ellison was very amazing. In fact, he was the best guy Vanessa had ever known. They were close friends from the time they were a year old, when his outgoing and boisterous mother, Cricket, lived down the street from Bill, Gloria, and Vanessa when they moved to the Rosemary Beach area after her...after her mother *fake* died.

She shook off the thought, lingering on Noah's role in her past. The two of them had grown attached at the hip, childhood buddies, preteen pals, and then, as teenagers, he of course became her boyfriend.

They loved each other, far more seriously than most kids their age, and they trusted each other wholly and completely. It was no surprise they became more and more physical as hormones crashed into the picture and it only took a blanket, some stars, and the bed of a 1993 Ford F-150 to turn into...Emily.

The pregnancy shocked their families, but it shook Bill Young to his core, and he vehemently and furiously disowned Vanessa. When she ran away to California to stay with a distant cousin, she swore to Noah she'd come back after high school with their baby. She'd promised.

But things took a turn. She couldn't handle a baby,

she was lost and alone, and she opted for adoption, never able to face Rosemary Beach or the people in it again. She devoted her life to her career, married and divorced a fairly prominent actor and certifiable jerk, Aaron Aldridge, and tried her hardest not to look back on the pain she'd caused Noah.

"How was it for you?" Emily asked eagerly, breaking Vanessa out of her thoughts. "I mean, first time seeing each other after so long. Was it weird?"

"It was..." Awful. Empty. Sad. Disappointing. A catalyst of serious and major regrets about things that could never be undone. "Fine. You know, awkward, I guess. I don't think he ever actually forgave me. I don't...I don't think I ever actually apologized." Her throat tightened.

"It was so many years ago," Emily whispered gently. "But it's never too late. For anything."

Vanessa winced a bit at the idea of a thirty-year-old apology for broken promises and decades of radio silence. She didn't even know where she'd begin and, frankly, didn't really want to.

"I'm ashamed," she admitted to Emily on a soft sigh. "It's so painful to think about the immature and selfish way I handled everything."

"You were just a kid."

Vanessa lifted a shoulder. "Still. I don't know how to apologize for that. I think it might be way too far gone."

Emily leveled her gaze, her eyes warm and encouraging, knowing Vanessa deeply despite their relatively new relationship.

"It can't hurt to try. You came here for forgiveness

from your dad." She shrugged. "Maybe what you need is forgiveness from Noah."

Vanessa nodded, taking a steadying breath. "Maybe. It's a complicated history. Honestly? I'm sort of hoping I don't have to see him again for a while."

Emily froze mid-fold, cringing apologetically.

"What?" Vanessa asked.

"He's...kind of...on his way here right now."

She tried her absolute hardest to deny the tiny shiver of excitement that zipped up her spine and focused solely on the large cloud of dread that instantly followed.

"Here? Why?"

"He needed to go over some things with me in the divorce paperwork. It's funky because of the whole expedited process, so there are some hoops to jump through. But don't worry." She held up a hand. "We're going to a coffee shop to discuss it all there."

Vanessa swallowed, nerves fraying in her chest.

Maybe Emily was right. Maybe she could apologize and clear the air and finally let bygones be bygones with Noah.

Noah Thomas Ellison had always been cute, through every stage of life, but forty-five years looked darn good on him.

He walked through the front doors of Young at Heart, his gaze instantly darkening as it met Vanessa's.

Wow, he didn't look happy to see her. And why

would he be? Still, the reality of it stung.

Of course, Emily had to slip away and answer the phone mere seconds before Noah showed up, leaving Vanessa alone with a six-foot-two living, breathing reminder of her damaging past mistakes.

"Hi," she said awkwardly. "Emily had to take a quick phone call from one of our suppliers with a shipping issue, but she'll be right out."

"No problem." Noah's blue eyes leveled with Vanessa, then darted away.

She wiped her palms on her dark jeans, attempting to swallow the lump of nervous tension in her throat.

"This place looks great," Noah said as a glimmer of a smile pulled across his clean-shaven face.

"Thank you." Vanessa moved closer to him, grateful for the segue and the fact that he wasn't so mad he couldn't speak to her.

They had talked at the party last night, after all. Maybe forgiveness wasn't so far out of reach after all.

Maybe Emily was even wiser than Vanessa realized.

"Listen, Noah..." She pushed a strand of hair behind her ear, her heart thumping in her chest and echoing through her brain. "I need to tell you something."

He turned from his perusal of the store, dark brows furrowing slightly. "What's up?"

"I..." She pressed her lips together, her stomach churning slightly as she drew in a shaky breath. "I'm really, really sorry."

Noah drew back, blinking as his face paled. "What?" He nearly whispered the word.

"I'm sorry," Vanessa repeated, steadying her voice. "I'm sorry that I left when I was pregnant and didn't take Cricket up on her offer to stay with you guys. I'm sorry I disappeared and didn't call. I'm sorry I had Emily adopted and I'm sorry I never came back like I said I would."

Her words, thirty years too late but sincere and scary nonetheless, hung in the air between them as Vanessa held her breath, waiting for a response.

Noah's jaw went slack and he looked away, his chest rising and falling hard as he processed Vanessa's apology.

She waited breathlessly, frozen with anticipation for his response.

Would he forgive her? Hug her? Laugh it off? Tell her it was water under the bridge and things happened the way they were supposed to, and all was well?

"Noah..." Vanessa said softly after way too many beats of silence. "Did...did you hear me? I said I'm very —"

"You're kidding, right?" He cocked his head, familiar blue eyes flashing as he met her gaze. "You can't be serious right now."

Vanessa's heart thumped as she inched backward. "I-I said I was sorry. Of course I'm serious, Noah. I...I...I really...am sorry."

He stepped forward, his expression shadowed with hurt as he ran a hand through his salt-and-pepper hair. "Do you seriously think that some awkward, casual apology tossed like small talk thirty years later is enough to fix...what...what you did?"

Shame punched as he dragged out the last three words, as if what she "did" was so big and bad that he couldn't even describe it.

"Of course not, but I just figured that I'd, you know, clear the air a little."

He snorted. "There's no air left between us to clear. No air, no apologies, no...nothing, Vanessa. I waited and hoped and prayed and you never came back. You never contacted me. You never...cared. I was wrecked. I couldn't sleep, couldn't eat, I quit baseball, everything. Just ask my mom."

"I know." Vanessa clenched her jaw, her eyes downcast as the metallic taste of regret and remorse filled her mouth and pressed down on her chest. She was so, so sorry. She'd been a kid—scared and alone and three thousand miles away and cutting all ties made sense then.

But now, to him? It had been small and selfish, but wouldn't he let her apologize?

"Noah, please—"

"No," he barked harshly. "I thought I'd never recover from losing you. And Emily. But I did recover. I went to college and law school and now here I am as a partner in my dream firm, and the entire time, every milestone, I was still thinking about you. I couldn't trust anyone to stay with me, even my ex-wife. Hence the 'ex.' We were everything, Vanessa."

She didn't know how to respond to that, so she stood stone still and quiet, letting him say what was clearly bubbling up, needing to be said.

He swallowed hard, his eyes narrow. "You and me...

we were best friends. We were soulmates. And you just ran away from me the second things got hard. And never once, in twenty-nine and a half years, did you think to call or show up here. And now you want to apologize because you're starting over and you want a clear conscience? No, Nessie. Not a chance."

The use of Vanessa's old nickname was like a dagger to her gut.

Tears sprung in her eyes as her throat tightened, and she suddenly felt unstable on her feet.

"Noah," she whispered in a reed-thin voice. "I—"

Emily bounced back into the main store, emerging from the back hallway that led to her office with even more pep in her step than she'd had the day before. "Oh, hi," she said to Noah. "I didn't realize you were waiting. I had to deal with a shipping wrinkle. It's all smoothed out now, though." She looked from one to the other, the awkward moment palpable. "Uh, everything okay out here?"

"Oh, yes, yes. We were just...catching up." Vanessa waved a dismissive hand, unable to even look at Noah. "You two go...do legal things. I'll...be here."

Just wallowing in shame, she added silently.

Emily split her attention again, looking curious and worried.

"Then let's get to it," Noah said quickly. "We can find somewhere...else to sit down and go over this paperwork."

Without saying goodbye, he walked toward the door and Emily hustled to join him.

"Bye," she said with a pathetic wave.

Then the two of them—father and daughter—walked toward the front door of Young at Heart and opened it, sending a chime echoing through the building.

"Bye," Vanessa croaked.

She stood frozen in the middle of the boutique, reeling. The shock of finding out her mother didn't die in a car accident forty-five years ago wasn't even at the forefront of her mind anymore.

The past pain with Noah ran far deeper than she'd even realized. Was she that short-sighted? Had she seriously been that selfish?

Of course, Vanessa knew she'd hurt Noah. She knew she'd broken her promise and disappeared, and she was not proud of that. But only in the past twenty-four hours had it become clear just how deep those wounds were. And somehow, after decades of separation, still raw.

Guilt gripped and a few warm tears slid down her cheeks as she walked into the back office of the store, closing the door behind her.

"There's no air left between us to clear," she repeated his cold words, shaking her head as she flopped down into the desk chair and swiveled around. "No nothing."

That's why he hardly wanted to get to know Emily. That's why he'd left Rosemary Beach and never come back, despite his mother's best efforts.

It was all because of Vanessa. She'd wrecked his life, and never even bothered to say sorry.

Sadly, Emily had been wrong about one thing. It was, in fact, too late.

Chapter Three

Emily

Emily Young had never had a father before, not for one single day of her life, so walking side by side next to Noah Ellison—her full, biological dad—was a bit more of a thrill than she'd let on.

It wasn't like Emily had had some gaping hole in her life or longing in her heart for a father all of these years. She'd been more than happy with Grandma Gigi growing up. Then, of course, meeting Vanessa and bonding with her birth mom had been an unexpected joy.

But now, she was in the presence of the man who'd given her life and half her DNA, and she felt a little giddy as they walked out onto the bustling corner of Rosemary Beach.

"Figured we could just go to Gloria's place," Noah said, nodding toward the next building.

"Sure." The diner was familiar territory for her, since she'd worked there for her first month in town, before she and Vanessa went full-time on Young at Heart.

She stole a glance at his profile, searching for a clue as to what made him tick and maybe looking for something that looked...well, like her. But she didn't resemble this man with a strong profile and angular jaw at all; she was a carbon copy of her mother and wondered if that's what Noah saw when he looked at her.

Emily was not dumb. She could certainly sense that Noah didn't come here to launch some daddy-daughter relationship with the baby his girlfriend had when they were sixteen. She understood that and wanted to be respectful of it.

He didn't come here to get to know her. He was just doing Emily a favor. Really, he was doing his mother, Cricket, a favor. She and Emily had grown close, since Cricket loved her role as Emily's grandmother. So much so that Cricket's meddling but loving hands were clearly all over Noah's unexpected return to Rosemary Beach.

Still, he was her...*dad*. A foreign concept, really. An exciting idea that Emily never in a million years dreamed she could experience.

"So, how long are you in town?" Emily asked as the silence became a beat too long.

"Hopefully, just until this afternoon," he replied, pulling open the door to the diner. "I really need to get back to my firm, but I wanted to make sure all of this stuff is correctly processed and filed before I leave."

A bit of disappointment sank in Emily's chest, but she pushed it away, reminding herself that any time with Noah was a gift, even if it was short and he had walls up higher than the Miami skyscraper where his law office was.

"For sure, I get that," she said, following him into the cozy, local eatery that had easily become a second home for her here in Rosemary Beach. Liz, the darling hostess, was a fast friend and, of course, Gloria was the greatest aunt of all time.

"Hey, girl!" Liz looked up from a menu she was wiping down at the hostess stand, her expression bright as she saw Emily. "You looking for Glo?"

"Actually..." Emily notched her head toward Noah, who was a few steps behind her. "We're gonna grab a bite and some coffee, if that's cool. This is my..." She cleared her throat awkwardly. "This is Noah Ellison."

Liz's brown eyes widened, knowing full well who Noah was and how he fit into the Vanessa Young-Rosemary Beach town lore.

"Welcome in, Noah," she said slowly, grabbing two menus and silverware packets. "Y'all can follow me."

The tables and booths of Gloria's buzzed with life, laughter, and conversation, and Emily weaved her way through them to a small booth in the back where Liz set up their menus.

As she was nearing the booth, Emily heard a man call her name.

She turned, her gaze landing on the dark, intense eyes of Reed Collins, who sat at his usual two-top with his usual ballcap and his usual...gorgeousness.

"Hey, how are you?" Emily walked over and smiled, wincing as she remembered the first time she'd met the mysterious stranger at this very table. "Don't worry, I'm not carrying iced tea this time."

Reed laughed at the shared memory of her clumsy accident, inching the monitor of his laptop down to look up at her.

Neither one of them would forget her first day on the job, when she'd slipped and spilled iced tea all over his expensive computer and darn near ruined it and some very important work. Fortunately, she had a tiny bit of IT experience from the past and she'd been able to help him recover the document. And, in the process, she'd learned his secret.

Emily was the only person in town who knew Reed's real identity—well, technically, his fake one. The handsome man who spent hours in the diner with his fingers flying over a keyboard was really R.C. Anderson, pen name for the bestselling mystery and thriller novelist. For his current work-in-progress, she'd learned, he was researching Panama City Beach and lived there on a houseboat, just a few miles up the road. She'd been there to fix his computer and learned the truth about his identity.

Even though they'd only met briefly and seen each other a few casual times since, Emily and Reed shared a big, big secret, and it made her feel like they knew each other better than they actually did.

"No apron today." Reed jutted his chin toward her denim shorts and tank top. "Just can't stay away, huh? Even on your day off?"

Emily smiled. "Actually, I don't work here anymore. I quit last week."

His brows rose. "Really? One too many tea spills?" he joked.

"Working here was temporary," she told him. "I'm

actually running the new clothing boutique next door, Young at Heart. My mother and I opened it together."

"Ah." He nodded and smiled, giving her a chance to take in his handsome jaw dusted with the slightest shadow of whiskers. "Very exciting. I'll have to stop in and check out your merchandise."

She laughed. "Unless you're in the market for a resort chic maxi dress, I don't think we'll have anything you'll like."

He narrowed his gaze, dark eyes locked on her. "I don't know. I might find something I like."

Emily felt her face flush. Was Reed flirting with her? The cute, famous but totally anonymous brilliant author?

When she'd stopped by his houseboat a few weeks ago to salvage his lost documents, he was awfully friendly, but she attributed that to the fact that she had saved his valuable lost work.

He couldn't actually like her, could he? And even if he did, he wasn't in town for very long. And even if he was...

She was still technically married. To a monster.

"Well, you're welcome to stop by the store anytime." She grinned, suddenly aware of Noah walking up to her and standing by her side.

"Hello," Noah said pointedly, looking at Reed. "Are you a friend of Emily's?"

"Oh, this is Reed." She gestured between the two men as she introduced them. "Reed this is Noah. My, uh..."

"Her father," Noah interjected, holding out his hand to shake Reed's. "Noah Ellison."

Holy cow. Did he just introduce himself as my father? It tilted her world a little, she had to admit.

Maybe Noah *did* want a relationship with her. In his own, slightly distant, closed-off, uncertain way. And she'd take it.

"Oh, hello." Reed's eyes widened a bit at Noah's words, and he stood up to shake hands. "Nice to meet you. Reed Collins."

Noah nodded, glancing back at Emily after their hands dropped. "How do you two know each other?"

"From when I worked here," Emily explained. "I spilled iced tea all over his laptop on my first day."

Reed laughed. "Quite the first impression was made, but it was impossible to forget about her, I'll give her that."

"I didn't know you worked here." Noah frowned.

Reed arched his brow, no doubt confused that her father wouldn't know she'd worked at the diner.

"It was just for a few weeks," she said quickly.

Noah nodded and gestured toward an empty booth. "I'll get all this paperwork ready," he said, giving Reed a nod before he stepped away.

Once again, Reed looked a little confused—or maybe curious. He was a novelist, after all.

"We're finalizing my divorce," she said, trying to offer a simple explanation although nothing about her relationship with her father was simple. "Noah's an attorney and

I guess there's lots of paperwork involved." She gave a wry finger twirl. "Yippee."

Reed gave a sympathetic smile, still looking just a little...interested. In her? She couldn't tell.

"Anyway, I'll see you around."

He gave her one more smile and she pivoted, heading to the booth where Noah had already pulled out some files and spread them on the table like they were in a conference room.

For a moment, she watched him, remembering all that Cricket had shared about her son—he was ambitious, focused, driven, and loved his job to the point of being a workaholic.

Emily had no complaints about that side of the gene pool. He was smart and good-looking, obviously he had a heart, since he'd come to help her. But did he have a sense of humor? A favorite sport? A weakness for pasta or any bad habits?

She ached to know who her father really was. But he had big, impenetrable, concrete walls around him, and she doubted it would be easy to break them down in the short time they had together.

"So, what's the deal with that guy?" Noah looked up from a file and flicked his gaze in the general direction of Reed's table.

Dang it. Now she had to lie to her father because she'd promised a stranger she'd keep his secret.

"There's no deal," she said, purposely vague as she dug her fingernail into the paper napkin on the table. "I spilled a drink on his laptop, he lost some documents, but

I was able to recover them. We've been friendly ever since."

Noah nodded slowly as he flipped open another file. "You should be careful. With, you know, dating and all of that."

Emily nearly choked. "Dating? I'm not even divorced yet."

"I know, but you will be, very soon. And you could..." He swallowed. "You could get hurt again. You need to be careful, and you really should take time to recover from what you've been through. It's not smart to jump into a new relationship after something like...." He tapped the stack of papers. "This."

Emily inched back, toying with the corner of her napkin. Was Noah seriously trying to give her, dare she say, *fatherly advice?*

She expected his warning to irritate her, or make her want to respond with, "Excuse me, I'm thirty and you don't even know me..." But why? He knew her well enough to help her out of a crappy marriage, and...he cared.

That was worth a lot.

"I'll tread lightly," she assured him. "And thank you. I appreciate the advice."

"Yeah, of course. I don't want you to end up hurt again," he said quickly, sincerity slipping like a ray of sunshine over his icy exterior.

They looked at each other across the table for a few beats of silence, as if neither one of them knew what to do or say or how to handle this situation.

Riding the high of his dad-like attitude when it came to Reed, she decided to take her shot. "So, um, before we dive into all of these depressing divorce logistics, can I ask you something?"

"Of course," Noah said, folding his hands like a lawyer about to listen to a confession.

"Did you think it was crazy that Vanessa and I found each other?"

"Well, I..." He scratched the back of his neck as he pondered the question. "I mean, I was really surprised. I was always under the impression that Vanessa implemented a closed adoption, and never thought she'd want any kind of relationship with you. No offense," he added quickly, lifting a hand. "But you're here now, working with her. Business partners thirty years later."

She heard the bitterness in his voice and, on one level, she understood it. But she'd had a good life and was grateful she'd been adopted, plus, she'd spent six weeks with her mother and Vanessa had her loyalty now.

"I'm just so glad to be here," she said, hoping to communicate that to him. "Vanessa's amazing, and we've gotten close quite quickly."

Noah's eyes darkened momentarily, and he glanced away, then back at Emily. "I'm glad you guys have found each other. Just, you know, be careful."

"You say that a lot." Emily narrowed her gaze, studying the deep layers of her father's expression.

"Vanessa is a...leaver." The bitterness sounded a little more like hate. "No matter how attached you think she might be, think again. She could disappear on you."

Emily chewed her lip, sensing the decades-old hurt that still stung Noah Ellison to his core.

"She seems pretty set on staying here to me," she said softly, not wanting to get in the middle of their problems...even if her conception was the cause of them.

"Well, she may surprise you." He flicked his brows, sipping a glass of iced water that Emily had hardly noticed Liz come over to pour. "I'm sure she's told you about the history, what all happened after we found out she was pregnant."

"I know the gist. And, honestly, I understand why you both made the choices that you did. I don't hold any resentment or anything." She picked at a frayed piece of denim in her jean shorts.

"Well, that's good. But just for the record, I agreed to the adoption, but it wasn't what I would have done."

The words hit Emily like crashing glass as her mind raced with thoughts and images about what her life would have been like if she hadn't gotten adopted. "But ultimately, it's what you guys decided to do."

"It's what we *had* to do. She made it clear she wasn't coming back from L.A., despite our agreements and promises. She left and she changed, and it was...not easy."

Emily swallowed. "I'm sure it wasn't."

"Anyway." Noah waved a hand, shaking his head as if trying to shake off the pain of the past. "I'm happy to hear she's turned over a new leaf and everything, but I can't go anywhere near it. Vanessa Young is nothing but chaos and confusion for me. I hope you can understand."

Emily nodded, although she wasn't sure if this was his way of politely telling her he wanted nothing to do with her, either. "I understand completely. But we can be...friends?"

Noah, for the first time all day, cracked a sincere smile that reached his eyes. "Yes, we can be friends. Now, let's get you divorced so you're free to date Mr. Ballcap who hasn't stopped looking over here since we sat down." He rolled his eyes.

Emily laughed, shaking her head and resisting the urge to glance over her shoulder at Reed. "No worries, Noah. I'm single, and it's going to stay that way."

Noah looked up from the paperwork he was skimming, giving her a dubious look. "We'll see about that. You've got quite the blend of genetics working in your favor. Mostly from my side, of course."

"So that's where I get my insufferable ego from," Emily teased, wagging a finger at him, happy to chip away at the concrete wall. "Anything else I've inherited that I should know about?"

"Well, I'm good at math. Your mother? Not so much."

"Oh, me, too!" She let out a little giggle. "And, yes, she has me handling the books at the store. Anything else?"

He thought for a moment, studying her long enough that she swore she could feel the first threads of a bond form.

"I love music," he said.

"Oh, yes, but not the stuff that's popular now," she said. "I'm weirdly partial to classic rock."

His jaw loosened. "Seriously? I have every Led Zeppelin, Pink Floyd, and Rush album ever made in vinyl."

She gasped, lighting up. "No! Rush? I've loved Rush ever since I was a kid—thanks to my Grandma Gigi, who raised me on rock-and-roll. I asked Vanessa once about music, and she just laughed and said she can't stand rock music."

"Listen," Noah said, leaning closer. "I sat front row at the Vapor Trails tour in '02 and caught Neil Peart's drumstick when he threw it into the crowd. It's framed at my condo."

Emily hooted in disbelief. "That is so insanely cool."

"I can't believe you're a Rush fan," he said, chuckling to himself. "That's...wow. That's awesome."

Emily sighed, soaking up every moment with Noah, knowing her time with him was fleeting, but determined to make the absolute most out of it.

It felt like she was piecing together the puzzle of herself, getting little hints and clues from both Vanessa and Noah about why she was who she was.

When they got back to the paperwork, he was still rigid and serious and focused. But she just knew their connection as father and daughter was undeniable. And all she could do was pray this was only the beginning.

"Hello, my darling granddaughter!" Cricket floated over to give Emily a big, warm hug as she walked through the front door of Cricket's, the beauty salon that was a mainstay of the Rosemary Beach downtown.

"Hi, Cricket." Emily hugged her back, glancing around at the empty chairs. "No appointments today?"

"I just finished my last client." She pushed her pink, cat-eye-shaped glasses up the bridge of her nose. "I have the afternoon off, and Paula and Shelly are coming over for knitting and gossip."

Emily laughed at the thought of the three older women sitting around chatting with their knitting needles in Cricket's loft apartment above the salon. "Sounds like fun."

"And how are you? One day closer to freedom I take it?"

"All thanks to your son," Emily said with a smile, walking around the salon chairs, running her hands along the soft pink leather, perfect for this blast from the past salon and the 1950s vibe Cricket had created.

"My son? You mean your father." Cricket arched a dark, drawn-on brow as she waltzed over to the front desk, shuffling some paperwork. "You can call him that, you know."

"Well, I..." Emily lifted her shoulder, unable to hide her pulling grin. "I don't want to get too ahead of myself. He isn't here to get to know me, and I get that he doesn't necessarily want to be too...involved."

Cricket rolled her eyes, flicking her fingers dramatically. "He doesn't know what's good for him. Thinks he wants to be some rich bachelor living in a Miami high-rise in his forties. He thought he wanted to marry

Rebecca! Talk about a mistake." She huffed out an exasperated sigh. "He'll learn, though. I just need to figure out how to show him."

Emily frowned curiously, angling her head as she studied her grandmother. "Show him what?"

Cricket pushed her pink glasses up the bridge of her nose again and eyed Emily, as if the following statement were completely obvious. "That he needs to stay here and be with Vanessa, of course."

She drew back with shock, her mouth falling open with a laugh of disbelief.

"Is that...is that a possibility?" she whispered, barely able to imagine the two of them "with" each other after the ice she'd felt when they were in the same room.

"It could be. It *should* be." Cricket lifted her chin as she closed and locked the drawer of the front desk before she walked back out to finish tidying up the salon.

Grabbing a broom and dustpan from the corner, she handed it to Emily. "You mind sweeping?"

"Not at all." Emily was barely able to move, but she slowly began to brush up all the strands of hair and dust from the linoleum floor, staring at Cricket. "Has he said anything to you about that? I mean, is there really a chance of that happening?"

She knew she'd better not get her hopes up but whoa, it was hard not to.

"It's my dream, you see." Cricket sighed wistfully as she rinsed out the hair washing basins and shook her head. "But it's not just me being selfish." She pointed a finger in Emily's direction. "Believe me. It's because I know my son, and I know what's best for him. And what is, and has always been, best for him is Vanessa Young."

"Wow." Emily swept up clumps of hair into the dustpan, trying to imagine what Noah and Vanessa would be like as a couple. "I know they were best friends growing up and everything, but that was so long ago. Do you really think they could rekindle? After all that happened?"

"Yes, I do." Cricket flicked off the faucet. "And I'll tell you why."

"Why?"

"Because of you, little lady."

Emily laughed. "Me?"

"You're my newest hope," she announced, shameless in her joy. "With you in the picture, their biological daughter, the very thing that bonds them eternally, they will surely remember how perfect they are for each other and stop making such silly and childish decisions and grow up and be together! Just as they were always meant to."

This was Cricket's ultimate dream? Sure, she knew—like everyone else in this town—that Cricket wanted Noah out of Miami and home in Rosemary Beach.

But this was new. Noah and Vanessa together? Seriously? Well, Cricket would know better than anyone how good they were for each other…if they could manage to let go of the past.

Emily didn't even know this was an option.

And as she helped her new grandmother clean and

close up the shop, chatting about the past and the future, she realized that Cricket's dream...might be hers, too.

Crazy? Maybe. But if there was any remote possibility that she, as a twenty-nine-year-old woman, could have a real, whole family?

How could she not be on board with that?

Chapter Four

Cricket

Cricket curled the purple yarn around her needle, letting it slide into the next loop with ease and speed, but her mind wasn't on knitting. She was rather enjoying Paula and Shelly's reaction to the story she'd just finished telling them.

"So, Emily likes the idea?" Paula asked.

"Likes it?" Cricket hooted. "That young woman's face lit up like the Fourth of July when I told her about my not-so-secret ultimate dream."

So now, more than ever, it *had* to happen. Emily would be dancing with joy. And what grandmother didn't want to give that to their granddaughter?

But Paula shook her head and lowered her needles. "Sure, she's enchanted by the idea. But what if it goes south, Cricket? Then what?"

"South? Noah and Vanessa are destined to be together!" She clucked at the pessimism. "It's not going to...go south. Whatever that means."

"It means bad," Shelly murmured, getting a deep sigh of frustration from Cricket.

Shelly and Paula shared a look, then both turned back to face Cricket.

"Cricket, honey, we love you," Shelly said warmly, finishing a stitch on her tote bag. "But we don't want you to get your, and now Emily's, expectations too high."

Cricket tsked. "They are not *too* high. They are right where they need to be."

Paula arched a dubious brow, pushing back a thick silver curl over her shoulder. "We know you want Noah here, and you think he should be with Vanessa again."

"I don't think, I *know*," she confirmed with certainty. "He hasn't been truly happy since the day she left. I don't care how fancy his car is, or what his address is, or how much money he makes. I'm his mother. I know what his real happiness looks like."

Paula sighed softly. "Just because he came back in town for a day or two doesn't mean he's changed his mind about anything."

Cricket swallowed, knowing that her smart friend was tragically correct. No, Noah didn't have some massive change of heart and decide to give up the big law firm and come home forever. She wasn't daft. She knew that kind of drastic switch was out of the question.

"Of course, I know. But...it could happen over time." She twirled a knitting needle around in her fingertips, scrunching up her face as she thought about this. "If I had more time, if I had him here for a bit longer, he could see. He could be reminded of what a wonderful place this is and how much he truly belongs here. And if he falls back in love with Vanessa in the process..." She leaned back. "Well then, that's just an added bonus, isn't it?"

Shelly shook her head and chuckled. "You are something else, Cricket Ellison."

"But I'm right, aren't I?"

"Hmm..." Paula pursed her lips. "I do think if Noah spent more time here, he'd see the charm of small-town life and maybe realize that it could be better outside of the city. I'm willing to give you that much, Crick."

"One problem, though." Shelly wagged her needle at Cricket. "He's leaving tomorrow morning."

"I know," Cricket said on a frustrated groan. "And I've hardly seen him since this morning. He's staying at The Pearl, of course, and he said he was so behind on work he's been writing briefs or depositions or whatever the heck he does all day and all evening. It's criminal, really, to work that much."

"Well, he does make a cool million, I'm sure." Shelly said. "Ain't that criminal."

"Doesn't matter," Cricket said quickly. "Money doesn't buy happiness, nor does it guarantee it. Family, however, that's a different story."

She returned to her cardigan, starting on the scalloped edge of the cuff, considering how she could possibly get Noah to stay in town just a little bit longer.

"I could suddenly fall ill," she suggested, looking eagerly at Shelly and Paula for their approval.

"Lady, you need help." Shelly rolled her eyes.

"Not horribly ill." Cricket raised her brow. "Just, you know, sickly enough for him to want to stay and look after me. Noah has a good heart. He won't leave if I'm sick."

"But you're not sick," Paula gently reminded her. "In

fact, you're in actual perfect health. And you can't fake sickness, honey. It's wrong."

Cricket wrinkled her nose, hating that they were right. She could finagle—no one could do it better—but she couldn't *lie*.

"If Noah is meant to stay longer"—Shelly lifted up her knitting needles, giving Cricket an encouraging smile—"God will provide a way."

Cricket sighed, sinking into her chair and returning to her purple cuff. "He'd better hurry."

The women laughed and continued chatting, shifting the conversation to Paula's granddaughter, who had her first serious boyfriend in high school and he, evidently, had a sports car.

But Cricket barely heard about the boy and his car.

How could she concentrate on that when she had a problem to solve? Noah would get in his own sports car tomorrow and drive all those hours south to Miami. How could she stop him?

Maybe there'd be a reason for him to come back. Perhaps he'd be less of a stranger now that Emily was in the picture, but truthfully, Cricket had no idea how all of this would unfold. Worst of all, maybe things would just continue on as they always had—with him busy and buried in work, and far, far away, all alone.

"Isn't the Class of '97 celebration coming up? The First Class Bash?" Shelly asked, changing the subject from Paula's granddaughter. "They always do it around graduation time, which is in a few weeks."

Cricket nodded, knowing that every May, Rosemary

Beach High School—with the sponsorship of small businesses in town—held some event to honor the graduating class of 1997, which was, of course, Noah and Vanessa's class.

They had been part of the very first graduating class when Rosemary Beach High became an official school in 1996, right in the earliest days of the transformation of the area into the tourist mecca it now was. The annual First Class Bash always gave Cricket the blues, because Noah never, ever went to the event.

Vanessa hadn't graduated with the class but was still considered part of it. Either way, it was tragically hopeless, because Cricket knew her son well enough to know that he would never stay in town for something he'd so intentionally avoided for the past twenty-six years.

"I wish that mattered." Cricket clicked her tongue. "But Noah refuses to go to the celebration. Of course, he'll be long back in Miami by then, and he'll ditch it like he does every year. The memories haunt him, and I can only imagine they're even worse for Vanessa. I doubt she'd attend."

"You're sure it's not something that could keep him in town?" Paula asked, lifting her brows hopefully. "Just for a few more weeks?"

"Not a chance," Cricket said, wishing the words weren't true. "He has no interest."

Paula pursed her lips, thinking hard. "What if you came up with something that you need his help to plan? For the '97 Bash? Then he'd have to stay."

Cricket sighed. "Well, I certainly could offer the

salon's sponsorship this year. I never do, because the event itself truly bums me out. But who knows?" Cricket glanced at the sky. "Maybe this year could be different. Noah won't attend, though. Maybe if he were already here, but he won't stay in town for something he can't stand so much."

"That makes sense," Shelly admitted. "You'll think of something, Cricket."

"Maybe I will. Your tote bag is looking fabulous, Shelly." Cricket smiled, admiring the cream-colored tight-knit tote that Shelly had nearly completed, trying to focus hard on her sweet friends and their company, and not on her unrealized dreams.

"Oh, you're too kind." Shelly held the bag up, examining it with a critical eye. "The handle is a bit lopsided, but hey. My niece is going to love it either way. I'm going to stitch sunflowers on it to jazz it up."

"Gorgeous!" Paula exclaimed.

"That'll be just lovely. Can I get you darlings anything? Some tea? Treats, perhaps?"

Paula nodded. "Ooh, tea sounds lovely."

"And those little cupcakes if you have 'em." Shelly grinned. "You know the ones."

"Salted caramel chocolate from Sweet Henrietta's." Cricket smiled slyly as she stood up and walked into her little corner kitchen off the living room. "You know me too well, Shelly."

As Cricket willed her mind to stay focused on all the good in her life—like her adorable little kitchen and wonderful friends and booming business—she put together a plate of goodies and a tea kettle on the stove.

Just as she was warming the kettle, she noticed her slipper socks suddenly felt very, very damp.

What in the world?

Cricket looked down at the floor and saw the butter-yellow tile in her kitchen rapidly becoming covered in a fast-moving layer of...

"Water!" Cricket shouted. "Oh, my heavens! There's water everywhere!"

Shelly and Paula came rushing down the hall at the sound of Cricket's shriek, but she couldn't even look up from the pool that seemed to be coming from the walls.

"Oh, no! Cricket!" Paula gasped, holding her hands in front of her mouth as they watched in horror. "Your apartment is flooding!"

It was getting deep as it spread into the living room and hallway, and for a very brief moment, Cricket felt as if she might faint.

"The water line. The water line." She turned, panicking briefly, then remembered the water valve in the pantry from when she'd updated the kitchen a while back.

"Should we get towels?" Shelly asked, sloshing back toward the living room, which was certainly ruined.

"We're gonna need a lot of towels," Paula said softly, giving Cricket an apologetic look.

After shutting off the water line, Cricket stood frozen and silent in an inch of water, staring at her sweet and beautiful—if a bit old—loft apartment that she so deeply adored.

"It can be fixed," she whispered to herself through a steadying breath. "Everything can be fixed."

"Yes, it can." Shelly walked over and put a tight arm around her. "And you will fix it. We're here to help you."

"Of course we are," Paula added, wrapping her arm around Cricket's other shoulder and giving her a squeeze. "It's going to be okay. Who should we call right now?"

"A water damage company, I imagine," Shelly answered, lifting her finger. "I think my husband knows of one. Let me give him a call."

"Good idea, and maybe the insurance company, too..."

As Paula and Shelly prattled on, grabbing their phones out of their purses and discussing an action plan to get Cricket through the night, everything became shockingly clear.

If Noah is meant to stay longer...God will provide a way.

A sudden sense of peace washed over Cricket as quickly as the water had covered her old wood floors.

She felt a smile spread across her face and calm joy fill her heart. Cricket could faintly hear Paula and Shelly going back and forth about what insurance would cover and how stingy they could be and how water damage was the main concern.

Cricket walked—or sloshed, rather—into the living room and held up both hands, grinning from ear to ear. "Ladies, I know who we're calling."

"Who?" Paula asked eagerly.

Shelly arched a dubious brow. "And why do you look so happy when your entire home is underwater?"

"I'll call Noah," she explained, lifting a victorious shoulder. "And he'll have to stay until this all gets fixed and sorted out, because who would leave their dear old mother in a flooded, damaged apartment to fend for herself with insurance agents?" She held a dramatic hand to her forehead, making the other women laugh.

Paula wagged a finger, slowly walking toward Cricket and nodding, impressed. "Whew, you are good, my friend. Darn good."

"Hey, I didn't flood my house." Cricket held her hands up defensively. "Although had that idea come to me..."

"I wouldn't put it past you," Shelly teased.

"But I didn't even have to meddle or manipulate or calculate. This was all destiny. Which just continues to further prove my point that Noah needs to be here."

Shelly moved her foot around in the water, splashing it about on the living room floors. "I guess I can't argue that."

Cricket looked happily at her damaged home. "I've been wanting new floors for quite a while, anyway."

"These kinds of things can take ages, you know," Shelly warned her. "Remodels and construction and all that."

Cricket laughed softly, wrapping her arms around her waist. "It wouldn't be the first time God changed the plans of a man named Noah, would it?"

"Do you have any idea what caused it?" Noah scratched his head, stepping through the water-soaked floors in bare feet.

Of course, he'd sped over from the hotel as soon as Cricket called and promised to help her in any way he could.

"Not a clue. One minute I was in here knitting with Shelly and Paula and the next there was two inches of water spreading out all over the place."

"We're so lucky this part of your apartment is only over the laundry area and breakroom of the salon," he said. "There's some damage, but you can keep the place open."

Cricket pursed her lips, trying not to smile or at least act like that was what made her happy. But the truth was, he had to stay, right?

Noah would surely not leave her and go back to Miami so long as her place was in this much of a mess. But the floors would get fixed, the water would dry.

What really needed to be fixed was her son's life, and this was her chance.

"It seems like a main line must have burst, Mom." He let out a frustrated sigh, bending over to check underneath the dishwasher for any clues. "This isn't a small amount of water."

Cricket sighed, feigning stress and dejectedness. "Oh, heavens. Surely this will take ages to fix, and it'll be so long until I feel safe and comfortable again."

Noah checked the fridge, washing machine, and bathroom, but couldn't find any visible cause of the flood.

Every brick wall Noah's investigation ran into was a victory to Cricket. The harder this was to figure out, the longer it would take to fix it.

"Well, you shut the water line off, right?" he asked, glancing around for any clues.

"Yes, I sure did. Just like Gene taught me all those years ago. And it only is the water for up here. The salon has its own water supply. Your dad was the one who thought of that. Oh." Cricket pressed a hand to her heart at the memory of her late husband, knowing how Noah felt about his late father. "If only he were still here. He'd know exactly what to do. He was so handy, and I am so... helpless."

Noah snorted softly. "You're a lot of things, Mom, but helpless isn't one of them."

"But I'm old and widowed and..." And pulling out all the stops. "And scared, Noah. This is kind of overwhelming."

On a sigh, he put an arm around her. "Water remediation is on the way, and they'll fill this place with fans to make sure there's no mold or deterioration. Once the immediate damage is dealt with, a plumber should come and figure out what pipe burst and how to fix it. And for you? You want to call your homeowners insurance and file a claim. They'll send someone out here to assess the damage and give you a payout to fix the loft."

Surely, he didn't expect her to handle all of this on her own, did he? That simply would not do.

"Okay." Cricket drew in a slow breath and let out the softest, truly the most pathetic sob she could muster. "It's just that..."

"Mom, you're going to be okay."

"Yes, yes. I will be." Cricket fanned herself as if fighting tears, lowering herself into her velvet swivel chair in the living room. "This is all just very overwhelming and stressful. You know, Noah, I've been starting to feel my age a bit more lately, and..." She looked up at him. "It's scary. I don't know if I can handle plumbers and insurance agents by myself. I'm...weaker these days. A bit frail, even."

Noah's eyes softened with sympathy as he crouched next to the chair, placing a strong hand on Cricket's shoulder. "You are the furthest thing from weak and frail."

"But this is too much, Noah. I can't manage all of this on my own. My home is ruined and...and..." She looked away, her voice breaking. "Maybe I should just find an assisted-living home now."

"Okay, okay. How about I stay?" Noah took her hand. "At least until all of this is squared away."

Somehow, through the grace of God, she managed not to cheer.

"Oh, heavens, no." Cricket turned back to face him, conjuring up true worry in her expression. She hoped. "I could never ask you to do that with work and everything."

"I can work remotely and make a few day trips back down there." He pressed his lips together and shook his head. "I'm not leaving you alone with this mess. I'll deal with the plumber and the insurance people and make sure everything gets fixed and paid for and handled. Okay?"

"Oh, Noah, you are such a saint." She pressed her hand to his cheek. "Just like your father. He'd be so proud of you." Cricket felt her eyes fill, and this time they were real tears.

"Thank you, Mom. I'll take care of everything." He reached a hand out to help her up. "Now, let's pack you a bag and you'll come stay the night at The Pearl with me."

"Oh, I don't want to encroach."

"I have the executive penthouse suite." He glanced over his shoulder. "Plenty of space, Mama. Come on."

Cricket smiled as she walked down the hallway toward her bedroom, water squishing around her feet. Beautiful, beautiful water that would keep Noah right where he belonged.

Chapter Five

Gloria

Gloria had never been to a private investigator's office before, and wished she didn't have to do this alone, but Vanessa had an unexpected meeting with someone from the small business association in Rosemary Beach.

So, Gloria made the drive to Destin alone, practicing what she'd say to Jason Chang, who had great reviews and was apparently skilled in locating missing persons.

Missing...not dead.

She sighed and switched off the radio, which was just competing with her thoughts. She'd rather cruise through picturesque Santa Rosa Beach hearing nothing but the sound of her childhood.

All those years when she and Vanessa were motherless, relying on cold and tough Bill Young for their needs growing up. They used to stay up late into the night together, cuddled underneath the patchwork quilt their friend and neighbor Cricket Ellison had made them, wondering about their mom.

Starved for information and stories about who their mother had been, the girls had invented their own character for Violet Young. They decided she was sweet and quiet, with a fierce personality. They were certain she'd love to sing and would dance around the kitchen while dinner was in the oven.

They'd pray together, reminding God to always say hi to their mommy in heaven, and think about the day they'd get to hug her.

Gloria gripped the steering wheel tighter as the memories yanked at her heart.

Their mother had been alive *the entire time.*

It still didn't feel real. It couldn't possibly be real. And there was no one to take the blame now...unless they found her still alive. Would screaming at a woman in her seventies make Gloria feel better? Would it erase that childhood pain?

She wanted to find out badly enough that she was driving an hour and meeting a PI.

She'd been barely five when her mother "died" in a car accident that her father had steadfastly refused to talk about, ever.

Gloria had the faintest memories of Violet...vague flashes of soft blond curls, a musical laugh, a touch of a soft hand. She remembered a blue-flowered dress and platform shoes. She remembered her mother crying once because a stick of butter fell and hit the ground.

But maybe she wasn't crying over butter. Maybe she'd just wanted to leave and go be on "the Great White Way."

Puh-lease.

The pain punched. Maybe the radio was better than—

Her dashboard screen lit up with an incoming phone call from Daisy Bennett, and she darn near drove off the road pressing the button on the steering wheel she hoped would answer her twenty-four-year-old daughter's call hands free.

Normally, of course, a call from Daisy was a daily occurrence. But her daughter's wedding to Kyle Whittington was only three and a half months away, tensions were flaring, and their once-close relationship was rocky at best.

They'd barely spoken in the last few days, following a doozy of a fight over the zillionaire family trying to suck Daisy into their country club life and ditch Gloria in the process.

"Hello?" she said loudly into the car microphone, fumbling with the buttons and praying she hadn't accidentally turned off cruise control. "Daisy?"

"Hey, Mom." Daisy's voice was soft and somber, fitting for two people mid-argument.

Even though they'd been able to talk briefly at Cricket's party the other night, things were far from smoothed over since the epic blowup where Daisy suggested that Gloria shouldn't even attend the wedding.

"What's going on, Dais?" She opted for casual and warm. "Are you working tonight?"

"No, I'm off until Thursday, thank goodness." Daisy sighed with the relief of any nurse at the hospital. "These overnights combined with all the wedding stuff have been exhausting me. I might switch to day shifts after I'm married."

Gloria drew back in the driver's seat, surprised by the comment. Last she'd discussed it with Daisy, she wanted to stop working as a nurse completely once she was Kyle's wife, and just be a full-time...rich wife.

This change was encouraging somehow, like maybe Kyle wouldn't completely erase the bubbly, caring young nurse Gloria had raised.

"That might be a really good plan," she replied. "How is the, um..." She hesitated, knowing this was a touchy subject, but come on. This was her daughter and best friend. "Wedding planning going?"

Daisy was quiet for a few seconds on the other end of the call. "Actually, that's sort of why I called."

"Oh." Gloria perked up with interest. "It is?"

"Yeah, um, I have something today. In an hour, actually. And it's really important, and Linda was supposed to go with me but I..." She paused and added, "I'd rather go with you."

Gloria held back a moan of frustration. The one time Daisy wanted Gloria's help and she was half an hour away on her way to find out if her mother was dead or alive.

She hadn't told Daisy about the letters yet, but wanted to, since she and Vanessa had agreed to tell their girls.

Maybe she should tell her today—before she met with the PI. Maybe they could talk about it after...whatever she wanted her to do today. Maybe she should drop everything and make Daisy a priority because she was a good mother, unlike the one she'd been saddled with.

"It's my hair and makeup trial," Daisy said when Gloria didn't respond. "Linda set the whole thing up, of course, and insisted on coming with me to make sure it was all done exactly to her liking. But I told her just a few minutes ago that I'd..." Her voice broke a bit. "Changed my mind, and I want to go with my own mother."

Gloria felt tears stinging. How could she miss this?

"So, will you go? It's in town, so...we could meet there."

Gloria glanced down at the GPS navigation on her phone screen. If she turned around right now, she could meet Daisy at the salon in time. "Of course I'll go, Dais. I'd love that."

This call, this invitation...it felt like an olive branch. And Gloria knew one thing for sure—no matter how badly they fought, or how tense their relationship had gotten, she was going to grab on to this and hold as tightly as she could to get her daughter back.

It was no surprise to anyone that Linda Whittington had booked Daisy with the most high-end, over-the-top hair and makeup artists in Rosemary Beach and the surrounding area.

As Gloria walked into Prestige Glamour Lounge, she practically slid across the sleek white marble floor. The place screamed money, exactly what Linda would demand for "her" wedding.

Daisy rose from a velvet chair, offering a sweet smile

that Gloria responded to with a long hug. *No Linda-bashing*, she reminded herself. She was here and Linda wasn't, and that deserved a dance of joy.

She wasn't exactly sure what had shifted in Daisy's heart and mind to spark this sudden change of plans, especially since Linda had been completely in charge of planning the wildly extravagant wedding down to the napkin holders for the last eight months.

"Nice place, huh?" Daisy whispered into her ear.

"It's beautiful," Gloria agreed.

A young woman, barely thirty, wearing a light-pink tank top and black slacks came waltzing out of a back room to greet them. Flawless blond curls bounced around narrow shoulders as she gave a friendly smile.

"Hello, hello! Welcome to Prestige Glamour. I'm Trisha, and you must be Daisy and Linda."

Daisy stepped forward, reaching her hand out to shake Trisha's. "I'm Daisy, but this is actually my mom, Gloria." She glanced over at Gloria, her brown eyes flashing with emotions as she met her mother's gaze. "She came with me today."

"Fantastic!" Trisha clasped her hands together. "We are so excited you've chosen to book us as your hair and makeup artists for your wedding on..." She pulled a large phone out and tapped the screen. "July twenty-third, right?"

Gloria swallowed. Wow, that was soon.

"Yup, that's the one," Daisy confirmed, her joy sounding a bit forced.

"Perfection," Trisha sang as she guided them to the

styling chairs in the back, which were situated in front of a giant mirror. "Okay, so I am going to be your makeup artist, and Bethany is your hair stylist. She's in the back but will be out here any second."

Gloria made herself comfortable on a smooth, white leather loveseat near the chair where Daisy sat.

She was still shocked that Daisy had invited her to this—in place of Linda, no less—after everything that had happened. It had to mean progress, but Gloria didn't want to push things. She knew the best course of action was to act normal and be supportive.

All she'd wanted for eight long months was to be included and valued in planning this wedding, and maybe it took a big nasty fight for Daisy to take a step back and consider that.

For now? Hair, makeup, and love. Today should be an exciting day for both of them, she reminded herself.

"Can I get you some champagne, Gloria? We have Veuve." She lifted a slender shoulder. "A little bubbly with your baby?"

Gloria glanced at Daisy, laughing softly. "Sure, why not?"

Trisha hustled away to the back room, leaving Daisy and Gloria alone for a few minutes.

"So, do you know what you want for hair and makeup?" Gloria asked. "I'm sure they can do anything you could dream of at this place. It's, like, Hollywood level. How fun for you."

But Daisy didn't smile back. Instead, she turned to

the mirror, looking at her beautiful, natural face, dotted with freckles. "Linda set it all up already, apparently."

Gloria frowned. "What do you mean?"

"She chose the hairstyle and the makeup and sent the salon all of the information prior to this trial." Daisy sank a little in the chair, her mouth turned down. "She says the look is going to be 'soft luxury glam with a vintage undertone.'"

"Oh, my." Gloria bit back a laugh, swallowing. "Here I was thinking it was just a matter of eyeshadow color."

"I wish." Daisy pressed her lips together, looking at Gloria for a few seconds as if she wanted to say more, but didn't, appearing soft and a little sad.

Had the wonder of the Whittingtons finally worn off? Was her sweet daughter coming...back? Hey, a mother could hope.

"Okay." Trisha returned from the back, with another equally beautiful and elegant young woman wearing waist-length braids and a linen maxi dress. "This is Bethany, our premiere wedding day hair stylist."

Daisy and Gloria both introduced themselves with warm handshakes as Trisha passed Gloria and Daisy crystal flutes filled to the brim with champagne.

"How festive!" Gloria said, lifting her glass.

But Daisy didn't touch hers.

"Shall we get started?" Bethany walked behind Daisy's chair, flipping her long, dark plaits over the backrest. "Beautiful hair, my dear. Is this your natural color?"

"Yes, it is," Daisy replied, smiling kindly into the mirror. "I've only ever dyed it once, in, like, eighth grade.

Remember, Mom?" She caught Gloria's gaze in the mirror, suddenly looking very young and like that sweet little angel who'd been glued to her side for twenty years.

"How could I forget?" Gloria laughed and shook her head. "You wanted dark auburn, as I recall, so we hit up Walgreens and picked a box out."

"No!" Bethany gasped dramatically as she sectioned out Daisy's hair. "Not a box dye."

"Oh, yes." Gloria sipped her champagne, warmed by the fizzy drink and the dear memories. "It was a nightmare."

Daisy laughed, too. "It sure was. I ended up with this horrible purply red atrocity."

Gloria nodded. "It was bad. There were tears. But... we got through it." She held Daisy's gaze a few beats. "We get through everything together."

Her daughter's eyes brightened. "Yeah, we do."

Gloria felt her whole heart melt at the silent connection they shared. Relieved and hopeful, she settled back to sip and observe.

Trisha swiped swatches of makeup onto Daisy's face to get a color match, rummaging through a giant cart of foundations.

"So, Miss Bride-To-Be." Bethany patted Daisy's head. "I hear we're doing a voluminous fishtail updo with extra-long, curled side pieces and spiral tendrils in the back."

Spiral tendrils? Voluminous updo? None of this sounded like Daisy, who always wore her hair in natural soft waves with the occasional half ponytail.

But who was Gloria to question it? No one could

deny that Linda Whittington had elegant taste, so surely her hair and makeup preferences would reflect that.

"I guess." Daisy shrugged. "My fiancé's Mom sort of picked out the style that she's going for, so we'll just roll with it."

And, Gloria assumed, she was paying for it all, which had to cost a fortune with this place.

"Okay, sounds good." Trisha laid out a display of various makeup brushes and sponges and tools. "I also have all the preferences that were submitted prior to your trial appointment as far as makeup goes. Sounds like we're doing big Hollywood glam with a smokey eye and heavy bronzed contour."

"Sure." Daisy threw her hands up and laughed. "Let's do it."

As the process got underway, Gloria finally stopped thinking about her mother and the canceled appointment with the PI in Destin. She even let herself stop thinking about all of the harsh words that were exchanged when she and Daisy fought the other day.

Here and now, she simply wanted to lean into this special day. There was no Linda, no exclusive, high-end wedding planner, just mother and daughter doing a beauty trial together.

After about an hour of talking about Daisy's over-the-top four-hundred-guest wedding and how she'd met Kyle and all the usual small talk, her hair and makeup were finished. And they were...

Hideous.

A giant mass of curls swallowed Daisy's entire head,

with long tendrils falling around her shoulders. Her face was caked in heavy makeup that completely hid all of her naturally beautiful features.

She looked like someone else entirely, and Gloria truly had no idea what to say as she stared at her daughter, blinking in shock.

"Wow." Gloria cleared her throat, setting down the now empty champagne flute on the side table and forcing a smile. "It's quite the look."

Daisy slowly turned to face the mirror, her jaw falling slack as she looked at the bird's nest of hair and black eye shadow. "Oh, my gosh."

Gloria held her breath for a moment, having no clue what Daisy was about to say next.

Her opinion wasn't the one that mattered. If Daisy loved this look, then this was her wedding look.

Daisy stared for a few more seconds, and then did something Gloria never expected in a million years.

She burst out laughing. "It's awful! Mom, look at me. I look like a raccoon with a terrible wig!"

Laughter bubbled up in Gloria's chest as she got up and walked over to the seat and mirror to get a better look at Daisy.

"Well..." Trisha pressed her lips together. "We followed Mrs. Whittington's exact instructions to a T."

"It's true," Bethany chimed in, wrapping up her curling iron and shaking her head. "Can't say it's my favorite look I've ever done, but our job is to follow instructions."

"No, no." Daisy shook her head. "You guys are

awesome and did exactly what she told you. It's just..." She dropped her voice to a whisper, the laughter and smile fading from her made-up face as Daisy looked up at her mom. "I hate it."

Gloria's motherly instinct sensed Daisy's need for support and guidance, her mom-dar blaring loudly in her mind. "Trisha, Bethany, do you think you guys could give us a few minutes while we talk all this over?"

"Of course." The stylists nodded and smiled, walking out of the room and closing the door behind them, leaving Daisy and Gloria alone.

"Mom." Daisy locked eyes with her mother, the thick black rim of eyeliner distorting her expression. "What am I going to do?"

"You're going to choose different hair and makeup styles and book another trial," Gloria said calmly. "It's not like today is the day. You can change anything before the wedding. There's still time."

Daisy pursed her lips, turning to face the mirror and cringing at her own reflection. "I can't, though."

"What do you mean? Of course you can. Look up some hairstyles and makeup looks on Pinterest or whatever and have them give it another go. I'm sure they have availability to do another—"

"No, it's not that." Daisy's eyes dropped downwards, revealing an even darker and thicker layer of eyeshadow than Gloria had realized. "I can't go against Linda's vision. This is how she wants me to look."

Gloria felt herself tense up as irritation at the insufferable woman skittered up her spine. "Surely you can tell her you didn't like the beauty selections she made. It's *your* wedding day, Daisy."

"Uh-uh." She shook her head, glancing back up with tears in her black-rimmed eyes. "It's not, Mom. It's not my wedding day." More tears fell, streaking some dark makeup down Daisy's cheek.

Gloria crouched down next to the salon chair and placed her hand on top of her daughter's. "Dais..."

"It's her day." She sniffed, wiping her eyes, smudging black goo. "Not mine. She's made every decision, had every idea, picked out every last little detail."

"I thought you liked that she was planning it," Gloria said gently. "You told me you loved her vision and that she was handling everything."

"It's gotten so out of hand, Mom." She sniffled. "So, so out of hand. I don't know about eighty percent of the people on the guest list. Maybe more! I hate my dress, I don't understand the food, she insisted on black tablecloths, which I think feels like a funeral, I've never met the minister...I mean, for heaven's sake, we're having the rehearsal dinner on a *yacht,* and I get seasick! None of this is for me. None of it."

Gloria's heart ached as she reached for her sobbing daughter and wrapped her in loving arms. "Oh, honey."

"And now, the whole thing is so far gone, the wedding is in three months, and I hate everything about it. I mean, look at me!" She turned to face the mirror, crying at the horrible hairstyle and streaks of black makeup running down her face. "Couldn't they use waterproof?" she asked on a blubbery laugh.

"Seriously," Gloria agreed. "What do *you* want for hair and makeup?"

"Something simple," she answered without hesitation. "With my hair in pretty waves and my makeup natural. I wanted to get married at the beach, with people I love, with sunflowers. Which of course I couldn't have because Linda declared them 'too pedestrian.'" She looked skyward, laughing a bit through her tears.

Gloria shut her eyes, shaking her head as she processed Daisy's words.

The fact was, since the wedding planning had begun and the role of Linda became clear, Gloria had anticipated this breakdown from her daughter. But as the months passed and the plans were made, Gloria had started to think this realization would never come.

She'd truly thought she'd lost Daisy to the Whittington family and the luxurious lifestyle, and as much as it broke her heart to see these tears on her daughter's sweet face, Gloria couldn't deny the well of gratitude and hope that sprang up in her chest.

Daisy—kind, authentic, independent, down-to-earth Daisy—was not gone after all.

"Okay, well, where do you want to go from here?" Gloria asked. "I could talk to Linda, if you want. I'm not afraid of her."

Well, maybe a little, but she'd go into battle if it was for the sake of Daisy's happiness.

"I don't know." Daisy huffed out a sigh, toying with the tight, spiral curls that fell around her face. "She'll just bulldoze you. She's paying a small fortune for this event, and that means she can do whatever she wants. I tried to get on board with everything and embrace it all, but this..." She gestured at her hair and face. "This won't do."

"No, it won't." Gloria patted her shoulder. "But we can figure something out."

Daisy nodded, sighing into the comfort.

"Look, let's find you some better hair and makeup ideas and schedule a new trial," Gloria said. "And I know you don't like your giant, frilly ball gown, but I bet we can get you a second dress to change into after the ceremony. And as for the tablecloths, I hear what you're saying about black being depressing, but if we can add some pops of color in the flowers—"

"Mom." Daisy leveled her gaze with Gloria's, her lip quivering a bit as her eyes filled once again. "I am so, so sorry."

Gloria's throat tightened. "Daisy..."

"I was so awful to you. I've treated you horribly throughout this entire thing, and I feel just terrible about it. I don't even know who I am anymore. The way I've been acting...I'm a certified...B-word. I can't believe I said such mean things to you and pushed you away and made you feel like you can't be a part of this." She wiped her eyes. "Honestly, I wish we'd done this whole thing together. I really, really messed up badly."

Gloria stood up, pulling Daisy from the chair to give her the most loving embrace they'd shared in months. She felt a few tears slip down her cheeks as she embraced her daughter tightly. "I forgive you, honey."

"You shouldn't, though," Daisy said, her voice

muffled as her face was buried in Gloria's shoulder. "I acted unforgivably. I don't know how to fix it."

Gloria pulled away, wiping Daisy's tears and holding her beautiful face in her hands. "It's okay, Dais. I'm just glad you finally broke down and found yourself again."

"I got lost in all of it."

"I know you did. It's okay, it happens." She patted her daughter's damp cheek. "I'm not going anywhere."

"This wedding is going to be awful." Daisy laughed, shaking her head.

"We'll do what we can. Have you tried talking to Kyle about any of this?"

Kyle, of course, was a completely separate issue. No, Gloria was not terribly fond of the entitled trust-fund kid her daughter had chosen to marry, but that was an argument for another day.

Daisy's shoulders sank. "She's his mother. He says that this is her dream, and I should basically just shut up and let her do what she wants because she's paying for it all."

Of course that was his response. What kind of husband would he be? Selfish? Thoughtless? And a mama's boy to boot.

Not now, Gloria. Not the time.

She swallowed her anger and focused on this breakthrough with Daisy. "Well, we can figure things out together, okay?"

"You'll help me, Mom? Even after how awful I was to you?"

Gloria squeezed her daughter's hand. "Forgiven and

forgotten, sweetheart. But I really think you should talk to Linda."

Daisy tensed up and shook her head.

"Just hear me out. She is going to be your mother-in-law. That's like a second mom. I know that she's a little intimidating, I get that, but she clearly does care about you. At least I think she does. She's just flexing her muscles over this wedding, but your relationship with her has to last a lifetime."

Daisy groaned as if the very idea of that pained her.

"I do think you can have an honest conversation with her, Daisy. Maybe you can discuss some of these wedding details and find a way to compromise so it feels a bit more 'you.'"

"I don't know..." Daisy glanced away, her expression worried.

"Honey, if she's going to be in your life, you're going to have to learn how to handle her and communicate with her."

"Okay." Daisy took a deep breath and nodded, squeezing her eyes shut. "I'll try. But first...I love you, Mommy."

Gloria let the words she'd been dying to hear for eight months wash over her. "I love you, too, baby. Oh, and when you get that goop off your face and fix your hair, let's get coffee. I have to turn your world upside down."

Daisy's brow raised. "I like the sound of that."

Chapter Six

Vanessa

"I'm so glad you two were able to talk openly like that." Vanessa turned in the passenger seat of Gloria's car, taking in the whole hair and makeup debacle story of the previous day and Daisy's change of heart. "I know things have been tense, and it's been so hard for you."

"This really felt like a turning point, Nessie." Glo let out a contented sigh as she sped along the highway to Destin, a million times happier than she had been these last few weeks. "I didn't realize just how much I needed it."

"You and Daisy have always been close," Vanessa said. "Much closer than you are with Jeremy."

"Pffft." She flicked her hand and let out a sad sigh. "You mean my son who hasn't called or texted in..." She rolled her eyes. "I honestly cannot remember the last time I heard from him."

"Does that bother you?" Vanessa asked. "You never talk about it."

"I keep telling myself he's in the middle of his baseball season at Boston College, and he's either traveling, practicing, or playing. Maybe even going to class. When he needs a parent, he's got Christian up there and they're close."

"Will he come home for the summer?" Vanessa asked, hoping for a chance to get to know her nephew. They'd met, of course, but all she really knew about the young man is that he was a baseball superstar, destined for the pros like his father, Christian Bennett, who'd played for the Red Sox.

"I don't know," Gloria said on a sigh. "Highly doubtful. His life is up there, although to be honest, I don't feel like I even know much about that life."

"I thought you guys were pretty close," Vanessa said.

"We were until this year, his junior year. He just seemed to drift off, but he's twenty-one now, so I guess he doesn't need his mommy anymore, sad to say."

"That's the way of things," Vanessa mused, looking left and right at the gorgeous scenery. "Nice drive up here. I'm glad you had to reschedule with the PI so that I could join."

"I hated the idea of doing this without you." Gloria placed a loving hand on her sister's arm. "I don't even know what our goal is here, but I didn't want to start this process alone, that's for sure."

"Well, you don't have to." Vanessa flipped through the tote bag in her lap, which contained every possible document they could find that would pertain to the mystery of their mother—the letters, the weird will, some old pictures they'd scared up. "Do you think this guy is going to be able to figure anything out about her whereabouts?"

Gloria shrugged. "I have no idea. But we can't do nothing after finding out that our entire motherless childhood was a total lie."

"Things could have been so different. I mean, can you imagine?" Vanessa closed her eyes. "Maybe Dad wouldn't have kicked me out when I got pregnant. I probably wouldn't have given Emily up for adoption. We would have had a mother, Glo. She was alive, walking this earth, the entire time."

"I know. I still can't believe she went chasing some... some acting dream when she had two kids!"

Vanessa pressed her lips together, knowing that people did run away—they ran away from Bill Young, like she did. Nothing in those letters indicated that she was mad at him, or afraid of him, but they really didn't know everything, did they.

"Maybe not all the blame falls on her shoulders," Vanessa said softly.

Gloria shot her a look. "You read the letters, Nessie. She didn't leave because she didn't love her husband. She left because she loved herself more than anything."

"I'm just glad I'm here now." Vanessa squeezed her sister's hand, not wanting to argue. "Hey, she'd only be seventy-two. Easily still alive. And if we find her, we get answers."

Gloria sighed. "Just be prepared not to like those answers, Ness."

"I know." Vanessa craned her neck to see the navigation screen on Glo's phone. "How much time do we have left?"

"Not long, and we'll be ten minutes early."

"Good." Vanessa leaned back in her seat, kicking her feet up onto the dash. "We'll have time to gather our thoughts and materials for...what's his name again?"

"Jason Chang."

"Right."

"I say we spend these last few minutes *not* thinking about Mom or the PI or the car accident that never happened." Gloria glanced at her sister. "Let's talk about other stuff."

"Like Daisy's wedding?" Vanessa asked.

"Like Noah Ellison."

Vanessa cringed, groaning loudly as she buried her face in her hands. "It's a total trainwreck, Glo. He wants nothing to do with me. And Emily is all jazzed about meeting her birth father and getting to know him, but you know he's not going to stick around. Which, of course, is entirely my fault. And, honestly, maybe that's why I'm not as mad at Violet as you are. We don't know the whole story."

"Don't beat yourself up over mistakes you made as a teenager, Ness," Gloria said. "Look what you have with Emily and this new chapter of life. It all worked out the way it was supposed to."

Vanessa chewed her lip, knowing that Glo's sentiment was absolutely right, and she did truly appreciate her sister's support.

But it just wasn't that simple.

"It's kind of hard to ignore my past mistakes when they're right in front of me, standing in the doorway of

Young at Heart, building a relationship with my daughter —*our* daughter," she corrected, still uncertain of how much or little Noah even wanted to be Emily's father.

"I get that, I really do," Gloria said. "Maybe it wouldn't hurt to not dance around the elephant in the room, you know? Lay it all out there and just talk to him about it."

"I tried!" Vanessa exclaimed. "The other day, when he came into the store to pick Emily up so they could go handle divorce paperwork, we had a few moments alone."

"And you brought all of this up to him?" Gloria's eyes widened with surprise. "How did it go? And excuse me, but *how* could you not tell me this?"

Vanessa felt her heart sink at the memory of her failed apology and Noah's cold rejection of her attempt at the most basic reconciliation.

"Because it didn't go well. At all. It went, like, horribly bad."

"Oh, shoot. Nessie. What happened?"

"I told him that I was sorry. I pushed past the tension and awkwardness and told him that I felt bad about how I treated him back in those days, that I was selfish and a bit impulsive, and I was sorry." She shrugged, slumping down in the passenger seat. "But he basically responded with, 'No apology will ever be enough, and I'll never forgive you.'"

Glo was quiet for a few moments, her eyes on the road for a good long minute or so.

"What?" Nessie prodded, studying her older sister's

expression, which was tough to read. "What are you thinking?"

"Well, look, honey. I love you. You know I'm always on your side, one hundred percent of the time."

Why did she not like the sound of that? "What's the but?" she asked.

"*But* I don't know if an apology like that is really going to cut it." Gloria turned to face her for a quick second, giving a sympathetic smile.

"I really meant it, Glo. It was sincere."

"I don't doubt that! I know you feel terrible about hurting him and I know regrets about those years have haunted you for a long, long time. But I've been around Rosemary Beach since you left. I was here for all those years when you'd disappeared, and you know I spent a lot of time with Cricket."

Vanessa's mind flashed back to a conversation she'd had with Cricket a couple of weeks ago, where she'd gotten a glimpse of the depth of pain she'd caused not only Noah, but his whole family.

Suddenly, her eyes stung with tears and her throat tightened. "Glo, I...I've made so many mistakes. I came here searching for forgiveness from Dad on his deathbed, and I didn't get it. And now, I'm not getting it from Noah, either."

Gloria let out a soft sigh, reaching over to give her sister's hand another squeeze. "Cricket forgave you. In fact, she adores you."

Vanessa laughed through her sniffles as she wiped a tear. "For reasons I do not understand."

"Because she sees how amazing you are. It takes a really, really strong woman to do what you did. To come home, and mend fences and rebuild your life after everything that happened when you left this place. That was not easy, Nessie. But you did it for yourself, and for Emily. And you've given me an enormous gift in the process."

Vanessa felt a swell of gratitude in her heart. Thank God she'd come home. "Despite all the terrible choices I've made, coming home was my best one yet."

"I couldn't agree more." Glo smiled. "Give it some time with Noah. He's got a good heart, and as much as he wants to act like the super serious big-city lawyer who's too focused on his life to go near yours, he can't deny his own heart."

Vanessa shook her head, not very convinced. "Of course, I agree that Noah has a good heart. I just know how badly I broke it. Hence him wanting to stay far, far away from me."

Her sister lifted a shoulder. "With Emily in the picture, though? All of that could change. And your apology was just a start. You broke the ice, which is good."

"But it's not enough."

"No, sister." Gloria laughed softly. "It is not enough. But like I said, give it time. I never thought Daisy would come around and go back to her old self, and now I feel like it might be starting to happen. People can surprise you."

"They sure can." Vanessa glanced out the window as

they entered the gorgeous, beachside city of Destin. "Like how Mom surprised us by not actually being dead."

Glo snorted. "Let's go get some answers, shall we?"

Jason Chang worked out of a small, private office in a small industrial park tucked away in a wooded area of Destin. They waited in a tiny reception area after texting him that they'd arrived, and he'd said he'd be right out.

While they sat in gray leather chairs with sunlight streaming in, Gloria shifted a few times, visibly uncomfortable.

"What's wrong?" Vanessa asked her.

She crossed and uncrossed her legs. "Are we sure we want to do this? Maybe we should let sleeping, dead or alive dogs die. Because being rejected by her *again* could really, really hurt us, Nessie. Even more than those letters."

Vanessa stared out the window, not seeing the sun or palm trees, but a glimpse into her future.

"We've spent our whole lives wondering about her, Glo. Now we know, at least a little bit, what she was like and why she left. And if she's still around, we need to find her. We'll always regret it if we don't. Besides, don't you think we were meant to find those letters? If Dad didn't want us to find them, he would have destroyed them."

Glo nodded slowly. "I hadn't considered that but, yes,

you're absolutely right. Maybe some part of him wanted us to know that she wasn't really dead."

Just then, a man walked out and greeted them with a warm smile. He was stocky and young, stretching his hand to shake Vanessa's first.

"I'm Jason Chang. It's great to meet you."

After quick introductions, they followed him to a sunny office down the hall, where he sat behind a large, clean desk and they took the two guest chairs.

Looking around at what could have been an accountant's office, Vanessa clutched her tote bag, her mind racing.

"So." He placed his hands on the desk and smiled at each of them. "Gloria, we spoke on the phone a few days ago. You're here about your mother, yes?"

"Yes, that's right." Gloria nodded. "After our father passed away about five weeks ago, we discovered some letters she'd written to him over a period of about thirty years. The thing is, they start almost the day we were told by our father that she was killed in a car accident."

He nodded, his expression sympathetic. "So, you think she faked her own death, and your father went along with it."

"Exactly," Vanessa said. "She says in her letters that she was following a dream to be an actress and lived in New York and Los Angeles. I guess what we really want to know is if she might still be alive. She'd be seventy-two."

"I can understand wanting know that," he said. "Are you willing to share the letters, or copies of them?"

"Of course." Vanessa dug out the stuffed, open envelope from her bag and set it on the desk, sliding it across the wooden surface. "There are almost fifty, written from 1979 to 2014."

He flicked his brows, maybe surprised by the volume. "And the last one?"

"No explanation," Gloria said. "She said she had a callback or audition or something and then we heard nothing."

He looked at the top letter. "Violet Young?"

"Well, we think her legal name was Clarinda, and her maiden name was Smith," Gloria said. "We unearthed a second will my father had signed before he died giving his property to Clarinda Smith."

"How did you figure out she was one and the same?" he asked, flipping open a laptop to type as he talked, presumably taking notes.

"I found their old wedding invitation in a scrapbook." Vanessa reached back into the tote bag and pulled it out, sealed in a plastic bag. "Where it said her name was Clarinda 'Violet' Smith. So Violet was a nickname, but we didn't know that."

"We didn't know anything about her," Gloria added. "I was five and Vanessa was a baby when she took off."

"Interesting." He typed rapidly, then looked at Vanessa with a curious frown. "So, he left the property to his wife, in her legal, maiden name?"

"Yes." They nodded.

"His wife who, according to your father—"

"Bill," Vanessa supplied.

"According to Bill, his wife passed away in a car accident in 1979." He narrowed his gaze, typing some more. "So if she's still alive, he would have known that."

Vanessa and Gloria shared a look, then nodded. Vanessa could see the pain in her sister's eyes. Dad had been so complicit in this lie, and that had to hurt her after all the years Gloria had taken care of him.

"Did you all live in Rosemary Beach at the time of your mother's alleged death?" He frowned. "Did it even exist then?"

"It was Inlet Beach, actually," Gloria said. "We didn't live there, no. When she 'died'"—she air-quoted and added a look that said just how she felt about all this—"we were in a small town in Georgia. Then we moved to what became Rosemary Beach to start over."

"Gotcha." More typing, more thinking. "Never found a death certificate, I take it."

They both shook their heads.

"Does she have other relatives? Sisters or cousins? Anyone else she might have stayed in touch with over the years?"

"We just were never told a lot about her," Gloria said.

"Have you searched any online databases, looked through IMDB for her names, since you said she was an actress?"

"We haven't done much of anything except come here," Vanessa told him. "If you could do all that..."

"I will," he assured them. "Leave me any documentation you have and let's get all our information exchanged and set up payment."

Vanessa handed over the entire tote bag, which contained the very, very small amount of evidence they had of their mother's life.

"Thank you." Jason reached into the bag and started pulling out the meager pieces of Violet's life that they still had. "I'm going to get started on this right away. In the meantime, if you find anything else out, anything at all, please call me. No detail is too small, and nothing is irrelevant."

"Sounds good, Jason." Gloria nodded. "Thank you."

He looked from one to the other. "I can find her," he said with soft confidence. "I'm pretty good at this. The question is, when I do, what do you want to do about it?"

"Meet her," Vanessa said.

"We don't know yet," Gloria said at the very same moment.

He gave a kind smile. "While I work, you should give that some thought, but I will tell you, this is not unusual."

"It's not?" Gloria asked.

"People orchestrate their deaths for many different reasons, and, oddly enough, spouses and family members go along with it. Maybe for financial reasons, maybe for protection, maybe for emotional reasons. But believe me, I've seen things like this before."

After they signed a contract and gave him a retainer, they said goodbye and walked out into the blinding sunshine to their car.

Vanessa turned to Gloria, who pulled sunglasses out and slid them over her face so fast, it made her wonder if her sister was fighting tears.

"You okay?" she asked Gloria.

"'People orchestrate their deaths for many reasons,'" she quoted, echoing Jason's tone. "Crazy, mean, thoughtless and selfish people," she said.

"Also desperate," Vanessa added.

They stood for a moment, both of them entirely uncertain where their mother fell on that scale. With Jason's help, they might soon find out.

Chapter Seven

Emily

Emily couldn't remember the last time she'd had a pedicure, but it was something she knew she'd never, ever take for granted. When she was married to Doug, he never wanted her to spend money on things like nails and hair—he didn't want her to have that kind of freedom. Then, after she ran away from him, she didn't have the money for a luxury like this.

But today, with Young at Heart completely ready to open and Vanessa gone off to Destin with Aunt Glo, Emily accepted Daisy's spontaneous invitation to meet for mani-pedis in town.

The two cousins, only five years apart, had quickly become good friends, and Emily was grateful for the chance to be a big sister of sorts to Daisy as she navigated her early twenties and complicated upcoming wedding.

They'd picked their colors, got pedi seats next to each other, and were leaning close while the bowls filled, ready to catch up—starting with a quiet discussion on the reason Gloria and Vanessa had gone to Destin.

"The whole thing is so insane." Daisy lowered her feet into the hot water basin, turning to face Emily to continue the chat. "We might have another grandmother! What craziness."

"It's bizarre," Emily agreed.

"I mean, that story is so deeply ingrained in our family history, I can't wrap my head around the fact that my Grandpa Bill lied about it." She let out a noisy sigh. "Sometimes you really don't know people until it's too late, huh?"

Like her ex-husband, Emily thought as she placed her feet in the hot water, moaning with pleasure. Instead of bringing Doug into the conversation, she just nodded.

"I hope they figure it out," Daisy said. "But then again, we don't know this woman. What if she's awful? Maybe we don't want her in our lives. Maybe she doesn't want to be. Or maybe she did die since she wrote the last letter. Who knows?"

Emily shrugged. "I just don't want them to get hurt."

"Agreed. My mom's been hurt enough lately," she said under her breath.

Emily frowned as she studied Daisy's pretty features. "What do you mean?"

"Come on, Emily." Daisy shot her a look, glaring up through thick, dark lashes. "You know full well how awful I've been to her about the wedding and…in general."

Emily wasn't sure how to respond to that. She couldn't deny that Daisy had caused some serious friction with her mother, but she wasn't sure she knew the extent of it. Plus, Emily liked Daisy a lot, and definitely saw good in her.

"I know things have been tough between you guys," she said, keeping it vague.

"Understatement," Daisy said with an eye-roll. "But..." She held up her finger. "We had a bit of a breakthrough, I'm happy to say. I brought her to my hair and makeup trial instead of Linda, and we talked."

"I bet that gesture went a really long way, especially after the fight you guys had last week."

"Well, it wasn't exactly what I'd hoped it would be, but I do think my mom and I got somewhere. I finally felt like I could just be real with her, and I sort of broke down about Linda and the entire thing. I told her how hard it's been, and how I got lost in all of it, but now I'm starting to realize what's really happening."

Emily sighed softly. "It's that bad, huh?"

"Atrocious."

As the nail techs started to work, Daisy whispered a horror story about Linda's choice for hair and makeup, and how that was just one of dozens of decisions the woman was making that were sure to ruin the day.

"She sounds absolutely awful, Daisy."

"She is. If I let her, she'll suck the joy out of this wedding."

"Then you can't let her." Emily said. "Although I'm sure that isn't easy."

Daisy snorted. "You have no idea. I just keep having this awful feeling in the pit of my stomach. Like, I know this isn't what a bride is supposed to feel like three months before her wedding."

Oh, boy.

Emily swallowed, glancing in the other direction to hide her expression from Daisy.

She remembered that feeling. She remembered that Doug yelled at her more frequently as the wedding approached. His temper freaked her out, but she chalked it up to stress because she didn't want to call the whole thing off.

But the closer it got, the more she had the same feeling in the pit of her stomach.

Was it right to tell Daisy that? Surely, she had some pre-wedding jitters. After all, her problems were with Linda, not Kyle.

But then, Kyle wasn't exactly a fan favorite around the family.

"Where is Kyle in all of this?" she asked, playing off the question as casually as possible. "I mean, have you talked to him about these feelings? Could he maybe have a conversation with his mother and tell her to back off a bit?"

"As if," Daisy said glumly, tilting her head back in the leather massage chair. "Kyle will stand up to his mother when hell freezes over. Not happening."

Emily wrinkled her nose, watching the nail tech paint smooth, even strokes of turquoise on her big toenail. "Does he know you're having a hard time, though?"

"I don't know." She shifted and switched feet. "He's very preoccupied, and last time I tried to talk to him about his mother, he totally blew up on me."

Emily's stomach rolled. "Blew up how?"

"Just yelled and cursed and all of it." Daisy sighed. "It sucks that we fought, but I guess I sort of instigated it. I mean, I wasn't exactly sweet in the conversation, so, you know."

"He should never yell at you, Daisy." Emily turned to face her cousin, her voice serious. "He shouldn't treat you like that."

Daisy gave a casual shrug. "It's just a fight. Couples fight."

"Yes, they do, but you just..." Emily paused, digging for the right words. "You have to be so careful, okay? He should be doing everything in his power to make you feel loved and cherished right now. And always. Because men..." She swallowed and forced herself to finish the thought. "The wrong man, I mean, can be awful."

Daisy went silent for a while, watching her toenails get painted, her growing anxiety palpable.

"I don't know what to do," she finally admitted. "I love him so much, but the stress of all of this and his psycho mom has just made everything bad. I've ruined my relationship with my mom, and I know I can fix it, but will it all happen again? And with Kyle...well, do I just resign myself to the fact that Linda will always come first?"

No, no, and no, Emily thought, but chose her words very, very carefully.

"You can most definitely fix it." Emily reached her hand over to Daisy's pedicure chair to underscore her point with a gentle touch. "First of all, you and Aunt Glo are tight, and you already started the reconciliation with that hair and makeup day."

"Yeah, that's true." She huffed out a breath. "I hope. But the whole wedding, and Linda, and Kyle...I don't know, Emily. I'm kind of freaking out. I'm going to take my mom's advice and try to have an honest conversation with Linda, but I'm low-key terrified. Maybe not low-key. I'm fully terrified."

"I'm sure she's intimidating, but it's a good idea. Maybe she'll listen to you."

Daisy cocked her head and gave a "get real" look. "She doesn't listen to anyone about anything."

Emily took a deep breath, thinking hard about the best advice to give her younger cousin in this situation. Besides telling her to run for the hills, because she knew that her own trauma and horrific marriage was definitely giving her a bias.

After pondering for a few minutes, Emily turned to her cousin. "Is there anyone else you can ask for advice about this? Maybe someone who's not so close to the whole situation—someone with a little more of an outsider's perspective? Like a friend or a..."

"My dad," Daisy blurted out, her eyelids shuttering closed as she said the words. "I need to talk to my dad."

Emily's knowledge of Daisy's father—Aunt Glo's ex-husband, Christian Bennett—was limited, to say the least. Baseball, Boston, and...that was it.

"I honestly don't think I've ever heard you mention your father," Emily said.

Daisy shrugged. "We hardly talk. He's Jeremy's go-to parent, Mom is mine."

"Was it hard when they got divorced?"

Another shrug, leading Emily to surmise that Daisy was pretty good at sliding over emotional things if she had to.

"Mom had to stay here to take care of Grandpa Bill. My dad wanted to follow his dreams and play for Boston." She made a face. "Oh, these people and their dream-following. Can't anyone just be satisfied and stay put?"

Emily gave a sad smile. "Sometimes, staying put isn't an option, but I know what you mean. From everything I heard, the divorce wasn't ugly." She grimaced. "Unlike mine."

"It was...not bad, I suppose," Daisy said. "I was young, and they protected me."

"Would you talk to your dad?" Emily asked. "And do you think he could help you?"

"I don't know. I see him once a year out of pure obligation, and we talk on the phone maybe once a month. If that."

It still sounded like a lot to Emily, who'd only met her biological father a few days ago, and wasn't even sure if he'd want much to do with her once this divorce was over and he headed back to Miami.

"It's whatever," Daisy said. "It was just sort of the way things happened when we were kids. It was always Dad and Jeremy, and Mom and me. Like two separate pairings. Dad and Jeremy lived and breathed baseball.

Dad was basically in charge of, like, the entire AAU league and their life was spent at tournaments. When they were local, Mom and I had to go." She groaned, rolling her eyes at the memory. "Want to know the two worst words in the English language?"

"Sure."

"Double header."

Emily laughed. "So, his attention was pretty focused on Jeremy, I take it."

"Slight understatement, but yes." Daisy chuckled, pushing some brown hair behind her ears and meeting Emily's gaze. "So, it left Mom and me together twenty-four-seven. We became best buds and were inseparable, just like Dad and Jeremy. When they split up, that's sort of how the family split. Right down the middle, half and half."

Emily suddenly understood all the more why it was so tragic that Gloria and Daisy had been fighting these past few months. "When was the last time you talked to your dad?"

Daisy pursed her lips, thinking about the question. "A few weeks ago, I guess. It's usually just a surface-level chat." She plucked at a thread on her jean shorts, her gaze downcast. "I'm not having him walk me down the aisle."

"You're not?"

"Nope. I'm walking alone." Daisy lifted her gaze back toward Emily. "We're just not close, and it feels silly to pretend."

"I guess I can understand that. But who knows? Maybe he'd be a good person to talk to about all of this.

He is your dad, after all, and he loves you and knows you."

Daisy nodded, not arguing that.

"I never had a father at all," Emily said softly. "So if it were me, I'd take the opportunity to get a dad perspective and keep that relationship as strong as you can. Plus, he should know the hornet's nest he's walking into with this wedding."

Laughing, Daisy nodded. "Fair enough." She reached her knuckles between the two chairs for a tap. "I'll call your Uncle Christian."

Emily laughed. "So much family I never knew I even had."

"Seriously," Daisy agreed, studying her for a minute. "You know what's funny and maybe a little sad?"

"Do I want to hear something sad?"

"Not sad, but...if I weren't getting married, I'd suggest we rent a place together. We're too old to live with our mothers and we could have a blast on the beach."

Emily's heart folded at the idea, wishing Daisy hadn't planted it because...that would be a dream.

"Oh, well, in another life, I guess," Emily said.

Daisy smiled. "Thanks for your help, *cuz*. You're going to help me get through this ridiculous festouche of a wedding."

Emily cracked up at the word. "It's that over the top, huh?"

"Dude." She gave a look. "Multiple ice sculptures. Flowers imported from Europe. Four hundred people.

And the dress..." Daisy laughed through a mock cry, shaking her head. "The dress is awful."

They spent the rest of the time talking about the wedding, the boutique opening on Monday, and Daisy meeting Noah...and all the things cousins and girlfriends talked about.

Emily simply couldn't remember enjoying a pedicure that much.

Later that afternoon, Emily was back at Young at Heart. Somehow, four days before the grand opening, just about everything was done and ready to roll.

Vanessa was in and out with her final finishing touches, including another jewelry stand and a pretty shoe rack display.

Emily was in the back office, tapping away on the computer, verifying all of the revenue projections for their first quarter as an LLC and entering expenses into a profit-and-loss spreadsheet.

She was deep in her element, and Vanessa would be back any minute with those last couple of touches for the store.

The sound of the front door opening hardly registered. She figured that Vanessa was back with what promised to be the world's cutest shoe rack.

"I'll be right out to help you!" Emily called through the open office door, hoping her mom could hear her from the main store.

She finished up and saved her document before hurrying through the back hallway to give Vanessa a hand.

But Emily was stopped in her tracks when she saw that the person who had walked into Young at Heart and made the front door chime was not, in fact, her mother.

"Reed?" She drew back, brushing her hair behind her ears and angling her head in confusion. "What are you doing here?"

"Sorry, is it not a good time?" He lifted a shoulder, glancing back toward the front door. "It was open, but I can come back later, if—"

"No, no." She smiled and shook her head, brushing the wrinkles out of her sundress. "It's a good time. I'm just working on some bookkeeping stuff in the back before our official opening on Monday."

"This place looks awesome." Reed looked around with genuine enthusiasm. His dark brown hair brushed the top of his collar as he lifted his gaze upward to admire the chandeliers Emily and Vanessa had picked out. "It's quite a vibe."

"Thank you." Emily locked her hands behind her back and stepped closer to him, gazing at the clothing store through his eyes. "It's been so much fun getting it all set up. Mostly cosmetic stuff, since it was already a retail store."

"So just the fun part, no construction involved."

She laughed softly. "Yes, basically."

"That's awesome." He nodded, brushing a hand

against his jaw like he was...a little nervous. Why? "This is going to be very successful here."

"Fingers crossed," she said brightly, waiting a beat for an explanation as to why he was there. When none came, she took a step closer. "So, what brings you into the boutique? Still interested in that floral maxi?"

He laughed, the smile reaching his espresso eyes. "Actually, I wanted to ask you something."

Emily leaned against the register counter. "Sure, what's up?"

"Would you maybe want to grab dinner sometime?"

Holy...cow. Was Reed Collins, a.k.a. R.C. Anderson a.k.a. world-famous bestselling author, asking Emily *on a date* right now?

And why did that give her a kind of unholy thrill? She wasn't legally divorced yet, so was it acceptable to go on a date? Because, dang, she liked the idea.

He knew she was getting a divorce, because she'd mentioned it at the restaurant, but, whoa. Reed Collins didn't let any moss grow. Of course, he didn't know the ugly circumstances, that she was escaping an abuser, so...

Oh, stop it, Emily. Just say yes.

"Um, sure, yes." She smiled, inching forward. "I'd love to."

Reed nodded like he was relieved. "Awesome, I'm glad to hear it. I really need to pick your brain."

Wait...what?

"About...something in particular?" she asked.

He shifted from one foot to the other, definitely

uncomfortable. "Well, the fact is, my series revolves around one main character—"

"Sam Steele," she answered. What did his book series have to do with their dinner?

"Yeah, that's right. You said you knew the books."

"Well, even if I hadn't, I'm pretty sure everyone knows the Sam Steele books, Reed. Do you forget that you're famous?" she asked on a laugh.

"Sometimes. But anyway, in the midst of trying to crack the case of a serial killer in Florida's Gulf Coast in my current book, Sam's getting a divorce. His wife, Alyssa, is leaving him because he's married to his work."

"That's sad," Emily remarked, still wondering where in the world this was going.

"So, anyway, I submitted the first ten chapters to my editor last week, and she came back with one massive note." He held up his hands to imitate scribbling across the air in front of him. "'Not. Enough. Emotion.' Sam is getting divorced and, evidently, it's not nearly emotional or sincere enough. I love the crime-fighting and bad guy catching. I kind of suck at the feely stuff. So that's where you come in."

"The feely stuff?"

"More or less." Reed gave an uncertain smile. "I kind of need a divorce expert."

Her heart dipped a little. "A lawyer?"

"No, a person going through a divorce. If you don't mind, I would really love to talk to you about what it feels like. I don't want to cross any boundaries, of course, but as a writer, it sometimes helps a lot to sit down with someone who has experienced the same thing as my character." He furrowed his brows. "Does that make sense?"

Emily felt a strange and unexpected punch to her gut.

Reed Collins didn't want to date her. He wanted to *interview* her. As a divorcee to help deepen his character development. It was a well-intentioned request and there was nothing wrong with it but, whoa, she was more disappointed than she should have been.

"Oh, um, yeah..." Emily shook her head, gathering herself and stifling the sinking feeling in her chest. "Of course, I'd love to help you."

"Thanks so much, Emily. I really appreciate it. I have your number from the whole laptop thing, so I'll text you and we can set something up over the weekend."

Emily nodded stiffly. "Sounds good."

"All right..." He jutted his chin toward the door. "I've got to go comb through more oceans of red scribbles in my poor, sad manuscript. I'll catch you later."

She gave a one-handed wave as he headed out the door, chimes ringing. "See ya."

As Emily walked back down the hallway to the office, she rolled her eyes at herself. How silly could she be, thinking this gorgeous, successful guy was interested in her romantically?

Plus, Noah was right in the concerns he'd expressed at the diner. It was way too soon for her to even think about getting involved with someone. Not to mention, someone who was only in town temporarily before he headed off to whatever setting was up next in the Sam Steele series.

She sighed, slumping back down at her computer. Emily had been given a tough hand in life, but this was by far the best things had ever been for her.

She had to remember that, and not screw it up by developing the worst possible thing that could happen right now...

A crush.

Except it might be too late.

Chapter Eight

Cricket

Once it was decided that Noah would remain in Rosemary Beach until Cricket's house was patched up and water free, she was all systems go in strategy development to get him to stay...permanently.

Now that he was here, surrounded by the wonderful people and undeniable charm of this town, she was determined to come up with an absolutely foolproof plan to show Noah why this was home, and home was where he belonged.

Not that crowded, loud metropolis filled with skyscrapers and nightclubs.

The flood was proof that she had God on her side, and...Cricket and God? That was quite the unstoppable team.

After staying up late into the night considering all her options, Cricket had developed an idea that was absolutely certain to soften Noah's heart and show him the true beauty of family and home.

And now? It was time to present that idea and make it happen. Her ticket to fixing her son's life and securing his future was only three weeks away, at the Class of 1997 annual celebration—the First Class Bash.

Which would be sponsored, for the first time ever, by the generous and thriving local business of Cricket's Beauty Salon.

As she strode down Main Street toward Amavida Coffee Roasters, Cricket mentally prepared her pitch but couldn't help but admire the scenery on her way.

Cricket never did get tired of this painfully adorable town, even if it hadn't grown "organically" like other small beach towns. None of them had European-inspired architecture with color and style brightening every street.

Striped awnings shaded the mullioned windows; picnic tables dotted the grassy areas for people to eat, sip, and enjoy the glorious weather and Gulf breezes.

But this morning, she couldn't dawdle and chat with some locals she recognized. She was on a mission to meet the small committee in charge of planning the First Class event every year, which always coincided with the normal high school graduation.

They would usually host a small gathering—a buffet lunch or tea—to honor that first graduating class. But not this year. With Cricket Ellison as the business sponsor, this year's "bash" was going to be a genuine *bash*.

And it was going to bash some common sense into one stubborn lawyer she knew and loved.

Of course, it would take some finagling, which really ought to be Cricket's middle name.

"Good morning, Shannon," Cricket greeted Shannon Banks, who had been the class president in 1997 and helped organize this event every year.

Noah should have been class president, of course,

but with everything that had happened with Vanessa and the baby, student government had not been on his mind.

"Cricket." Shannon opened her arms for a hug. "It's wonderful to see you. How are you?"

Shannon was always a sweet, friendly woman with a big smile and short curly hair—that could use a root touchup, Cricket couldn't help but notice.

She'd married the boy she had dated all through high school, and they had a couple of teenagers and a house near the beach.

"I'm well." Cricket smiled. "Very excited to be here."

Shannon's blue eyes glimmered. "Well, I have to say, we were all just overjoyed when we got your message that you wanted to sponsor the First Class Bash this year! Your salon is such a community staple, and of course, with your own son being a member of the first class, it seems like a perfect fit."

"I am honored and thrilled to be a part of the event this year." Cricket walked over to Terrence Hunter and Catherine Yates, who were other members of the Class of '97 and worked with Shannon every year to keep the annual celebration alive. "Wonderful to see you both again."

"Mrs. Ellison." Terrence, with his wide, warm smile, had been a friend of Noah's back in the day, when they played baseball at the high school together.

"Oh, please, honey. Cricket is just fine." She hugged him. "You're all grown now."

"You're still Noah's mom to me." He chuckled,

gesturing to the woman next to him. "You remember Catherine, right?"

"How could I forget the cheer captain?" Cricket hugged the slender woman who still looked, in fact, like she was the cheer captain in high school. Pretty little thing, just like she'd always been.

After introductions and pleasantries, the four of them sat down in a corner booth with iced lattes, ready to work.

"So, Cricket." Shannon sipped her coffee. "What did you have in mind for the First Class Bash this year? Usually the sponsor decides what sort of event they want to put on, but if you don't know yet, we're happy to brainstorm some possibilities."

"Oh, that won't be necessary." Cricket pushed her glasses up the bridge of her nose and folded her hands on the table. "I would like to elevate the First Class Bash this year and make it something really special and memorable."

"Sounds wonderful!" Catherine smiled, brushing her auburn hair behind her shoulders. "A dinner party maybe? Might be pricey."

"Or a brunch?" Terrence raised his brows. "Everybody loves brunch, and it won't be as expensive."

"It's true," Shannon said, nodding.

"Actually..." Cricket leaned back in the leather booth seat, pressing her lips together. "I think you—all of the Class of '97—deserve a chance to relive your high school prom."

The three committee members blinked in surprise,

exchanging looks as Cricket's idea hung in the air between them.

"A...prom?" Catherine angled her head, turning to Shannon. "Can we do that? It sounds kind of fun."

Shannon laughed. "Of course you'd think that, prom queen."

"It's true." Catherine pretended to place a crown on her head. "I was the 1997 Rosemary Beach High prom queen. I can't say I'm entirely opposed to this throwback to the glory days." She turned to Cricket. "Tell us more."

"Well, I'm thinking we go all out. And don't worry about funding—the salon is your sponsor and I'm feeling quite generous." She gave a sly smile and arched a brow. "Just like you said, Catherine, we'll throw it back to the nineties. Decorations, music, clothes...it'll be like reliving the prom night for our most special class."

The prom, Cricket thought to herself, that Noah and Vanessa never got to have.

Yes, sure, she imagined this would be a nice reunion and celebration event for the entire class, but that wasn't exactly Cricket's primary concern.

Of course, Noah hadn't gone to his senior prom. That night, she'd stayed home with him, and they watched a *Star Wars* marathon to get his mind off of it. She hurt for him, and for some reason, that particular letdown never left her.

And now was her chance to fix that with the prom night of his dreams and Vanessa as his date.

If Cricket could make this night absolutely magical and perfect, maybe Noah would come around. And if

Vanessa attended, too? They could share it together and rekindle their feelings for each other, and well...

She'd leave the rest to God. But Cricket could make a prom happen without divine intervention. She just needed to sell this committee on the idea.

Shannon nodded slowly, processing Cricket's description of the prom night. "I mean...usually we just do a luncheon or something."

"Oh, let's go bigger this year." Cricket leaned forward. "The graduates are in their forties with families and busy lives. They probably never get to dress up and dance to their favorite music from the era. People will love it!"

The others considered that.

She held up her hands, spreading her fingers wide. "A romantic night under the stars. People can bring their spouses, there will be punch and a DJ, and it will all be so festive and fun. Prom is a very special occasion, and the First Class Bash is an important event." Cricket held up her latte and took a sip through the straw. "You with me?"

Terrence, Catherine, and Shannon all exchanged looks from their side of the booth, smiles growing on their faces.

How could they object to this? The three of them, Cricket remembered, were stars of Noah's graduating class, and are now deeply involved in the Rosemary Beach community. Shannon the president, Catherine the cheerleader, and Terrence the athlete—of course they would want to relive their senior prom.

"Well, I think it sounds great," Shannon said first. "We can make it super cheesy and fun."

Catherine nodded. "Hit the nineties theme hard. Good ole days, baby."

"Wonderful." Cricket stirred her latte, feeling victorious and excited.

Terrence leaned forward. "My wife has a friend who does event decorations. I bet she can hit her up for some décor."

"Are we having it in the school gym?" Shannon asked.

Catherine arched a brow. "Would it be a true prom if we didn't?"

"Oh, yes, it will be so fun," Cricket added. "Just like it was back in the day."

"We love your ideas and your enthusiasm, Cricket." Shannon clasped her hands together and beamed across the table. "Welcome to the team."

"Thank you, darling. Let's make this First Class Bash the best one yet."

And it would have to be.

The good news was that Cricket had Noah here at least for a bit longer while the flood damages got handled, and she could use her time wisely to convince him to attend. With Vanessa. And leave his job and stay forever.

One thing at a time, Cricket. One thing at a time.

"Hey, Mom." Noah scratched the back of his head, having to shout over the sound of the giant industrial fans that sat in every corner of Cricket's tiny loft.

She walked in, feeling so encouraged and excited after her meeting with the First Class Bash committee that the ugly, dirty fans didn't even put her in a bad mood.

They'd been running for a few days already, but evidently the water damage was severe, and the remediation company wanted to be sure no mold would grow.

It was fine with Cricket. In fact, everyone could take their sweet, sweet time.

"Hi, honey." She set her purse down and looked around at her place, which was, admittedly in shambles. "These things are just blowing nonstop, huh? Don't you think it's dry by now?"

"Allegedly, the water seeped into the subfloor, which is like forty years old." He gave an apologetic expression, letting out a soft sigh. "Tough to get it all fully dry. But the guys were here a little while ago and it seems like they're doing their best."

"All right. Well, I do appreciate you being here. Thank you." Cricket glanced at her kitchen table, where Noah had set up his laptop with an extra screen and keyboard.

It touched her heart that he cared enough to spend the day working in her little loft, battling the sound of the fans and the workers marching in and out at all hours.

"Did you get in touch with the contractor? Marco?"

she asked, pouring herself a glass of ice water from the fridge.

Noah sat back down at his computer, shaking his head with defeat. "I did, but unfortunately, it's not good news."

"Oh, no." She turned around, holding a hand to her chest. "What did he say?"

"He can't get to this job for four to five weeks." Noah ran a hand through his hair and groaned softly.

Oh, dear, Cricket thought to herself with sarcasm in her own internal voice. *Three to four weeks, what a travesty.*

"The insurance guy should be coming by in the next few days to assess the damaged property and write you a check, but you won't be able to do any actual renovation until Marco can get started." Noah shook his head. "I'm sorry, Mom. It's the best I could do."

"Oh, it's okay, honey." She sat down at the other seat across from him, resting her chin in her palm. "It's just that...I'm not so sure what to even do. How do I go about all of this? Insurance and contractors...it's all just too much."

"Well, I'm so involved now, I really should just handle it and stay until the whole process is done." Noah smiled. "Like we talked about."

She tried her hardest not to grin. "Are you sure? With work and all, I hate to be a burden..."

"You are never a burden, Mom. I told you, I'm not leaving you alone to handle all of this by yourself. I'll stay until you're standing on brand-new floors with no water damage that was completely paid for by insurance. And if at any point in the process I need to do some arguing, well, it's a good thing I went to law school." He gave a teasing wink.

"Oh, my dear son." She reached across the table and squeezed his hand. "Where in the world would I be without you?"

He gave a tight smile. "I think you'd be just fine, but honestly, I don't mind."

Which was a huge change from the last decade or so when he'd steadfastly refused to be here.

Was it because Vanessa was here, she wondered with a punch of hope.

She rubbed her fingers on the glass, smearing the condensation. "I know this isn't easy for you. I know you're not the biggest fan of Rosemary Beach."

"'Sokay," he said, suddenly preoccupied with whatever was on his computer screen.

"But it's a nice change. And you'll get to know some... people."

He looked up over the monitor and she braced for the way he usually told her to back off. Never unkind, but quite clear.

But his expression seemed softer and maybe a little bit more open. "Yeah, some people."

She studied him, quiet for a moment.

"I mean, now that Emily's here..." He let his voice trail off. "It doesn't hurt to, you know, follow up on the divorce stuff for her."

Emily! Of course! That's why he wanted to stay. And this flood had given him the perfect cover.

"I think that's so sweet," she said, choosing her words carefully. "There's nothing like...a daughter."

"Well, yeah, I don't think we'll be...you know, heading off to the Daddy-Daughter Dance, but yeah. I don't mind getting to know her."

The Daddy-Daughter Dance! Her mental wheels spinning, she forced herself to stand and play everything casually. "Well, I'm just delighted you're helping me handle the insurance and construction. I'd be lost without it, Noah."

He nodded. "So, where have you been, Mom? Busy day at the salon?"

"I actually had a meeting with some people at Amavida after my last client." She inched forward, bursting to tell Noah about the prom.

He narrowed his eyes suspiciously. "What people? Why do you look like you have a secret?"

"Well, it's not really a secret." She shrugged. "Do you remember Shannon Banks?"

"From high school? Yeah, I do. She was class president or some such nonsense."

It hadn't been nonsense when he wanted that role but then gave up on that dream. She let that slide.

"Yes, she was. And I met with her First Class Bash committee because the salon is sponsoring it this year." She smiled brightly. "Isn't that exciting?"

Noah's entire demeanor instantly shifted. His blue eyes darkened and his shoulders sank down an inch.

"Mom...you're...why?" He frowned, shaking his head with confusion. "You've never gone near that stupid event. Why now?"

"Well, because." She lifted her chin. "I run a prominent local business, and I felt it's time I give back. It's *your* graduating class."

He swallowed, his jaw clenching. "Yes, I'm aware."

"And I know you've never gone to the Bash before because you're always so busy with work and Miami—"

"Among other reasons."

"Right, well...yes. But you're here now for at least the next few weeks, and I'm putting on the event this year." She locked eyes with her son. "It would mean the absolute world to me if you'd attend."

Noah sucked in a breath to respond, but paused, looking away. "Mom, I...I don't go to that stuff. You know that. And you know why I don't go."

"I know, honey, but you're here now!" She raised her hands. "Right here in Rosemary Beach. And you were a part of the first ever graduation class of the high school. It's something to celebrate!"

"It was just by chance that they made it an official school the year I was a senior." He raised his brows. "It's not like there's anything actually special about the Class of '97. Our twenty-fifth is past and..." He looked down at his work like anything was more important than that. "The whole thing is dumb."

"Well, I beg to disagree, my dear son. I think the first ever graduating class of Rosemary Beach High School deserves a fabulous celebration, and that's why...I'm... sponsoring an event."

Noah eyed her with open suspicion. "What are you up to now, Cricket Ellison?"

"Just trying to plan a fun party, that's all." She raised her hands and leaned back defensively. "It's a prom."

"A what?"

"We're recreating the 1997 senior prom. Night under the stars, punch bowl, terrible dresses, the whole nine."

Noah's jaw fell a little slack, and Cricket could practically see the flashbacks of his sad and broken prom night dance across his eyes. "Doesn't that seem a bit over the top?"

"Not at all." Cricket lifted her shoulder. "I think it will be wonderful, and since you'll be here in town on the big night..."

Noah shut his eyes. "Mom, I'm sorry. But...no. Drop it."

"Noah, please. It's for the salon this year!" Cricket exclaimed. "Won't you just make an appearance? Oh, how silly I would look if my own son didn't attend the very event I'm putting on for his class."

He inhaled slowly and leveled his gaze, his dark eyes shadowed. "Look, I don't want to hurt you, but I'm not going to go to a prom or anything related to high school. I wish you the best with planning this whole thing. But I have to keep my distance. You know that."

"You're not keeping your distance from Emily," she reminded him.

"She's not..." When he didn't finish, she knew what he was thinking.

She's not Vanessa. And Cricket knew when to drop a subject.

"Of course, Noah." She stood and picked up her water glass. "I completely understand."

For now, she'd let it go and pretend to have accepted defeat. She had weeks to change his mind and make this happen.

She wasn't worried. Not in the slightest.

Chapter Nine

Gloria

Gloria loved her job at the diner every day—she loved the people, her staff, the small-town charm where everyone knew each other and, of course, the delicious aromas and cozy atmosphere.

Even at 6:30 in the morning, when she always arrived, Gloria was ready for a wonderful day at work.

Aside from raising Daisy and Jeremy, the diner was her greatest accomplishment, and today more than ever, Gloria needed it to fill her spirit and bring her joy.

"Hey, Liz." She greeted her sweet hostess, who always wore a bouncy ponytail and a big smile and came in even earlier than Gloria to set up.

"Morning, Glo! Happy Saturday!"

Gloria sure hoped it would be. She walked past the kitchen to her small office where she ran the administrative side of the business. Things would be busy today, and Gloria needed to contact some of her suppliers and iron out a few shipping issues.

"Time to focus, Glo," she whispered to herself, pulling up her spreadsheets and order forms.

First up was the beef supplier. Gloria needed to contact them to change their delivery window to—

A knock on the door of the office startled her, and Gloria looked up to see who was standing there.

"Hi, Mom." Daisy, dressed in light-blue scrubs with her hair pulled back, gingerly stepped into the office and smiled.

"Daisy!" Gloria sat up, everything forgotten with the unexpected arrival of her daughter.

Gloria couldn't even remember the last time Daisy showed up spontaneously at the diner just to say hi or talk to her about something. This was *progress*. And Gloria was thrilled to see her.

"Come on in, honey." She gestured at the small chair in the corner of the tiny office. It wasn't much, but it was her space. "What's going on? Are you on your way to work?"

"Yeah, I've got a twelve-hour day shift today, but I'm early, and...I wanted to talk to you." She twirled her thick ponytail, chewing on her lip nervously.

"Okay." Gloria swiveled in her desk chair, crossing her legs as she turned to face Daisy and give her daughter her full attention. "Is everything all right?"

Gloria prayed the answer was yes, because she wasn't sure she could handle another crisis.

"Yeah, yeah. I'm fine." Daisy walked over to the corner chair, folding into it with her legs under her, like a little girl sitting criss-cross-applesauce. "I'm going to have that talk with Linda tonight. You know...*that* talk."

"Ah, yes." Gloria clicked her tongue. "The 'please back off because it's my wedding not yours' talk."

"Yeah." Daisy rolled her eyes and laughed. "That's the talk. And honestly? I'm kind of freaking out."

Gloria nodded, understanding Daisy's trepidation. Heck, she was kind of scared of the woman, too.

She couldn't help but take note, though, of the fact that Daisy had come to her for guidance and advice. She didn't go to Kyle, or the new, trendy, wealthy group of friends—or acquaintances—she'd made through him. She'd walked into the diner, just like she always used to, looking for support from her mom.

And she had to get it.

"Do you know how you're going to express your feelings?" Gloria asked. "I think the most important thing here is not what's said, but how you say it."

Daisy nodded, listening.

"Hate to be a cliché, but as always, honesty is going to be your best friend."

Daisy sighed noisily. "But if I'm honest with her and tell her how I really feel, she'll totally flip out. She's put so much into this extravagant wedding. Money, time, energy. More money." She snorted softly. "Did I mention money?"

"Okay, so clearly you're feeling some pressure because of Linda's generous spending on the wedding."

"It makes me feel like I can't have any of my own opinions or ideas." Daisy sank back, shrugging her shoulders. "Like if I'm not paying for it, I don't get a say."

"You're the bride. And they offered to pay for everything, it's not like you ever expected that or even asked for a dime. Did you?"

"Nope. I never asked for anything but, you know, a chance to call the shots on my own wedding day."

"Dais, tell her exactly what you just told me." Gloria rolled her desk chair closer, leveling her gaze with Daisy's. "Tell her that she's so incredibly generous, and you are infinitely grateful for that, but it's made you feel like you can't have your own opinions about the wedding. And since you're the bride, you'd like to make a few changes to have it feel more authentic to who you are, instead of just who Linda is."

Daisy huffed out a breath. "You said that so nicely. I don't know if I'll be able to recreate that without sounding like a total brat."

"You're not a brat." Gloria straightened her back and lifted her chin. "Here. Let's practice."

Daisy arched a dubious brow. "Practice?"

"Yes. I'm Linda Whittington." Gloria flipped her hair dramatically, lowering her voice to jokingly imitate Linda's sophisticated drawl. "Wife of renowned gazillionaire Arthur Whittington, Pilates princess, fundraiser planner extraordinaire, and Botox advocate."

Daisy giggled, her eyes dancing with amusement. "Mom, you can't be serious."

"No, no." Gloria wiggled her finger. "Not Mom. Future mother-in-law. Now, Daisy, you mentioned you have something you'd like to address with me?" She teasingly batted her eyelashes, making Daisy laugh some more.

"Okay, *Linda*." She glanced down and her smile faded as she tried to consider what to say and how to say it. "I wanted to tell you that I really appreciate your generosity—"

"Oh, please, honey. It's a drop in the bucket for us. Have you seen the yacht?"

"Mom!" Daisy tilted her head back, cackling with laughter.

"I'm sorry, I'm sorry." Gloria raised her hands defensively. "I couldn't resist. I'll be serious now." She swiped her hand in front of her face, settling into a serious expression. "Go ahead."

"Okay. Anyway, Linda, I'm so grateful for how generous you've been with the wedding and everything, and I feel so lucky to have you as my future mother-in-law."

Gloria tilted her chin up and flipped her hair again. "Is this going somewhere, honey? I have my daily facial in half an hour."

Daisy snickered, rolling her eyes at her mom's humor, but it was visibly cheering her up, and that was Gloria's intention.

"Yes, I just...I just feel like my own ideas and style have been sort of lost in the shuffle of everything, and I was wondering if maybe we could change a few things for the big day, so it feels more...me?"

Gloria gave an exaggerated frown, still in character. "Well, what do you want to change?"

Daisy took a deep breath. "I was hoping we could pare down the guest list just a little, since there are so many people invited who I've never met. And I know you had my ceremony dress custom made—and it's beautiful!

But maybe I could change into something a little more relaxed for the reception?"

Gloria paused, thinking hard about what the real Linda would say in response to Daisy's polite and perfectly reasonable requests for her own wedding. "Well, I suppose I can remove a few extraneous parties that we haven't spoken to in a long time... Invites haven't gone out just yet."

"That would be great." Daisy smiled. "Just to make it a little more personal."

"As for the dress..." She angled her head, certain that Linda would be okay with Daisy wearing a different dress at the reception. Celebrity brides did it all the time! "Yes, I'm comfortable with you having a second look for the night, as long as the ceremony pictures are taken in your Vera Lang."

Daisy giggled. "Wang. It's Vera Wang."

"Oh, well, you get it." Gloria laughed, finally breaking character from her impression of Linda which, admittedly, was quite fun and brought Daisy some joy.

"How was that?" Daisy asked, flipping her high ponytail over her shoulder.

"It was great, Dais. Everything you want to say to her is completely fair and understandable. At the end of the day, Linda is a mother, and she loves her son. You're going to be her daughter-in-law, and I imagine she is starting to really love you, too."

Gloria tamped down the twinge of irritation and jealousy that rose in her chest as she said those words. She truly did want Daisy to be accepted and adored by her in-laws, but Linda in particular just didn't have the warmth and sincerity that Gloria believed Daisy deserved in her new family.

That aside, people could grow and maybe, over time, she'd start to see a different side of Linda. After all, they'd be in each other's lives forever.

"I think she likes me, I really do." Daisy leaned over to grab her work bag, a dark green tote with patches sewn onto it that she'd had for years. "I just know how fixated she is on this wedding and everything being perfect."

"Daisy." Gloria got up and placed her hands on Daisy's narrow shoulders that were carrying so much weight. "Just be your honest, authentic self. Linda is a mom, she has a heart. She'll understand where you're coming from and want to help make you feel better."

"You think so?"

Gloria nodded with certainty. "I know it. It's not in a mother's DNA to let their kid be unhappy. And you're sort of her kid now."

Daisy pursed her lips as she rose. "I'm your kid."

"And thank God for that." Gloria wrapped Daisy into a tight hug, holding her daughter close for an extra few seconds. "Okay, go be awesome at work and keep me posted on how tonight goes."

She smiled and opened the office door to head out. "Thanks, Mom. I love you."

"I love you, too, honey."

Gloria sat back down in her chair, feeling much lighter and more joyful than she had a few minutes ago.

Once she finally hit her stride on her paperwork and order forms, Gloria's phone buzzed with an incoming call. Pulling herself from work, she grabbed the phone to see if she could ignore the call.

Incoming Call: Jason Chang

Oh, no. Could not ignore him. She swiped the screen and swiveled away from her desk, standing, because she'd probably have to pace her tiny office for a conversation with the private investigator.

"Jason, hello."

"Good morning, Gloria. I hope I didn't catch you too early on a Saturday."

"Oh, please, I run a diner. I don't know the meaning of 'too early,'" she said on a soft laugh, aching to skip the pleasantries and hear if he'd discovered anything about Violet.

"So, I've looked over all of the letters and documentation that you and your sister provided, as well as run a couple of initial searches and early stage investigations into your mother's two different names."

She bit her lip. "And?"

"Don't get too excited, because I don't have much yet."

"Anything is helpful, Jason," Gloria said. "What did you find out?"

"All I can tell you so far is that I have confirmed, with only a minimal margin of doubt, that your mother is still alive."

Gloria froze, her throat tightening as she tried to gather herself. "Oh. She's still...oh. Wow. Okay."

The news hit her harder than she'd expected it to. Of course, she and Nessie had discussed the possibility that their mother could still be alive somewhere. But, for whatever reason, hearing it confirmed—even with a minimal margin of doubt—hit hard.

All these years, all this time, she was still out there. She'd never showed up, never looked up the daughters she'd left behind, never wanted to change her past mistakes.

"How do you know?" she asked. "And do you know where she is?"

"Not yet, but I have access to some of the most comprehensive databases in the country, including vital records, Social Security death index, filings from every funeral home and obituary notification, Legacy.com, credit reports, utility records, that sort of thing. If she'd died, there'd be a record of it and there is none."

"Oh, okay. Even if she used another name?"

"Clarinda Smith is her legal name. There's a birth certificate on file, a Social Security number, and a marriage certificate to William Young. In my professional opinion, she's not dead."

Gloria sighed, processing that. "Now what?"

"The next step can take a lot longer. Having bots comb a huge amount of data, frequently hitting dead ends, old addresses, and bad information. I'll need more time."

"That's fair," she said. "Please take all you need and we'll...wait."

What else could they do?

Jason cleared his throat. "In the meantime, please don't hesitate to reach out with anything, okay?"

"Okay." Gloria swallowed. "Thank you, Jason."

"Of course. I know this is difficult, but eventually, we'll find her."

The tenderness in his voice struck a chord in Gloria's heart, and she wondered if he was this kind and gentle to all of his clients, or if their case was just that devastating. "Thank you, Jason. Keep me posted."

"Will do. Try to enjoy your day, Gloria. Bye."

"Bye, Jason. Thanks again." Gloria set the phone down, dropped her head into her hands, and started to cry.

She was out there, Violet Young or Clarinda Smith or whatever she called herself now. She'd been out there this whole time. She'd written Bill all those letters, and never once, in all of her lonely nights or quiet moments, did she ever think about her daughters.

Gloria Bennett was a forgiver. She forgave those she loved quickly and with joy. But this? This level of selfishness and short-sightedness and downright evil?

Gloria didn't care who or where her mother was, she was never, ever going to forgive her.

Chapter Ten

Vanessa

Vanessa had had a feeling in her gut this whole time that her mother was still alive, but a small part of her didn't want to believe it was true.

She didn't want to believe that the woman who wrote those letters, who ran away and let her children believe she'd died, was continuing on, year after year, never reaching out.

She'd really committed, Vanessa had to give her that. But after Gloria's call to tell her that Jason had discovered that their mother wasn't dead, Vanessa needed a break. Thankfully, Emily was a total godsend and everything at Young at Heart was completely ready to roll for opening day on Monday.

As she walked through town, scoping out a place for an afternoon coffee and something sweet, she tried to focus on the positive.

It was overwhelming, all of this happening at once. The discoveries about their mother, the opening of the store, and, of course, Noah being in town and spending a little bit of time with Emily.

It was all weird and scary and confusing, but as Vanessa wandered through the achingly adorable streets of Rosemary Beach, she was certain she wouldn't have it any other way.

She thought about her life in L.A., the endless struggle to move up, climb the ladder, stay relevant. Here she could just...be. Even through the ups and downs and drama of it all, she had so much more peace.

Vanessa stopped at the order window at 3rd Cup, treating herself to an iced caramel macchiato and a croissant, which she took to an empty picnic table under the awning of the shop.

Truthfully, she didn't quite know what to make of the fact that her mother was still alive. Did it really matter at this point? It wasn't like they were all just going to forget everything and find her and rekindle a relationship.

No, that was out of the question. Still, the harsh reality stung, knowing that if her mother had been around, Vanessa probably would have kept Emily.

Heck, she probably would have married Noah. Her life would be completely and totally different. But would it be better? It was impossible to say.

She sipped the sweet coffee, stirring in the dollop of whipped cream on the top when she noticed a text pop up on her phone screen.

Cricket Ellison: *Hi, dear. Would you mind stopping by the salon for a few moments? I could really use your young and hip second opinion on something.*

Vanessa snorted to herself as she tore off a piece of croissant, tempted to reply that the real young and hip opinion would have to come from Emily.

But she knew darn well that Cricket didn't do

anything without a good reason, so there was surely a motive behind her asking Vanessa about...whatever this needed opinion might be.

She typed back, "*Be over in ten,*" and finished her croissant.

The walk to Cricket's Beauty Salon didn't even take the full ten minutes, and Vanessa relished the hot summer air and her sweet afternoon coffee the whole way there.

"Hey, Cricket." She swung open the doors of the salon, greeting Cricket.

"Nessie, there you are." She was standing behind a salon chair, carefully painting caramel highlights on a woman's dark hair.

The client gave Vanessa a polite smile, and Vanessa did the same.

"What can I do for you?" She walked over to give Cricket a hug and admire the artistic work she was doing on her client's hair. "Those are going to be beautiful."

"Aren't they?" Cricket brushed the dye onto a strand. "We're doing five different shades of blond. Perfect for summer, don't you think?"

"How fabulous." She smiled in the mirror at the woman.

"Anyway, Ness, honey, I need you to run up to my loft and help me out with something."

"Sure, what is it?"

"Well, I know you've heard about my devastating flood."

She stifled a laugh. "Uh, yes, the whole town has heard. How is the remediation going, by the way?"

"That's sort of what I need your help with." She lowered her dish of hair dye onto a rolling table next to her and pushed up her glasses, eyeing Vanessa. "Upstairs there are several floor samples, and I simply can't decide which one to choose. My old floors were the original wood, and I simply don't know how to replicate that. Would you mind going up there and just taking a look at each of them? Give me your thoughts? You are a designer, after all."

"Of course, I'd be happy to. But...I'm a stylist, you know. Not an interior designer."

Cricket waved a dismissive hand, as if that small detail didn't matter in the slightest. "You've got an eye, and that's what I need."

The point was fair enough. "Okay, I'll head up there now."

"It's unlocked." She began removing foil from the freshly colored hair. "Thank you, darling!"

"No problem."

Vanessa walked through the back door of the salon, which opened up to an old brick hallway and a flight of stairs. She'd been to Cricket's loft before, though not since the flood happened, so she wasn't sure just how much disarray to expect.

When she reached the second story, she walked up to the front door of the little apartment—which was pink, of course—and opened it.

"Yikes," Vanessa whispered to herself, instantly taken

aback by the sight of gigantic fans and plastic tarps. "Poor Cricket."

She set her purse down on a table by the front door and began to slowly walk around on the dusty subfloor. The carpets had already been ripped up, it appeared.

Vanessa looked for the flooring samples that Cricket wanted her to take a peek at, but she didn't see anything anywhere.

That was odd.

Vanessa tiptoed across the exposed floorboards and turned the corner to peek into the kitchen, thinking maybe she'd left them on the counter.

"Vanessa?"

The man's voice startled her, and she gasped as she jumped back, shocked to see Noah sitting at Cricket's kitchen table in front of a laptop.

"Oh, my gosh, Noah, you scared me." She laughed softly, shaking off the jolt of adrenaline that had kicked up her heart rate.

"Sorry, I didn't know you were coming by." He leaned back, somehow making black-rimmed reading glasses look way too attractive.

"I hadn't planned on it, but Cricket texted me and asked me to come up here and give an opinion on samples for her new floor." Vanessa quickly attempted to smooth down her hair. "She's with a client."

Noah frowned, his dark brows pulling together. "The samples haven't come in yet. They're not expected for a week."

"Huh." Vanessa crossed her arms, confused and

slightly uncomfortable. This was the first time she and Noah had been completely alone together since, well, she'd left him thirty years ago. "That's weird. She said they were here. She was really specific."

Noah chuckled softly, and it relieved Vanessa a little to see that he was relaxed. "She must have been confused."

"Very unlike her."

"No kidding." He flicked his brows, standing up and rounding the counter to refill a water glass at the sink.

Vanessa clenched her jaw, rocking back on her heels as she racked her brain for ways to diffuse this awkwardness.

It didn't seem possible. Not after her rejected apology and Noah's clear stance that he wanted nothing to do with her.

"I didn't know you were working over here," she said randomly, feeling dumb but desperate for the silence to be broken. "I figured you had a hotel or something."

"I do," he explained, taking a drink from the water glass and propping a hip against the countertop. "But I'm spending the day here so I can handle the workers coming in and out. Mom's not really cut out to deal with all of this on her own, plus, she has hair clients and all that. I'm staying until everything's finished."

"Oh." Vanessa wasn't sure how to feel about that. Excitement mixed with anticipation and a definite splash of dread. Would she run into him frequently?

Well, she hadn't exactly run into him now. She'd been...*sent* here.

Oh, Cricket.

"I'm sure your mom is loving having you here."

He smiled. "Just a little."

Vanessa nodded awkwardly, her gaze flicking across Noah as she tried to forget how deeply she'd once loved him, how close they'd been, how much he meant to her.

That was another lifetime. And in this lifetime, he'd been polite, and she needed to leave.

"Anyway, sorry for interrupting your work." She gave a little wave and turned on her heel. "I'll tell Cricket the samples aren't in yet and, uh, be on my way."

Noah inhaled slowly, holding her gaze for a few beats longer. "All right, Vanessa. Good luck with the store."

She looked back and smiled over her shoulder, nearly tripping on the cord of one of the giant blower fans. "Oh, thank you! Okay, bye then. I'll see ya—" She tried to turn the front door handle, but it wasn't moving. "What the..."

She shook it and shook it, but the front door of Cricket's loft was...locked? How was that possible?

"Um, Noah?"

He came closer. "What's up?"

"The door handle won't turn." She whipped around to face him. "It's...locked."

"What?" He laughed with disbelief. "We're *inside* the apartment. How can it be locked from the outside?"

Vanessa stepped out of the way, gesturing at the gold door handle for Noah to give it a try himself.

He grabbed the handle and tried to turn it, shook it, and gave it a tap. "What on Earth?"

Together, they pushed on the door, jiggled the handle, but...nothing. It was locked.

"Okay, that's bizarre." Vanessa stepped back.

Noah pulled out his phone and tapped the screen. "I'll call her."

Vanessa listened, but it rang twice and went to voicemail. "Her phone's off," she said softly.

Noah closed his eyes, pinching the bridge of his nose as he shook his head. "Well, we're stuck until she comes up here."

Vanessa walked away from the front door and back into the living room, pacing around.

A week ago, she would have been excited about the idea of some unexpected alone time with Noah. She would have seen it as a chance to really apologize, clear the air, get forgiveness and leave the past in the past.

But now? She knew how deep his resentment ran, and she knew full well he didn't want even a civil relationship with her, or any kind of relationship at all.

The last thing she needed was to be trapped in here for God knew how long with him...the man who was once her best friend, her greatest love. The man who fathered her only child. The man who knew her better than anyone on the planet.

The man who wanted absolutely nothing to do with her.

Great.

"I'll just, um..." Vanessa perched awkwardly on the edge of the sofa, pulling out her phone. "Wait here."

"You want something to drink? Water, iced tea?" He

lowered his voice to a sarcastic grumble. "Vodka, perhaps?"

Vanessa laughed, half considering taking him up on that. "I'm all right. You keep working, I'll just...be here."

He shot her a look, something familiar twinkling in his blue eyes. Something she hadn't seen in a long time. "You'll just sit there and stare at the wall until my mother comes back up?"

"I have my phone." She wiggled her cell. "I can keep myself busy."

He lowered his gaze, taking off his reading glasses and setting them on the table next to his computer. "I could use a break anyway." Noah walked over to the living room and sat down in the chair across from her.

Vanessa blinked, drawing back in utter shock.

Had she heard him correctly? Was he actually voluntarily spending time with her?

"Oh, okay." She set her phone down, giving a tight smile. "How's work going?"

"Look, Ness."

The sound of his voice using the decades-old nickname made her wince. "Yeah?"

"I'm sorry for how harsh I was the other day." He swallowed. "This has all just kind of turned my life upside down. You coming back here is one thing. But then adding Emily into the mix...it's just been a lot to take in. Your apology sort of hit me out of nowhere, and to be honest? I don't really know the best way to process all of this. So I'm doing what I do know how to do." He jutted his chin toward the laptop. "Put my head down and work."

Vanessa nodded, feeling as if she was frozen in place.

"I really appreciate you saying that. And I completely get that a random, surprise apology for something so massive and so long ago was...weird. And definitely not the best way to handle it. I'm sorry about that."

"No worries." He lifted a broad shoulder and smiled. "I'm here for at least a few more weeks, you live here, and we share a grown daughter. We might as well find a way to be cool with each other, right? At least until I head back down to Miami."

Was he serious? Vanessa opened her mouth to respond but was nearly too stunned to speak. "Right, yes. I would like that."

"Good." He nodded.

It certainly wasn't forgiveness. But it was...something.

She stared at him for a moment, realizing there was about a mountain of stuff she wanted to say to him. About her life, her work, the years they'd been apart. And her mother! Oh, how she'd love to break her promise to Gloria and tell him what they'd discovered.

He was so smart, he could help. And he'd understand how she felt, but—

"Did you hear about the prom?" Noah asked.

"The prom?" Vanessa cocked her head, not sure she'd heard him correctly. "What are you talking about?"

"You know how, for whatever reason, there's some celebration every year at the high school for our 'special' Class of 1997?"

"Oh, yeah." She frowned. "The First Class Bash. I've heard about it but never even been invited. Not that I would have gone."

"You haven't been invited?" He seemed surprised.

"I didn't graduate, remember?"

"Right." His gaze darkened a bit with the memory of Vanessa's absence at graduation, right before she'd promised she'd come back and never did. "Anyway, my mom is sponsoring the whole thing this year, and she's taking it entirely too far."

Vanessa laughed softly. "Cricket? Taking something too far? I'm stunned. So what does this have to do with the prom? Or I guess kids these days just call it prom." She'd styled a few of her clients' kids for the event and remembered noticing that change over time.

"The prom that Cricket's doing for the Bash," he explained, giving a subtle, loving eye-roll. "She's putting on a 'prom' for the Class of 1997 so they can relive their glory years or whatever."

Vanessa felt her jaw go slack as she laughed with disbelief. "You're kidding."

"Dead serious. Dresses, decorations, the whole nine. Oh, and plenty of Elton John and Backstreet Boys."

"Isn't the Bash usually, like, a lunch at Olive Garden or something?"

"Not when Cricket's in charge." He gave a rueful laugh. "Now it's...a night under the stars. And in the high school gym."

"No!" Vanessa hooted a soft laugh. "Hey, the woman has a vision. She gets what she wants."

He arched a brow. "You don't say."

"So are you going?" she asked.

"To Prom 2.0? You're kidding, right?"

She lifted a shoulder. "Cricket's salon is sponsoring it. I'd imagine she's full-court-pressing you to make an appearance."

He sighed, shaking his head. "No, I'm not going. I don't exactly care to relive anything about high school. Well, not the latter half," he added softly, his gaze catching hers.

Vanessa thought back to those years, the first two years of high school spent in a juvenile but very real romance with Noah. The year before that, in middle school, their close friendship had gone to the next level when he kissed her at a birthday bonfire for one of their classmates.

They'd walked into high school as a couple, and Noah walked out of it alone and shattered.

No wonder he didn't want to relive the prom they'd missed going to together.

"Did you go?" Vanessa asked. "To your senior prom, I mean. The actual one."

He scoffed softly, as if the answer was obvious. "Uh, no. I did not. I stayed home and watched *Star Wars* with my mother."

Vanessa flinched, shutting her eyes tightly as she thought of high school Noah, sad and at home on prom night. "Maybe you should go to the First Class Bash. Get the magical prom night you were robbed of in '97."

Noah practically choked. "I think I'll pass. Maybe I'll

throw on an old *Star Wars* movie while I work on my latest case, though, just to relive the spirit of the night."

Vanessa chuckled, but her heart felt heavy. "I'm sorry, Noah. I'm sorry you didn't get to go to our prom. I'm sorry I stole so much from you."

For a moment, he studied her, maybe—just maybe—accepting the apology this time.

But he just flicked his hand. "Hey, Ness, I told you. Let's just drop all that stuff and get through the time we have to coexist here with minimal tension. I'm fine."

She swallowed, averting her gaze from his, landing on the bookshelf in the corner of Cricket's living room.

In front of all the books, facing forward, was their 1995 high school yearbook, featuring a giant sand dollar on the cover. It was still called Inlet High, since it didn't officially become Rosemary Beach High School until '96, hence the 'first class' of '97.

Noah, having followed Vanessa's gaze, let out a soft groan. "Why is that there? That was not there last night."

Vanessa frowned, getting up and walking over to the bookshelf. She picked up the hardback yearbook, wiping some dust off the embossed cover. "This was 1995," she said softly. "The end of our sophomore year."

Before things went bad. When life was still perfect and futures were still bright and things were so painfully simple.

When these particular yearbooks came out, Vanessa was not yet pregnant and would still have two normal months of summer before finding out about her surprise baby in August, when she ran off.

Good heavens, they'd been young. Why did she even have sex at that age, she wondered.

Once more, she thought of Violet. Would her juvenile decisions have been different—smarter, perhaps—if she'd had a mother to guide her? Emily might never have been born.

Pushing the thought away, she could smell the old paper and the dust on the book, hugging it against her chest.

"I remember the day I got this yearbook," she said softly, turning back to face Noah in the living room. "It was the last day of tenth grade. Summer was starting."

"It was before..." Noah's voice dropped, and his gaze fell to the floor. "Everything."

It was early that summer when Noah and Vanessa had so stupidly and irresponsibly gone "all the way." It was inevitable, she guessed, considering how close they'd been. Yes, they were kids. Young and dumb. But she trusted him completely and loved him with every fiber of her being.

Vanessa brought the yearbook over and sat down on the couch, patting the empty spot next to her. "Come on. For old times' sake."

"My mother set this up," Noah grumbled, getting up to move to the sofa next to Vanessa, close enough for her to smell a hint of woodsy cologne and clean shampoo.

"Ya think?" Vanessa laughed, rolling her eyes. "She's a bit of a...manipulator."

He sighed. "A bit? Yeah, she obviously wanted us to see this yearbook."

"Let's humor her." Vanessa opened it and began to flip through the pages, her mind and heart transported to 1995, when things were bright and happy and easy, and she would have bet her bottom dollar she'd be marrying the man sitting next to her.

"Oh, man." Noah laughed, stopping her at a page and pointing at a familiar-looking woman. "Is that Mrs. Goldenblatt? The music teacher?"

"Yes, it is." Vanessa smiled at the memory. "Remember how terrible we were in music class?"

"Hey, speak for yourself." He drew back. "I played that recorder like a boss."

Vanessa snorted. "What did we always say she looked like?"

"A poodle," Noah answered, a soft smile pulling at his mouth. "You always called her the poodle. And for some reason, I thought you were hilarious."

Vanessa looked at sweet Mrs. Goldenblatt's gigantic nest of honey blond curls. "I stand by that nickname."

They continued perusing the time capsule of memories, stopping in spots to laugh at age-old inside jokes or remember stories and classmates.

By the time they got to the team sports sections, they'd laughed and reminisced enough to break down the concrete wall of tension that had been stuck between them.

"Oh, look, your baseball picture!" Vanessa pointed at a quarter-page spread of sixteen-year-old Noah in a batter's stance, glaring fiercely into the camera with the bat over his shoulder. "Wow, I don't remember you taking yourself quite that seriously," she teased.

"Hey, I was the star player." He nudged her, leaning closer to see the picture.

"The star ballplayer and first chair recorder... What didn't you do?" she joked.

They flipped to the next section, where a group of girls holding up garments, one of them being Vanessa, grinned proudly into the camera, underneath the headline, "Fashion Design."

"That's what I didn't do," Noah said.

"I forgot about fashion design." Vanessa smiled, running her thumb across the glossy page. "It was an elective course. The boys did woodshop and they let the girls do fashion design. We had little sewing stations and everything."

Vanessa studied herself in the photo. Her smile was beaming and bright as she held up a pink-and-blue striped sweater with the other girls. Oh, if only she'd known what was coming that summer.

They continued on, and as they laughed and talked their way through every page of the yearbook, Vanessa grew more and more comfortable and at ease.

It was like a little break from reality, a tiny glimpse into the bubble of the past, where none of the pain and regrets of reality existed, and Vanessa and Noah could remember their roots as the very best of friends.

Before she knew it, Vanessa had flipped through every page of the yearbook, and somehow, someway, everything was different. The ice between them had melted away.

"Is that the end of it?" he asked, thumbing the last page.

"I think we've reached the end. We've successfully relived sophomore year." Without thinking, Vanessa turned over the last page of student pictures, revealing the blank sheets in the back of the book where other kids would sign and write notes to each other.

Before she had a chance to say anything or flip the page back, she and Noah were both staring straight at a one-paragraph love note written in bubbly, youthful print from Vanessa to Noah.

She held her breath, her gaze stuck on the words in front of them, which were decorated with pink highlighter hearts and smiley faces.

To the best boyfriend in the world! I love you, Noah Ellison! Thank you for being my best friend all the time, always making me laugh, and never letting me down. I hope this summer is filled with beach days, movie nights, and as many chocolate chip muffins as your mom will let us eat, ha ha. Not sure how I could get through life without you, but really glad I never have to find out! Can't wait to be your wife one day and live in a big house on the beach! Love love love forever, your Ness.

Oh.

Suddenly, the tension was back, and more palpable than ever.

Next to her, she felt Noah's whole body stiffen.

"I, um..." Vanessa slowly shut the yearbook, swallowing what felt like sand in her throat. "I really need to get going...maybe we can try calling Cricket again, or—"

"Vanessa." He turned to her, his steel-blue gaze pinning her.

"Noah." She croaked his name through the lump in her throat.

"We were so sure." He stared down at the shut book as he shook his head. "We were so darn sure. Everything could have been fine. Great, even. We were always meant to..."

When he didn't finish for three full heartbeats, she leaned a millimeter closer. "Meant to what?"

"Be together," he said, low and soft.

She patted the front cover of the yearbook. "Yeah, well, clearly I thought so too. You weren't alone in that." Vanessa squeezed her eyes shut, getting up quickly. "I'm trying the door again."

"Ness."

She walked to the front door, reached for the handle, and, sure enough, it turned and opened.

"It's unlocked now," she said over her shoulder, grabbing her purse and slipping out the door. "Bye, Noah."

Before she could hear if he said anything in response, she rushed down the staircase, tears springing into her eyes.

She really did ruin everything. Not by getting pregnant, but by leaving and refusing to come back. By letting Bill Young win. By being so darn stupid and stubborn.

She broke that boy's heart, and now he was a man with trust issues and resentment because of her.

That brief half hour spent looking through the yearbook was a slap across the face that reminded Vanessa just how special her relationship with Noah had been... and just how big of a mess she'd made when she ruined it.

And she'd have to live with the result of that for the rest of her life.

Chapter Eleven
Daisy

Daisy Elizabeth Bennett was no stranger to confrontation. As a full-time nurse at the hospital, she'd dealt with more than her fair share of unruly patients and nasty coworkers, arrogant doctors and hellacious administrators. So, Daisy could generally hold her own on the battlefield of life...or at least in the hospital.

She prided herself, in fact, on having a backbone and sticking up for herself even when it wasn't easy. Of course, sometimes she was a little hard-headed, and dug her heels in too much, leading to trouble.

For example, the fight she'd had with Mom a couple of weeks ago that even now made Daisy shudder when she thought about it. The horrible things she'd said in her anger and frustration still kept her up at night, regretting every word that hurt her sweet mother.

She'd felt absolutely terrible ever since and was trying her hardest to earn Gloria's forgiveness and show her how wrong she was, and how sorry she was. She was glad, however, that the confrontation led to such a breakthrough with Mom, that she was finally able to just melt the façade and fall into her mother's arms and...need her.

She'd been trying so hard not to need her mom, to be

an independent adult who was about to get married and could make all her own decisions. But it was lonely. And sad. And Daisy had gotten so wrapped up in the lavish lifestyle of her future in-laws that she'd lost herself in all the glitz and glam.

The fight with Mom had been a massive wake-up call, throwing her through a glass window of reality, and Daisy had suddenly realized what an absolute brat she had been.

She could only blame herself for her actions and words. But if she were really to step out and make progress toward maturity, she had to have this discussion with Linda Whittington.

She'd worked a 7-to-7 day shift for a nice change, so it was nearly eight o'clock on a warm summer night when she finished her patient paperwork. Taking one last check on Bob Hartmann's oxygen saturation—it was good—and filling in the night nurse on Margaret Horn's nausea and her medication, she was good to go.

She couldn't delay this any longer. Nerves crawled up her spine as she logged out of the employee portal on the hospital computer and tried to prepare for the conversation she was about to have.

As Daisy rode the elevator to the ground floor of the hospital and walked to the parking lot, she wondered why in the world she was so *scared* of Linda.

Maybe it wasn't fear, per se, but intimidation. Maybe it was just that Daisy had never truly felt good enough for Kyle, or the family as a whole, and she so deeply and desperately wanted to fit in. And, of course, fitting in would only happen with the stamp of Linda's approval.

But ever since the blowup with Mom, she'd hardly been able to look herself in the mirror, knowing how shallow and nasty and selfish this process—and the ultra-wealthy people around her—had made her.

Daisy had to clean up the mess she'd made in the past several months and make absolutely sure that things were different going forward.

She rolled her eyes at the electronic dings of her fancy Mercedes, which was Kyle's materialistic way of apologizing for their last massive fight. She couldn't lie, she loved the car. It was gorgeous.

But something about driving it just never felt quite right. Of course, if she ever admitted that to Kyle he'd flip out.

She cruised out of the hospital parking lot, heading down the main highway toward the luxury golf and beach community where the Whittington mansion sat proudly overlooking the Gulf of Mexico.

Daisy had already arranged to meet with Linda tonight to go over the current status of everything, now that the wedding was only three months away. She decided it was the perfect time to have a nice, respectful heart-to-heart with her fiancé's mother.

She could do that, right?

Daisy typed in the code she knew by heart now, watching the big, iron gates of the Whittington house slowly glide open, and she drove up the paved driveway and parked her car in front of the mansion.

Wishing her heart wasn't beating so fast and her palms weren't so sweaty, Daisy walked up to the front door and gave it a knock.

Melanie, the housekeeper, opened the door. "Daisy, honey! Welcome."

"Hi, Mel." Daisy slipped off her work sneakers and handed Melanie her purse to put away, always most comfortable around the ever-present housekeeper at the Whittingtons'. She was quite possibly the most real and down to earth person under the roof. "Thank you so much."

"You've just finished work?" Melanie glanced at Daisy's flowered scrubs. "That's unusual."

"I know. I scored a day shift for a change, but with all those doctors coming in and out? I think the overnights are calmer."

"Whatever time of day, you are a saint for being a nurse." She shook her head and leaned closer, lowering her voice to a whisper. "It won't be long until you are done working for good, yes?"

"That's the plan," Daisy agreed, but for some reason the idea of quitting work once she was married didn't sound quite as appealing as it had when she and Kyle first discussed it.

Day or night shift, she loved working as a nurse. It was the essence of who she was.

Maybe she could bring that up to Linda, too. Maybe staying at work would help Daisy stay grounded once she was a part of this high-flying family for good.

"Daisy, dear." Linda glided across the marble

entryway wearing a satin loungewear set that probably cost a month's rent.

"Hi, Linda." She leaned forward to give Linda their typical greeting, an air kiss on each cheek. "How are you?"

"Better than you, I'm sure." Linda frowned, looking Daisy's scrubs up and down. "You must be exhausted from a day in a hospital." She cringed, making Daisy wonder if she should have showered at home before coming here. Maybe day-old scrubs weren't clean enough for this house.

"I could never handle it," Linda said, gesturing her to the dining room table, where they always met for the business of discussing the wedding.

"It was an easy day, actually," Daisy said. "The worst thing I had to do today was take out a trach tube, so, all in all, a good day."

"I don't know what that is and I don't want to know." She arched a brow as best she could through the iron walls of Botox in her forehead. "Now, sit, sit. We have a lot to discuss."

Daisy scanned the table, which had papers spread all over it and Linda's laptop open at the head of the table to one of their many wedding planning spreadsheets.

"I heard about the hair and makeup debacle." Linda turned, taking off her Tiffany reading glasses and giving Daisy a look of concern that felt almost genuine. "Trisha called me and told me you didn't care for the look. See, this is why I should have come with you." She nudged Daisy. "I need to be there to handle these things!"

"I brought my mother," Daisy said, taking the seat to Linda's right.

"Yes, and that's...that's great, sweetie. But you must remember that a sophisticated opinion is very important in these matters. This is a very high-class wedding. I scheduled another trial that I simply insist on being part of. We're going to slightly alter the hair and makeup, but I do think we need to stick with—"

"Linda."

She drew back, surprised by Daisy's interruption. "Yes?"

"I need to talk to you."

Linda once again attempted to frown through her tight forehead, angling her head in confusion. "What about, dear?"

Daisy's heart thumped in her chest and she rubbed her palms over her thighs, wishing she wasn't so stupidly nervous.

"I really, really appreciate how much you've done for this wedding. You've been beyond generous with your money and time and energy, and I just want you to know I'm so grateful. I know it's going to be absolutely beautiful."

Linda hesitated, then gave a sniff. "Well, thank you, Daisy. But why do I have the feeling that's not all you want to say?"

"Because it's not." Daisy glanced down, picking at a hangnail. "Linda, I...I was kind of wondering if maybe I—well, my mother and I—could make a couple of changes to the wedding?"

Linda's blue eyes widened. "Changes?"

"Nothing major, of course. It's just that I feel like a lot of this isn't really...I don't know...but it's not *me*." She shrugged and offered a smile that was very much not reciprocated.

"This wedding is going to be a five-star black-tie *event*. An experience." Linda nearly ground out the words, heightening Daisy's humming anxiety. "It isn't your basic stamped-out wedding. You realize that, don't you? You may never have been to an occasion like this one."

And she didn't even want to go to *this* one.

"I totally understand that, and it's going to be amazing. But could we consider paring down the guest list a bit? There are so many people coming that I've never met, and—"

"Daisy." Linda held up a hand and closed her eyes, visibly digging for patience. "Arthur and I are hosting a luxurious banquet party to celebrate the marriage of our oldest son. It's proper etiquette in, well, *our* world to invite colleagues and associates."

"But I'm the bride," she whispered, hating that her voice sounded weak.

But she was weak, and this woman was a human bulldozer.

"And I'm the hostess." Linda swallowed. "We can't change the guest list, RSVPs have already been sent out."

"Okay, well, could I maybe have a different dress to change into after the ceremony? One that's not so...

ruffly?" She offered an awkward laugh. "I'm not really able to dance in the designer gown."

"Dress changes are tacky, sweetie. Getting all sweaty and sexy? No. Not your style and certainly not the image we're going for. I thought we discussed this already."

Frustration burned hot in Daisy's belly and finally she sat up straight and raised her chin.

"Linda, please listen to me. I know that you have a no-budget, unlimited credit card and five hundred first-class friends to impress and a taste for everything wildly expensive and fancy. I know that Kyle is your son, and you want this party to be the event of the season. But you have completely taken over everything and made it all about *you* and what *you* want." She stared at Linda's stunned expression and took a breath before continuing. "It's my wedding day. I'm the bride."

Linda stared at her in stunned silence, her jaw falling slack as she shuttered her long, thick, and probably fake eyelashes with a sigh of utter and complete irritation. Like she just couldn't be bothered with something so pesky as a *bride* when she was planning a *wedding*.

"I don't mean to offend you, Linda, and I really don't want to seem ungrateful—"

"Well, you certainly sound ungrateful." Kyle's voice startled Daisy, and she whipped around to see her fiancé standing in the hallway, staring at her with disdain and anger.

"Kyle...you're...what are you..." Daisy stammered, feeling her cheeks get hot.

"Honey." Linda stood up and gave her son a tight

hug. "I didn't know you were stopping by."

"Dad said I could borrow the Bentley tomorrow." His gaze slid back over to Daisy. "I came in through the pool door."

Of course, the Whittington mansion was big enough that someone could easily enter through the pool door off of the patio without anyone hearing or noticing.

Daisy locked eyes with her future husband. He was the right man for her, she knew it. He was funny and charming and smart, and he'd swept her off her feet like no one ever had.

She clung to his gaze now, knowing that this man, the man she was about to marry, was going to be on her side and in her corner. They were about to be life partners. He had to stand up for her. He *had* to.

"What were you two talking about?" Kyle frowned. "Daisy, are you unhappy with my mother's plans?"

"No, not at all," she said quickly.

"Yes, she's quite unhappy," Linda interjected, crossing her arms and giving Daisy a nasty glare she'd never seen before but somehow knew the woman was capable of. "Daisy feels that I've taken over the entire wedding and made it all about me. Do you think that, Kyle?"

Daisy held her breath and clenched her jaw, begging and praying silently for the words she needed to hear. Support. Backup. Love. Respect.

Kyle, please be the husband I want you to be.

She bit her lip so hard she tasted blood while her fiancé paused for a long time, glancing back and forth between his fiancée and his mother while Daisy's heart pounded.

"Of course not," he said finally. "Mother, you've been awesome planning everything, organizing everything. None of this would be possible without you. Daisy is just having some pre-wedding jitters. Isn't that right, Daisy?"

She swallowed, her throat thick with unshed tears.

"I just...I was not feeling...heard. I feel like the wedding isn't for me, or for us, but more to impress people. And a lot of it just doesn't feel very much like my personality. In truth, I got swept up in all the money and expensive things but now I'm about to have a wedding in a room full of people I don't know wearing a dress I hate, and my own mother hasn't even been a part of any of it."

"Daisy, come on." Kyle rolled his eyes, visibly inching closer to Linda. "Your mom is busy running a...a food place."

"It's actually called a diner," she said softly.

He didn't even hear her. "My mother plans events and parties like this all the time. It's her thing. She's good —no, she's *great*—at it. Why don't you just accept the designer dress and the bougie party and enjoy it?"

Linda drew back, sniffling as if she was upset, but Daisy could see the tiniest hint of a sly smile on her lips.

She'd won, and she knew it.

Daisy pinned her gaze on Kyle's, desperately trying to communicate with him to stand up for her and be on her side, but it was very clear where he stood.

"I'm gonna go." Daisy pushed past both of them and grabbed her purse off the oversized flower-covered table in the main entry, heading out the front door as a tear fell from her eye.

Before she could get to her car, she heard Kyle's footsteps running out onto the driveway. "Daisy, wait."

An apology? Had he changed his mind and seen her side and realized that his mother was a filthy rich control freak?

"What?" She turned around, breathing the word.

"What the hell has gotten into you?" He frowned, shaking his head with disapproval. "That woman has done everything for me, given me the world. And you just treat her with disregard and disrespect."

She choked softly. "Are you *serious*?"

"As a heart attack. Do I have to remind you my family is paying every dime for this wedding?"

The words hit like a gut punch so hard, she winced and stepped back. "I'm well aware of that, thank you."

"Then why would you tell her that you hate your dress and complain about the guest list and whatever other issues you're having? Daisy, she's done all of this for us."

"I know, and I'm really grateful!" she insisted, frustration rising in her voice. "I just feel like I got lost in the whole thing, and it's my wedding, not hers."

He lifted a smug shoulder. "I mean, she's paying for it, so it's kind of hers."

"Then I wish she wasn't!" Daisy blurted out, now fully emotional. "I wish we were just getting married on the beach with fifty people we know and love and had a taco bar and cupcakes."

He laughed, a smug, entitled, belittling laugh. "You're being ridiculous."

"How is that ridiculous? Our wedding is about our love for each other, remember?"

"Daisy, it's more than that. It's a big deal for the kind of people my parents associate with. It's a statement about who they are, and it demonstrates...something you wouldn't understand."

"It demonstrates that they're filthy rich," she muttered.

"Watch it, Daisy."

"How can this wedding mean anything except to tell the world we love each other and want to commit our lives to each other forever?" she asked.

She studied Kyle for a moment as he glanced off into the night sky, his jaw clenching.

Who is this man, she thought with a startled gasp.

He wasn't the enchanting and sophisticated and, yes, wealthy young man who'd swept her off her feet and opened up a world of new experiences she'd never thought she'd have. Things like country clubs and private planes and exotic vacations.

She was only twenty-four, and when she met Kyle, he'd offered her an entirely new way of life, filled with fun and extravagance and fanciness. It was captivating.

But now, the man in front of her just looked entitled and arrogant and mean. His shadowed, glaring eyes didn't look a thing like the dazzling blue ones she'd fallen so hard for, and his stiff body language felt a bit threatening.

"I'm going home," she announced, turning around to unlock her stupid overpriced car.

"Daisy." He grabbed her arm, clutching his fingers around her wrist. "Don't walk away from me."

The tone in his cold voice sent an icy chill up her spine.

"I have done so much for you. My family, and specifically my mother, has done so much for you. She's accepted you and embraced you and is giving you the wedding that every girl dreams of. You need to go apologize to her."

"I most certainly will not." She shook her arm free, giving him a nasty glare as she got into the Mercedes. "And for the record, not every girl dreams of this."

Daisy didn't cry on the drive home like she expected to. She rolled the top down on the car and let the warm, nighttime air settle into her skin.

She felt something shift as she made the turn to go to the only place she wanted to go in the whole world—to her mother.

Normally, when she and Kyle fought—which had been frequently in the last few months—Daisy instantly wanted to make things better. She'd cry and apologize and beg him to let it go and be happy again. And, after a time, he would. He'd apologize, too—sometimes with a lavish gift, if he'd been really awful—and they'd continue on and be happy.

But right now, Daisy felt different. She felt cold and mad and...numb. To her shock and terror, she wasn't sure what she wanted to do...and that included marrying him.

Chapter Twelve

Emily

"He said that to you?" Emily gasped in horror as she, Vanessa, and Gloria all sat in the sun-washed living room at Gloria's condo on Sunday morning, listening to Daisy share the latest update on the wedding planning saga.

And it was *not* a good one, underscoring her fears that all men were basically awful. She so wanted to let go of that belief and not let her abusive ex-husband darken her view of the world.

But Kyle wasn't doing anything to help that cause.

"Yes, that's exactly what he said." Daisy leaned back on the sofa, rolling her eyes as she sipped coffee from a Gloria's Diner mug. "He was completely in Linda's corner, backed her up the whole time. I felt so ganged up on. And then when I tried to leave, he came out into the driveway. I thought he was maybe going to apologize, but oh, no. I just got *another* earful."

Emily shifted her attention to Gloria, who visibly winced.

"He told me I should apologize *to her*," Daisy continued with a sigh of misery and a look at her mother. "I tried," she said. "I tried to have a productive and honest conversation with my future mother-in-law. Now I've just made a bad situation way, way worse. I should have just kept my mouth shut."

"Absolutely not," Vanessa chimed in, tucking her legs underneath her as she sipped her coffee and took a bite of one of the muffins that Gloria had put out for everyone. "You spoke your mind, Daisy. And you had every right to."

Gloria nodded in agreement. "It's true. I'm really proud of you for standing up for yourself."

"I don't feel proud of myself." Daisy's shoulders sank. "I thought that woman had a heart, you know? That she'd be loving—okay, not *loving*—but at least understanding. But now I feel like I messed everything up, and Kyle is mad and they're both mad and I seem ungrateful and... *urgh!*" She buried her face in her hands. "I don't know what to do."

Emily took a deep drink of coffee as she considered exactly what to advise her younger cousin. Without basically saying, "Run and run fast, Em."

She leaned in and tried a gentler approach. "Did he at least acknowledge that your feelings are valid, even if he doesn't agree with them?"

Daisy snorted dryly. "Uh...no. He told me I'm being ridiculous. I tried to leave, but then he grabbed my arm and stopped me, insisting that I—"

"Wait, *what?*" Emily could practically feel the hairs on the back of her neck stand up. "He *grabbed* you?"

Daisy opened her mouth to respond, waving a dismissive hand as the wheels clearly turned in her brain, remembering what Emily had gone through. "Well, it was just like a gentle grab. It wasn't like he was trying to hurt me or anything..."

"I do not like that, Daisy." Gloria frowned, turning to Vanessa and Emily for support, not that she had to.

"Look, Daisy." Emily sighed and steadied her voice. "I don't know Kyle Whittington. And I'm not going to make assumptions about your fiancé or your relationship. But physical aggression like that is really, really scary. And wrong."

And dangerous, she added mentally, but Emily was already about to break.

"I don't know if I would call it aggression..."

"It's a red flag," Emily continued, leaning forward in the chair and setting her mug on the coffee table, meeting Daisy's gaze. "And that aside, he shouldn't be siding with his mother over you."

"She's right," Vanessa agreed. "He needs to step up and be a man and treat you like the woman who is about to be his wife. With respect and love and understanding."

"And gentleness," Emily added.

"Listen to them, Em," Gloria said, having been surprisingly quiet but there was pain in her expression as she looked at her daughter. "If he truly loves you, Dais, and he is the man for you, then he will put you first. Above his mother, above his friends, above his money. You will be his number one."

Daisy pressed her lips together, a single tear falling down her cheek. She was silent for a few beats. "It was just a bad night, you guys. Tensions are high, everyone is stressed about the wedding and Kyle has had a lot going on with work."

Oh, no. The *excuses*.

Emily felt like she was looking in a mirror at her past self, listening to Daisy conjure up every imaginable reason for why it was okay that her husband acted that way and treated her that way.

It was always a game of excuse making. Until one day, there was no excusing his behavior.

Emily did not want to see Daisy go through anything even remotely close to what she'd endured in her marriage to Doug.

"Just be careful, Daisy," she warned. "Be sure you're not making a mistake."

Daisy grunted. "I'm not. It's Kyle. I love him so, so much. He's just, you know, loyal to his mother and wanted to defend her. Maybe it's not such a bad thing."

Emily cringed at the twisted logic, watching Daisy's eyes dart back and forth between the other women as she attempted to justify and rationalize her fiancé's behavior.

"He should have defended you," Gloria said softly, looking down at her coffee, as unwilling to hurt Daisy as they all were, but clearly aching for her to take off the blinders.

"You have to make sure you think long term," Vanessa said, just as gently as the others. "Because if him choosing his mother over you time after time becomes a pattern, that could really be a problem. Especially when it comes to big life things like where to live, what kind of house to buy, how to raise a family. You don't want to end up married to Linda, if you know what I'm saying."

Daisy's eyes widened with visible fear, her lip trembling.

"To be fair," Vanessa added quickly, "you're also sitting around with three divorced women, so maybe we aren't the best advice givers."

Glo snorted.

"Except you." Vanessa shifted her gaze to Emily. "Emily, I think you can offer the best input here."

Emily swallowed, taking a deep breath as she looked at the cousin who she'd grown to love in such a short time. What should she say to her?

The obvious, of course: *get out and get out now. Cut him off, block his number, be done, because you deserve so much more.*

But Emily knew one other thing about this situation —no one could tell Daisy what to do. The decision had to be hers, made with clarity, and it had to rise up from her heart. Hopefully, that would happen before she walked down the aisle in the gown she hated and married into a family she feared.

But it had to be Daisy's decision, and she was a smart girl. Blind at the moment, but smart. All they could do was ask her the questions that helped her see straight.

Daisy lifted her gaze, twisting the ends of her long, dark hair in between her fingertips. "I don't think it's going to be a pattern," she said softly. "The Linda thing. Maybe he just feels indebted to her because she's paying for everything."

"And won't he always feel that way?" Emily asked softly. "Because she'll always be buying him stuff. And you, indirectly."

"Is that something you really want?" Vanessa asked. "Because Linda is going to be controlling things, and Kyle is going to let her. I mean, don't take this the wrong way, Daisy, but do you want to stop working and be a rich wife?"

Daisy's face fell and she tilted her head back, visibly lost and overwhelmed by all of the uncertainty and second-guessing. "I thought so. They all made it sound so wonderful and appealing to live like that. I mean, isn't it every girl's dream?"

"Being a nurse was your dream," Gloria said. "When you were a little girl, you would put on a white hat and bring me a tray, pretending I was in the hospital and you were my nurse."

Daisy gave a dry laugh. "Now that's a weird little girl game."

"No, it wasn't," Gloria said. "You had a dream. You wanted to be a nurse."

"Then I wanted to be...living in a mansion on the beach, like Linda." She made a face of pure disgust. "God save me from being anything like her."

The comment gave Emily hope. "Daisy, all I can tell you is that you need to think really, really hard about the decision you're making. Not just with obnoxious Linda and all the money flaunting, but with Kyle. You have to be certain he's going to be your supporter and your partner and your best friend. Are you one hundred percent certain of that?"

Daisy blinked at Emily, her eyes filling with tears. "I'm not certain of anything right now. I think maybe tensions are just high and we're all stressed and it's hectic. But then I'm like...what if these are his true colors and I'm making a huge mistake and...and..." She began to sob, bringing them all instantly closer to hug and love her.

"We're all here for you, Dais." Gloria wrapped an arm around her daughter.

"Absolutely," Vanessa added. "You have our support."

Daisy looked at Emily expectantly, waiting for her to add in her unwavering support.

"I think you should be really careful, Daisy," she whispered. "I say that as your cousin, your friend, and a woman who's been through the hell of a husband who..." She swallowed. "I just don't want you to go through what I did."

Daisy nodded, sniffling and wiping her eyes. "I know. Thank you. Okay, okay, this is enough about me. Can we talk about something else? Anything? How about our *not dead* grandmother? I can't believe this investigator really thinks she's alive."

Since the four women were the only people in the world who knew what was going on with Vanessa and Gloria's mother, they delved into that topic next, and Daisy looked visibly relieved.

Changing the topic was easy...but nothing about

Daisy's situation was simple. It was dark and scary and took Emily back to places she never wanted to go again.

While they exhausted one subject and moved to the next, Emily considered telling them about her dinner plans to see Reed Collins and dive deeper into her dark past but opted not to.

Still, the upcoming appointment loomed, so she tried to just enjoy her new family and not think about what she had to do that evening.

Since Emily's dinner with Reed Collins was most definitely not a date, she wasn't going to dress for one.

She picked a casual white tank top and jeans, barely put on makeup, and tied her hair in a ponytail, which, to her, screamed, "I'm not trying to impress you."

Sure, it was hard not to have a mini crush on the guy. He was brilliant and successful and great-looking, probably not thirty-five years old. Plus, she had that connection of being the only person in town who knew his true identity as a mega successful author.

But Emily's divorce wasn't even completely finalized, and even in a few weeks after the paperwork went through, it was way, way too soon to date. Not that this was a date, she reminded herself. Anyway, if the morning with Daisy had taught her anything, it was that Emily had learned hard, hard lessons about trusting men and it would be a long time, if ever, before Emily Young let another man into her heart.

Since the restaurant where they'd decided to meet was only a couple of miles from Emily and Vanessa's beach house, she decided to ride her bike and enjoy the glorious day. There was a bike trail that ran parallel to 30A, the now famous strip that had given this whole tourist section of the Panhandle its nickname.

Riding west along the trail, she looked to her left and could see down the small side streets directly to the Gulf, which was glistening today. The breeze and speed whipped her ponytail back and forth, lifting her spirits.

What an amazing place she'd landed, she mused as she passed a beachfront resort. And she wasn't just another "30A tourist," either. She *lived* here.

Well, she was sharing a place with Vanessa, which was fun, but...

She remembered Daisy's throwaway comment about being roommates, the thought churning up very mixed emotions. For one thing, she knew in her heart that Daisy was making a mistake with this marriage, but it wasn't her place to smack sense into her younger cousin.

For another? The idea was a dream and Emily so longed for a chance to live like that—not that she didn't love living with Vanessa. But they worked together, too, and she wanted to be young and live like a thirty-year-old.

She was nearly at the restaurant—Crabby Steve's, it was called, right on the water—but she was early, even with biking. To kill a few minutes, she turned down one of the side streets that went to the water, planning to stop, catch her breath, and take in the scenes at the beach.

As she reached the end of a very small street, she looked left, her eye catching on a precious yellow house—a cottage, practically—on the corner so that one whole side faced the beach.

Something about the house caught her heart, making her ignore the water view and take in the two wraparound decks on both levels and the turquoise shutters that made the place so sweet.

And the For Rent sign in the front yard.

"Oh." She let out a little whimper of longing, squinting at the sign like it was...well, a sign.

"Two bedrooms, entire second floor, long-term renters only," she read out loud.

The whole second floor? What would that cost? A fortune for one person, she assumed, but that didn't stop her from taking out her phone and clicking the sign to save the number.

Because...it was a literal sign, and Emily wasn't about to ignore that.

Then she checked her watch and rode to the restaurant.

Crabby Steve's was essentially a beach shack, with a huge, weathered deck for umbrella-covered tables directly on the water. She peered up at the packed tables, happy to see Reed give her a wave from one of them.

She waved back and locked her bike, the whole time reminding herself that not only wasn't this a date, but she would have to recount emotions about her marriage. That wasn't going to be easy, especially after this morning's talk with Emily.

But she'd agreed to this—well, she'd agreed when she thought it was a date—so in she went to the lion's den and hoped Reed Collins didn't eat her alive.

"Emily." Reed stood as she approached. He wore a plain black T-shirt and khaki shorts. He didn't have his typical ballcap on, and his hair was long and perfectly tousled. "Hey, so glad you made it."

"It was easy." She smiled, gesturing out to the parking lot. "And fun on two wheels."

"Brilliant way to get around," he said, pulling out a chair kitty-corner from his. "I got here a little early to be sure we had a water-view table."

"That was nice of you," she said, settling into the chair and looking around at the lively tables and down a long wooden walkway to the beach, realizing they'd be here for the sunset.

Very romantic...except it wasn't.

A server came up to them with a glass of iced water for her. "And you didn't get stood up," she said, laughing with Reed as if they had an inside joke. "How about we start with some drinks?"

He ordered a beer, so Emily did, too, but she'd likely not drink much. She wanted to avoid anything that could make her emotional if she had to talk about her ex-husband during this "interview."

"I've been wanting to try this place," he said, scooting in and following her gaze. "It's apparently a staple when you come to Rosemary Beach."

"Why didn't you?" she asked.

"Oh, I don't have anyone to have dinner with," he

said matter-of-factly, lifting a shoulder. "Sitting alone at Gloria's Diner with a laptop is one thing, but even the loneliest of lone wolves can't come to a place like this solo."

"That's fair." Emily ran her fingers along the plastic menu without looking at it. "But haven't you met at least one person since you've been in this area?"

He shook his head. "Just you. I try to keep a *really* low profile when I'm staying somewhere for writing research."

"I remember," Emily said. "The alias and the hat and everything."

"Plus, no reason to make friends and get all connected to a place when I know I'm leaving."

A small thread of disappointment wormed its way through her gut. Of course Reed was leaving. He was only in Rosemary Beach—well, technically, he was living in Panama City Beach on a houseboat—until he finished writing his current novel, which was set here.

After that, he'd go to whatever random location he decided to set as the backdrop for the next Sam Steele book, and Emily would likely never see him again.

As if she needed *another* reason to remember that this wasn't a date.

"But I'm glad I met you," Reed said. "You're one of maybe ten people in the world who know who I am. It's refreshing to have a friend."

Emily angled her head, meeting his gaze. "You have no idea how much I feel that."

He looked curious at the comment, but the waitress

came back, gave them their drinks, and they ordered apps and some entrees. While they waited, they chatted easily, with Emily telling him about her family here—she gave him the shortest version of the story of how she'd been adopted and recently reconnected with her biological parents—and how excited she was for tomorrow's grand opening.

"Oh, that's a big day. Should you be at the store tonight?" Reed asked.

"Nope. We're so ready, it hurts. Honestly, we could have opened last week, but Vanessa wanted everything just so." She gave a grin. "It's cool. I'm glad not to think about it and just enjoy this."

"Well, I hope you enjoy it when I start, uh, interviewing you."

She picked up a conch fritter, inhaling the delicious sea scent. "You can start. I'll drown my sorrows in deep-fried heaven."

He laughed but his expression grew serious, and he averted his gaze down toward the table.

"I don't want to force you to go in-depth about anything if you're not comfortable," he started. "I just really could use some personal emotion to draw inspiration from. In the words of my editor, Sam's feelings about his divorce were flat, lifeless, and utterly one dimensional."

"Yikes." Emily cringed, dabbing the corner of her mouth with a paper napkin. "Well, normally I don't like to drone on about my sob story, but if the great career of..."—she lowered her voice and glanced left and right at the tables near them— "R.C. Anderson is on the line, well, I guess I'll make an exception."

He chuckled. "I trust you with my secret, Emily."

For some reason, the statement, which was genuine and warm, touched her. She scooted her chair in and nodded.

"And I trust you with my past, Reed. Hit me with your questions."

"Not to be a total weirdo, but is it okay if I take notes?" He pulled his phone out of his pocket and set it on the table, offering a sheepish smile. "I just want to remember all the little nuances."

Emily waved a dismissive hand. "I mean, you're interviewing me for research. Take whatever notes you need. I, unlike you, am an open book, no pun intended."

He smiled, and it reached his eyes, making them gleam and look even more handsome than before. "I really appreciate that. So, do you want to just give me some background context about your marriage? Why it didn't work, how it started out, how you felt when you knew it was over...that kind of thing."

Emily leaned back, taking a deep drink of the light, refreshing beer and wondering where in the world to begin.

"I guess I should inform you that I'm not your typical divorcee. For one thing, the ink's not dry yet, and the stamp of freedom hasn't been placed on the paperwork. But it's done. And my marriage didn't end because of arguments, or infidelity, or some sort of massive disagreements that we couldn't seem to get past."

Reed listened intently, studying her, his expression focused and interested.

"We didn't grow apart slowly or fall for other people or simply lose feelings for each other. My story is different, so it's probably nothing like your character's."

"That's fine. I have to believe the underlying emotion is the same."

Yes, it probably was, she thought. Sadness, regret, and shame.

For a second, Daisy's face flashed in her mind, but she pushed it aside, focusing on the conversation at hand.

"The truth is, mine is really, really dark."

"How so?"

Emily let out a long sigh, putting her fritter back on the plate as she gathered her thoughts. How honest should she be?

She looked at Reed, seeing something undeniably comforting in his eyes—something she'd noticed the day she'd met him when she spilled the tea all over his computer. He made her feel safe in a strange, confusing way.

This would be okay, she decided.

"Doug was physically abusive," Emily said softly.

Reed's eyes closed as he leaned back with shock. "Emily...I am so sorry."

"It's okay. I'm perfectly fine now, and he's out of my life."

"You don't have to talk about this anymore if you don't want to." He pushed the phone an inch away. "I feel like a jerk trying to interview you and record notes. I'm so sorry. I had no idea—"

"Reed, it's fine, really." She offered a gentle laugh and went to put her hand over the phone, but it landed on his. She added a little pressure before letting go. "I actually think I can help you. And I'm okay talking about it, I promise."

He nodded, gritting his teeth. "He hit you?"

"He did worse than hit me."

Reed clenched his jaw, narrowing his eyes at the impact of Emily's words. "What a...well, I'll go with monster out of respect. But there are worse things to call a man like that."

"Monster works." Emily took a deep breath and leaned back in the booth. "It started out with loud fights. Except, they weren't really fights. They were just him yelling at me and me asking him to stop. Then, about a year or so into our marriage, he hit me for the first time. Just struck me right across the face."

Reed swallowed, his face pale. "I want to beat this guy up. I can't believe you went through this, Emily."

"To make a long story short, the abuse spiraled over several years, finally culminating with me actually fearing for my life. He'd carefully and tactfully cut everyone off who I was close to and made me quit my job. I had no one. I'd frequently go weeks on end without seeing another soul besides Doug. Then, my Grandma Gigi died."

"Who adopted you?"

"Her daughter was my adopted mother, a single

mother, but she passed when I was young. Gigi raised me."

Once again, his shoulders sank. "Emily."

She smiled, lifting her brows. "I know, the stuff your novels are made of."

"Just...the kind of life that has probably made you a very strong woman."

The compliment warmed her. "Thank you."

"Were you close to your grandmother?"

Emily chuckled softly at the question, which was like asking if Mount Everest was tall.

"She was my world, Reed. She raised me and loved me and grounded me. And, in a sense, she saved me."

"How?" he asked.

"She knew—without me telling her—that things had really deteriorated with Doug. By the time she died, I was essentially trapped in the house and in the marriage, and I was scared. I had to sneak out just to see her, and sometimes..." She closed her eyes as she remembered the time he'd come home from work early and she'd been at Gigi's. Ouch. "He didn't like that."

She saw him squirm uncomfortably. "I apologize on behalf of the entire male population."

"Reed," she said softly. "I know all men aren't like him. At least, I'm trying to teach myself that."

He nodded slowly, holding her gaze, a silent message in his eyes. As if he wanted to show her that was true.

"But Gigi, yeah. I thought I did a good job of hiding it, but yes. She knew. I didn't realize she knew the full extent of it until she passed, when she left me a letter."

"What did it say?"

Emily sighed, remembering the day she read that letter with shaking hands, her tears falling onto the paper and smudging the ink. "It said that she knew how bad it was, much worse than I'd let on, and that she'd left me money—cash—in a safe place. She told me to take it and use it to escape him."

Reed's jaw went slack and his eyes wide, blinking with astonishment. "You ran away?'"

"I did. Which is more Nicholas Sparks than R.C. Anderson," she said, trying to make light of something that wasn't light at all.

"But why not just go to the police? Get him arrested?"

She winced. "If only I could. My ex-husband is a well-connected FBI agent who worked very closely with the local police. And, honestly, the whole lot of law enforcement is tight and, in some cases, corrupt."

"Now that I know from my research," he joked dryly. "But I understand how that could have made it difficult for you."

"Impossible," she agreed. "If I filed charges? No, the case would have been squashed and...I would have been...squashed, too." She gave a humorless smile. "By his fist."

"Emily." He dropped his head, letting out a groan. "I hate that you went through something so traumatic."

"Honestly? I hate it, too, but the whole thing made me tough and well, kind of fearless."

"How did you manage to get away from him?"

"With Gigi's cash, I made my way from Colorado to Florida with a fake ID and some terribly dyed and cut hair, trying to stay hidden. I ended up in Cocoa Beach, where I worked for a lovely family at their inn. I contacted my birth mother, and she showed up and brought me here."

Reed just stared at her, completely stunned as he tried to process the dump of information that was Emily's rollercoaster of a past.

"And now..." She sipped her beer, adding a smug and playful smile. "I'm drinking beer and eating conch fritters with you."

"What happened to Doug? Did he go to jail?"

"Oh, yes." She smiled, waving a hand. "Forgot to tell you the happy ending. Kind of an important part of the story."

"Yeah, slightly," he scoffed.

"Yes, I was working as a server at a wedding in Cocoa Beach and he showed up. He'd found me, somehow, despite all my efforts to leave absolutely zero trace. He gave me a good scare by waiting for me in my motel room, but thankfully one of the awesome women there was dating the chief of police. They arrested him and took him away. Fast-forward to now, my biological father is a lawyer and got my divorce expedited. Twenty-one more days and I'm legally free of him forever."

Reed ran his fingers through his brown hair, his eyes locked on her with a kind of fascination glimmering in his gaze.

"I'm shocked at how easy it was to tell you all of that,

honestly." She smiled, feeling a weight lift off of her chest. "I haven't told that story to anyone who wasn't family or a close family friend."

"I imagine it's really tough to talk about."

Emily lifted a shoulder, glancing to the side and watching a server carry a tray of burgers and fries through the bustling restaurant. "It's getting easier, actually. A lot easier."

"I'm so glad you're okay. I'm so glad you got away from that nightmare and you're free now."

"As a bird." She lifted her hands playfully.

Reed shook his head, chuckling softly. "I feel like such an idiot."

"Why?"

"Because I guess I'd just assumed you had some sort of normal, run-of-the-mill divorce. I asked you for an interview and...and I brought out *notes*. Only to find out you were a domestic violence victim." He angled his head, meeting her gaze with a serious expression. "I'm so sorry."

"Don't be." Emily waved a hand. "You couldn't have known."

Reed picked a fry off of his plate and took a bite, his attention still locked on Emily as his mind visibly spun. "You're incredibly strong, Emily."

"Thank you. I appreciate that. And, at the end of the day, divorce is divorce, so I'm still happy to share some emotions with you to help with your book."

"Are you sure?" He furrowed his brow. "I don't want to make you talk—"

"I promised you an interview," she reminded him with a smile, reaching across the table and tapping his phone. "Ask away."

Reed sucked in a breath, a slow smile pulling at his lips. "Okay, well, I'm not going to interrogate you. I guess if you could just give me a basic idea of the emotions that you felt from the divorce aspect of it all. Not the abuse and the running away, but...the ruined marriage. What was that like?"

Emily finished off her beer, setting the glass down on the table as she glanced around and pondered the question.

She'd always been so wrapped up in fear and pain and anxiety, she'd hardly had time to think about the broken marriage itself.

"Failure," she said after a long pause, letting the words fall out. "It felt like failure. I felt stupid and embarrassed for falling in love with such a soulless, evil person. I felt robbed of years of my life, years that were stolen from me. I felt, for a time, hopeless. Like this was a stain on my life that would never lift, and no matter what I did, I couldn't escape the horrible mistake of marrying the wrong person."

"You can't blame yourself," he said.

"I know, but I felt judged by the world for being divorced at twenty-nine. I grieved the life I thought I'd have—the life with a happy marriage and a house and kids. As hard as it is to believe, I'd visualized all of that with him before things got bad. It breaks my heart to think I might never have that, because I'm scarred and broken."

"Emily," Reed's voice was nearly a whisper. "You are the furthest imaginable thing from broken. You're an absolute badass who dyed her hair and got a fake ID and saved her own life. A literal heroine, if you ask me."

Emily couldn't help but laugh at his description of her, a soft flush warming her cheeks at the wonder and awe in his voice. "Well, thank you."

"And actually..." He leaned back, studying her. "That really does help me. I really appreciate you being so open and real about all of this."

She nodded, her heart feeling lighter than it had when she walked into the restaurant. "It feels good to talk about it so freely. To know it's in my past and not my present."

"And most definitely not your future," Reed added. "Which I have a feeling is really, really bright."

Emily's chest warmed with joy as she thought about Young at Heart opening tomorrow and all the good, exciting things in this new chapter of life.

"I think you're right." She nodded with certainty, straightening her shoulders. "I'm glad that we're friends," she added, meaning it.

Reed smiled, his dark eyes glimmering in the soft light of the fading sun. "I'm glad, too," he said. "I honestly have never met anyone like you."

She just smiled at him and turned to watch the sun disappear into the Gulf, gone like her old life, but leaving a glow of hope for the future.

Chapter Thirteen

Cricket

"You closing early today?" Noah walked into the salon, coming up for air after spending the morning working up in Cricket's loft while the flooring guys tore up her damaged old wood.

"As a matter of fact, I am." Cricket swept the floor, cleaning up all remnants of Sally Petrewski's split ends, which had desperately needed to go.

Cricket was itching to get her salon cleaned up and shut down for the day so she could head next door to the Young at Heart grand opening.

She had picked out a fabulous floral maxi, finished her hairdressing and bookkeeping for the day, and now was just about done cleaning up the store.

There was only one more task Cricket had to accomplish before she could go join in on the celebration for Vanessa and Emily.

"Noah, dear." She walked over to her son, who was reading something on his phone. A work email, no doubt. That wretched job.

"Yes? Sorry." He slid the phone into his back pocket, giving her his full attention. "Work stuff."

"I figured." She angled her head sympathetically.

"Speaking of, you work so hard. Is there any way you could take the rest of the afternoon off?"

He narrowed his eyes as if he knew this request likely had a Cricket-worthy ulterior motive. But it was a good one, so she powered on with a smile and a simple, "Please?"

"Um, no. It's Monday, and I'm swamped." He sighed. "I came down because I heard you vacuuming and thought you might need help. I have about five minutes until I have to hop on another call."

Well, it was a good thing Cricket didn't take no for an answer.

"Oh, of course, of course. I completely understand. It's just that...well...I'm going to a very important event this afternoon, and I was really just hoping and praying you'd accompany me."

"The opening of the boutique," he said bluntly, as a statement rather than a question.

"Oh." Cricket feigned surprise. "I wasn't aware you knew about that. Have you and Vanessa been talking more?"

He leveled his gaze. "Mom, I know you told Vanessa to go up to your loft the other day so that we'd run into each other, and I know you put out the yearbook so we'd reminisce about the good old days. And I know, although I still haven't figured out how, that you locked the door from the outside so she couldn't leave."

Cricket pushed her glasses up the bridge of her nose and lifted her chin confidently. "I haven't a single clue what you're talking about."

He laughed, shaking his head with slight amusement. "Okay. Look, I know what you're doing."

She frowned.

"I know you want me to fall for Vanessa again and remember all the good times we had as kids and be with her so that I'll stay here. Am I wrong?"

Cricket drew back, pressing her lips together, hating when she was quite *that* transparent.

Anyway, he was off a bit.

She didn't want Noah to be with Vanessa solely because she wanted him to stay in town. Obviously, that was a huge benefit. But no. Cricket wanted her son to be with Vanessa Young because she was the love of his life. Because they had a child together who was now an amazing grown woman.

It was because she was his mother and she always, *always* knew what was best for him.

"I just..." Cricket dropped her façade and opted for honesty. "I just want you to be happy, Noah."

"I am happy."

She stepped closer, reaching up and touching his clean-shaven cheek with her hand. "You may be forty-five with a couple of gray hairs, but you're still my son, Noah Thomas. Don't think I cannot read you like a knitting magazine."

He chuckled. "I promise I'm happy, Mama. Really."

"Not *truly* happy." Cricket shook her head. "Not how you were."

"What, when I was sixteen?" He cocked his head and

gave a half-smile. "Come on. I'm never going to be a kid again."

"It's not about age, it's about home. It's about belonging. It's about...love."

He huffed out a breath and inched back. "Nothing will ever happen again between Nessie and me, Mom. I'm sorry."

Cricket found that hard to believe, but she held her tongue.

"Anyway, I know that today is the grand opening of the store, and I figured you'd be going. You'll have a good time."

"Oh, won't you come, Noah? There's going to be champagne and cake and..."

"Vanessa." He quickly averted his gaze. "No, I can't. I'm sorry, Mom. I'm fine being civil and polite with Vanessa, but that's all it's going to be, okay? There's too much history there and weirdness."

Cricket sighed, making a dejected face. "I suppose I understand. I won't pressure you. Go on, get back to work then, lest the world stop spinning."

Noah chuckled, shook his head, and turned around to head back up to Cricket's loft to finish his ever-important duties.

She watched as he placed his hand on the door handle in the back of the salon and opened it. She waited one...two...three...

"But you know..." Cricket arched her brow, watching as Noah looked back to face her. "There is another woman involved in the opening of this brand-new business. Not just Vanessa."

Noah sighed softly, his face shifting into an expression that Cricket couldn't quite read.

She took a few steps closer to him, shrugging her shoulders as if she was just casually throwing out some random, extra information for his consideration.

"A woman who just so happens to be your daughter and would completely and totally explode with joy if you showed up."

Noah ran a hand through his hair, squeezing his eyes shut. "Mom, please."

Cricket raised her hands defensively, drawing back. "I'm just saying. It's Emily's business, too. In fact, she's the one running the whole operation. You should be quite proud of her."

"I hardly know her."

"You could change that."

The words hung in the air between them as Cricket studied her grown son. She watched as his expression changed from frustrated, to considering, to...soft. "I want to, but I'm worried if I get too close..."

"What? What will happen if you get too close besides having a relationship with this wonderful young woman who is your own flesh and blood?" Cricket asked gently, reaching forward to touch his arm. "That girl has never had a father. In fact, the only man she's ever trusted was a horrible criminal who deserves nothing but misery."

Noah's face fell and he shuddered. "I know."

"I'm just saying. It would mean a great deal to her if you showed an interest. But like I said, I know you have many important things to do, and I won't continue to harp." Cricket turned on her heel, heading toward the front door of her salon. "I'll just be on my way now."

"Mom. Wait."

She whipped around.

Noah sighed and shook his head. "I'll sign off for the afternoon. Come on."

Cricket gasped, pressing her hand to her chest and grinning widely. "Really? You'll come?"

He came closer and wrapped an arm around her shoulders, chuckling quietly to himself. "Let's go, you little manipulating...manipulator."

She giggled at that. "Been called worse."

"Well, the day is young," he joked.

But Cricket nearly danced. Noah had a weakness for Emily. He saw himself in her and couldn't help but want to have a relationship with his daughter, despite his best efforts to deny it and keep his distance.

Once again, her dear boy's heart of gold was shining through, and everything was lining up for him to finally understand what true happiness was.

With a little help from his mother, of course.

THE GRAND OPENING of Young at Heart was a delightfully feminine and elegant event, and the store itself looked like a showpiece.

Of course it did, because if there was one thing Vanessa Young had, it was style and taste.

Cricket had no doubt this boutique would be a massive success, especially in a walkable, cutesy, tourist town like Rosemary Beach.

"Oh, this place is simply fabulous, isn't it?" Cricket smiled at Gloria as the two of them stole away to catch up in the corner, champagne flutes in hand.

"They did an amazing job." Gloria smiled, sipping from her champagne flute and balancing a napkin with pink-frosted cookies on her fingers. "I'm so proud of Nessie. And Emily!"

"How wonderful that they did this together." Cricket sighed wistfully. "It's such a beautiful story, the reunion of mother and daughter after all those years."

Something imperceptible to Cricket flashed in Gloria's blue eyes, but she quickly smiled and nodded with enthusiastic agreement.

"Anyhoo, where the heck have you been, Glo? I feel like I've hardly seen you these past few weeks." Cricket smiled at the woman who she'd known since she was five years old.

"Oh, you know, life." Gloria waved a hand. "The wedding is getting close now and Daisy is...a bit all over the place. Plus, the diner is busy as always."

"Of course, of course." Cricked nodded. "And the wedding planning is going well? Are you feeling more involved now that it's approaching the date?"

"Well, yeah, I am involved." Gloria shrugged. "And Daisy and I have been able to really work through our differences, which has been a huge relief."

"What a gift." Cricked smiled. "I knew you two

would be fine. You're two peas. Speaking of your kiddos, how is my darling Jeremy? Is he a superstar pro athlete yet?" she teased.

Gloria flicked her fingers. "Pah. I hardly hear a peep from him these days! I know he's so busy, but a text now and then wouldn't hurt."

"Boys are that way," Cricked assured her. "I can remember long stretches where Noah hardly reached out. But then, when something magically happens that makes them need you? He'll be your best friend."

Gloria laughed softly. "If Jeremy's looking for a parent buddy, he has Christian."

Cricket spotted Emily from across the room, grabbing a small plate at the charcuterie board in the middle of the boutique, alone for the first time since Cricket had arrived.

Noah was around somewhere, but Cricket couldn't spot him. Young at Heart had a surprisingly large turnout and the boutique was packed.

"Chat soon, Glo." Cricket blew Gloria a kiss. "I'm off to be a grandma."

Her friend laughed. "Doing what you do best. And I don't mean...grandma-ing."

Did everyone know she was trying to be a puppeteer? Oh, well. Who cared? Just as long as it worked out.

"Hi, there!" Emily turned to Cricket, her blue eyes dancing like the waves of the Gulf, her pretty face framed with long, shiny waves that fell around her shoulders.

Her highlights were holding up nicely, Cricket thought with a smug smile.

"Hello, my sweet granddaughter." She placed a hand on Emily's back and led her to the side of the snack table. "I just had to steal my moment with the woman of the hour."

"Oh, please." Emily shook her head and blushed. "This is all Vanessa. I just look at spreadsheets."

"Emily, you must learn to take pride in your accomplishments. Look around you!" Cricket gestured around at Young at Heart, delighting in every colorful, elegant, and chic detail that made the store feel luxurious and cozy at the same time. "You are a success."

"That remains to be seen." Emily arched her brow, taking a bite of a cracker. "But thank you. That means a lot."

"I saw you talking to Noah." Cricket nudged her arm playfully. "Your dad."

Emily brightened. "Yeah, I was really surprised he wanted to come. I definitely didn't expect to see him here."

"Oh, he wouldn't have missed it for the world. He was eager to celebrate with you."

Emily blinked, raising her brows with surprise. "Eager?"

"Well, you know." Cricket gave an exaggerated wink. "I might have nudged a bit."

"You're quite good at nudging people, I've learned."

"You learn quick. And speaking of..." She jutted her chin toward the back corner of the boutique, where Noah and Vanessa were finally interacting. "Nudge, nudge."

They were alone in a conversation. Body language was...tense, but certainly not completely closed off.

Vanessa said something and Noah smiled. Actually, he laughed. Oh, this was good!

"Huh, look at that," Emily said, following Cricket's gaze to her chatting parents. "I think they're getting along."

"They'll be doing more than that soon," Cricket muttered under her breath.

"Cricket!" Emily gasped, laughing. "Seriously, do you really think there's a chance that they'll get together? They are both single and...wow. I still can't even wrap my brain around it. There's no way, though, right?"

"Oh, honey, there's always a way." Cricket sipped her champagne and watched Noah and Vanessa.

They were both laughing now, clearly enjoying some old joke from happier days gone by. Noah's walls were coming down even faster than Cricket had hoped.

"Because of their history and love for each other?" Emily guessed.

"Well, yes, fundamentally. And I'm not going to lie—I'm doing everything I can to get them to fell head over heels back in love with each other, as the whole world knows they should. I've been giving it my best effort. But even a master like me needs an assistant."

Emily fought a smile. "You hiring help in the nudging process, Cricket?"

She laughed and wagged her finger at her granddaughter. "You have immeasurable pull with both of them. Vanessa and Noah both have a soft spot for you, obviously, since they're your biological parents."

She brushed some hair behind her shoulder. "Well, I mean, I don't know..."

"Oh, yes. They do, trust me. How would you feel about helping me, you know, guide things in the right direction a bit?"

Emily chuckled, angling her head as she frowned with confusion. "What do you mean? Like, try to set them up?"

"In a way, yes." Cricket took another sip of the bubbly drink and lowered her voice. "I need you on my team if we're going to make this happen. I already made some headway locking them in my loft together the other day."

Emily drew back, her eyes wide. "You *what*?"

Cricket brushed off her shock. "We both agree it's for the best for the two of them. They just can't see past their own mistakes and hurt from a million years ago."

Emily shrugged. "I suppose that's true, but..."

"Can I count on you, Emily?"

"You're enlisting me to meddle?"

"To nudge, child!" Cricket grinned hopefully. "With a little force and a lot of finesse. That's my personal style."

Emily sighed, looking back at the sight of her parents together, her eyes glistening. "I'll...do a gentle nudge but I won't encourage my mother to do anything that makes her...not happy. She deserves to be happy."

Which Noah would make her, Cricket thought. "Perfect. And your first assignment, should you decide to accept it, is help on the prom."

"The...oh, yes. I've heard about this." Emily laughed. "It's so cheesy but kind of perfect at the same time."

"Right?" Cricket beamed with pride over her brilliant idea, turning to face Emily directly and give her a serious and stern expression. "However, as expected, both Noah and Vanessa are claiming they want nothing to do with it and will not be in attendance. And despite my best efforts, I've not been able to change Noah's mind. But you?"

"You want me to go to this prom?"

"I want you to convince him to go."

"Oh, I don't know if I can do that." Emily shook her head. "He hardly even knows me. He's been very kind and there are glimpses of a connection between us, but I don't want to push it."

"Even for true love? Push and push you must, my dear. He won't admit this, but he's fascinated by you. He adores you. I can tell."

A sincere smile pulled across Emily's face as her gaze darted over toward Noah. "Really?"

"Yes." Cricket knew that, and meant it. It was quite telling when he took the rest of the day off work to make an appearance for Emily. "All I'm suggesting is that you mention the prom to him and try to figure out a way where it makes sense to go. Vanessa, too, although she'll likely be an easier sell."

"I don't know." Emily huffed out a sigh. "She didn't

even technically graduate with the class. She practically shuddered when she told me about the event."

"She'll come around, especially since you're going to be there."

She drew back. "I am?"

"As my assistant. I'll need your help to set it up and take it down."

"Don't you have a committee?"

"I need you there," she said, knowing it would be a huge draw for Vanessa and Noah.

"Sure, I'll help." Emily finished her champagne. "And I'll see what I can do about convincing them. No promises, though." She gave Cricket a warning look. "Especially with Noah."

"Oh, I'm not worried. He's got a soft heart, my boy. It may take him some time, but he'll figure out what's right."

Chapter Fourteen

Gloria

Days after the grand opening, the conversation Gloria had with Cricket was still bothering her.

It was wrong to keep the truth about her mother a secret from such a dear friend, but she knew it was for the best. She loved Cricket—she was the closest thing to a mother Gloria'd had for the past forty-some years.

But she could not keep a secret and if she knew the truth, half the state of Florida would have known by the evening.

According to her last call with Jason, the investigation was coming up with nothing yet. There wasn't anything else to do until they found her, but he was hitting dead ends.

From what Gloria had heard, Vanessa and Emily's first week in business was going very well, and she was thrilled for her sister and niece. She tried to keep her attention focused on normal things—running the diner, being with Daisy.

Gloria was finishing up the morning work at the diner when she decided to pop in next door to Young at Heart and say hi to the girls. As she left her little back office, she pulled out her phone to send yet another text to Jeremy, which would undoubtedly go unanswered.

Of course, she thought to herself. *As soon as Daisy and I are close again, Jeremy is distant.*

But still, it hurt that he couldn't find two minutes in his busy baseball and college schedule to shoot her a text. Would he even answer this one?

Didn't matter. She had to keep the lines of communication open.

She typed on her phone as she waved to Liz at the hostess stand and walked out of the diner into the blazing heat.

Hey, Jer, I miss you! I know you're crazy busy, but I'd love to hear from you if you ever get a chance. Love you, honey.

She sent the message, not confident that it would get more than a three-word response, but she sent it anyway, because a day would come when Jeremy would need her, and she'd be there.

That's what mothers did.

Gloria opened the front door to the boutique, sending chimes echoing through the store. Even though this property had spent decades as Bill's Sporting Goods, Gloria could hardly remember what Dad's pro shop had looked like.

The gorgeous, newly pink corner property filled with light and fun didn't seem like it could have ever been anything but Young at Heart.

"Hey, you!" Emily rushed over to hug Gloria. "What's up?"

"Just popping over to say hi." Gloria glanced around. There were several customers in the store—sifting through racks, holding up folded sweaters, trying things on in the back behind tastefully selected curtains. "This is amazing, Emily."

"It's up and running," she said, looking around, then her expression grew serious. "Hey, what's up with Daisy? Anything new in the Whittington drama?"

Gloria sighed softly. "No. She went to his apartment the other night and is back to living there, so I guess they've worked it out? Who can even keep up these days?"

Emily wrinkled her nose. "It shouldn't be like that."

"I know."

"Daisy will make the best decision for herself," Emily said. "She's smart. And very capable. She'll do the right thing."

"Kyle Whittington sometimes makes her dumb, though." Gloria smacked her lips. "Is Nessie around?"

Right as Gloria asked the question, Vanessa emerged from the back room carrying three beautiful blouses on velvet hangers draped across her arm.

"Hey, sister."

"Hi!" Vanessa gave her a quick wave but kept walking toward the dressing room area in the back. "I'm helping a customer find the perfect summer office wardrobe."

"Don't let me get in your way!" Gloria watched as Vanessa walked back to the dressing rooms, where a woman emerged from behind one of the curtains in white slacks and a teal button-down blouse.

Vanessa offered her the options in her arms, and the woman lit up with excitement.

"She's killing it," Gloria said to Emily.

"People love her. It's like coming into a store and having a professional stylist dress you."

"I'm so proud of you two." Gloria wrapped her arm around her niece's shoulders and gave her a squeeze.

"Thanks, Auntie," Emily said with a playful smile.

Gloria felt her phone buzzing with a call from her purse. "Oh, let me take this. It might be Jeremy."

Emily gasped. "The elusive Jeremy? Go ahead."

Gloria walked out of the store and fished through her bag, finally grasping her vibrating phone.

She squinted in the blinding sunlight to see whose name was on the screen.

It was an unsaved phone number...local area code, but nothing Gloria recognized. So not Jeremy, darn it.

Figuring it was likely spam, she swiped her finger across the answer button and held the phone to her ear. "Hello?"

"Hello, I'm looking for Gloria Bennett," a woman said.

Yeah, spam. "You got her. What do you need?"

"This is Heather over at Bayside Pharmacy. I'm calling about William Young. I have your number listed here as his emergency contact."

No, not spam. Something about Dad? She sat on the bench out front of the store and held her hand up to block the afternoon sun. "Oh, okay, yes. I am. How can I help you?"

Why would a pharmacy have contact with Dad? The stubborn old coot refused to take so much as a Tylenol, even after his stroke, which was probably why he was dead.

The thought gave her a twinge of grief and guilt as she pressed the phone to her ear to hear over traffic.

"I'm calling because William hasn't picked up his usual prescriptions in over a month," Heather said. "We've called and texted his cell but haven't received any response."

What prescriptions? Gloria didn't want to come off as a terrible caretaker who didn't even know what meds her dying dad was on, but...he hadn't been on anything.

"Oh, well, I'm sorry, but my father actually passed away almost five weeks ago."

"Oh... Oh. I am so sorry, ma'am. You have my deepest condolences."

"Thank you," she said, still wracking her brain to think what meds he could have had.

"I'll just go ahead and cancel these then, no need to worry about—"

"Wait, actually. Heather?"

"Yes?"

"What medication was it, if you don't mind me asking?"

"I'm so sorry, Gloria, I can't release that information unless you come here in person with a valid photo ID. William was in a slightly complicated situation, and I'm happy to explain it to you, but I'm just not permitted to do it over the phone without identity verification. I'm sorry."

"No worries. Thank you, Heather. Have a good one." Gloria hung up the phone, dropped it back into her purse and sat in the burning sun for a moment.

A complicated situation? What did that even mean? And where the heck was Bayside Pharmacy?

She typed the name into her GPS and stared at the address, almost an hour away, well north of them. Dad was getting medication from a pharmacy that far away? Why?

Chills she couldn't begin to explain, especially in this heat, danced over her skin. Something wasn't right. Something...was not *right* about this.

She got up and went back into the store to find Vanessa standing behind the register typing on a laptop.

"Hey, Glo. Sorry, we got a crazy rush, and that woman was just desperate for help. Things have slowed down now, and—"

"Can you take a couple hours off? We need to take a field trip."

"I'm so busy, can we—"

"It's urgent, Ness. Can you trust me?"

Vanessa backed away from the laptop, two hands in the air. "With my life," she said. "I'll tell Emily she's on stylist duty."

Gloria spent the first five minutes of the drive telling Vanessa everything that the pharmacist had said to her on the phone.

The next forty-five minutes, all they could do was throw out theories and ideas about why Dad would take medication and keep it a secret, and why he'd get it in DeFuniak Springs, which was probably a nice little town in the middle of nowhere.

What they didn't mention—even though they were both thinking it—was if this had to do with their mother.

"It's just so weird," Gloria said, glancing at the GPS on her phone, which indicated they were almost there. "I saw him every day. I brought him groceries, cooked for him, handled everything. The only medicine I ever saw that man take was his blood pressure medication, and even that, he skipped it more than he took it."

"Did he get it himself?"

"No. I picked it up from Walgreens all the time. But other than that, he didn't take a thing."

"And yet, they have his medication at Bayside Pharmacy," Vanessa said, glancing at the mostly rural town around them. "Which has no bay to be beside, I might note."

Gloria let out a frustrated sigh. "I suppose anything is possible. Thank you again for coming with me. I know you're totally wrapped up in Young at Heart right now, but I did not want to do this alone. I have this weird gut feeling about it. Something isn't adding up."

"Of course I'm here." Vanessa placed her hand on

Gloria's arm. "I'm happy I was able to get away. And I feel you on the weird gut feeling. I have it, too. Why on Earth would he come all the way up here?"

"Because he didn't want me to know," Gloria said.

They shared a silent look as the GPS guided them to a small, weathered strip center that housed a pharmacy, a Dollar Store, two abandoned shops, and a Mexican restaurant called Hola Joes that made starvation look more appealing than eating there.

The whole place was dilapidated and depressing.

She shifted the car into park and turned to face her sister. "You ready for this?"

"I don't know," Vanessa admitted. "But we're together, so..." She took Gloria's hand. "Let's find out what he was taking and why."

They walked into the pharmacy, which felt like a drug store that was frozen in time in the 1980s. It was clearly family-owned and operated, with a small selection of over-the-counter medications and random needs.

The pharmacy counter was in the back, with an old-fashioned sign above it displaying an Rx.

"Come on." Gloria nodded toward the back of the store, and Vanessa followed her as they headed down the narrow aisle.

"Hello, can I help you?" An older woman with long gray hair and a pleasant smile stood on the other side of the counter.

"Hi. Are you Heather, by any chance?"

The woman nodded. "Yes, ma'am, that's me. What can I do for you?"

"I'm Gloria Bennett." Gloria reached into her purse and rooted for her wallet. "We spoke on the phone about my father, William Young."

"Oh, yes. I remember."

"Got it." Gloria snatched her wallet out of her purse and slid her driver's license out of the clear slot, handing it to the woman. "Here's my ID. I was wondering if you'd be able to give me some information about my father's prescriptions that were filled here? You mentioned something on the phone about a 'complicated situation'?"

Vanessa turned to Gloria, and they shared a look.

"Oh, yes." Heather, who was sweet but moving entirely too slowly, took the license and nodded. "Let me just go run this through the scanner and verify it with William's power of attorney and his HIPAA release form. Give me one moment, dear."

"No problem. Thank you." She turned to Vanessa. "Like Fort Knox, huh?"

"Well, she's following the rules."

Heather disappeared into a sea of shelves that were filled to the brim with medication bottles and boxes.

"You're sure he didn't take anything besides the blood pressure one?" Vanessa asked. "Maybe it was something specialized that only this place carried?"

"Maybe. But why wouldn't I know that, Ness? I went with him to all his doctor's appointments. He could drive, but I wanted to help him, so—"

"Gloria?" Heather stepped behind the counter, handing back Gloria's driver's license. "I verified your power of attorney, so I can share your late father's medical information with you."

"Great, thank you." Gloria tapped her hands on the counter anxiously.

"But, um..." Heather glanced at Vanessa. "Just... Gloria."

"Oh, sorry!" Vanessa waved. "I'll wait in the car."

Gloria almost laughed. As if she wasn't going to tell Vanessa the second she knew what the medicine was.

"Okay, I'll be out in a minute." She turned her attention back to Heather, concern growing. "Yes?"

"Okay." She set a piece of paper on the counter and spun it so Gloria could read it. "Your father, William Young, has picked up these medications on a monthly basis for the past four years."

Gloria frantically scanned the sheet, where the names of three different prescription drugs were listed.

"Donepezil...Memantine...Rivastigmine..." She sounded out the gibberish medication names, lifting her gaze back up to Heather. "What are these? I've never heard of these."

"They're all prescribed to patients with moderate to severe Alzheimer's. They help increase cognitive function and can slightly improve memory."

Gloria shook her head with confusion, not able to process what the pharmacist was saying to her.

"Alzheimer's?" she whispered the word. "My father didn't have Alzheimer's. I mean, he was a bit out of it in the last few months after his stroke, but he certainly didn't have any kind of memory loss or dementia."

Heather swallowed. "These medications weren't for him," she said. "He had the approval to pick them up for a patient."

"What patient?"

A patient?

For a moment, she couldn't breathe. Somehow, she asked, "Can you tell me the patient's name?"

"No."

"Please." She pressed her hands together. "My dad is dead, but..."

But her mother might not be.

"I'm sorry," Heather said, sticking to her guns. "I cannot tell you the patient's name."

Gloria reached over the counter and looked the woman in the eyes. "It might be my mother who I haven't seen since I was five."

Heather blinked, obviously not expecting that. "I can't—"

"Could you tell me if I guess the name correctly?" she pressed.

"Um..." Heather glanced at her computer screen, which Gloria couldn't see.

She had to know. She *had* to. "Is it Clarinda Smith?"

Heather let out a long, slow sigh, the sound of a woman who didn't want to break the rules but had to.

"Yes," she said softly, then clicked her computer off as if to say *that's all you get.*

But it was enough for the world to tilt and Gloria to nearly fall right off.

Chapter Fifteen

Vanessa

It was an hour to Jason Chang's office in Destin, but Gloria floored it and risked life, limb, and a speeding ticket. All Vanessa could do was stare out the window and try to figure all of this out.

She couldn't help but think about the fact that if Clarinda had dementia, she'd be deemed mentally unfit to inherit the store. Young at Heart was safe in Vanessa's hands, most likely, but that didn't bring her a whole lot of peace.

She and Glo didn't talk much, other than to recap the obvious—their mother was alive, taking medication for dementia, and Dad kept that from them, too. He died knowing where she was and...

Gloria was mostly quiet, too, blinking back tears and happily agreeing that they had to see Jason in person. A phone call wouldn't do. They had to see him, tell him, and make him understand they were desperate to know where she was.

Vanessa watched the scenery, but didn't really see the blue sky or the endless flat horizon of the Panhandle. All she could see was...the image of her mother she'd invented as a child. Yes, she'd seen pictures of Violet.

But in her mind, she looked different. Like a combination of Vanessa and Gloria, but younger and so, so vibrant. Her dream mother. Her dead mother.

"Why wouldn't he tell me?" Gloria whispered, her voice ragged. "If she has dementia, why shouldn't I know?"

"He dug so deep on that lie, Glo," Vanessa said. "How could he?"

"But you know what? It explains a lot." Gloria looked at her. "I mean, it might be the reason he was so nasty all the time. He was rotten from the inside because he carried a dark lie, which probably came with guilt and shame and a sense that when he died, he'd be quickly and efficiently turned away from the pearly gates."

Vanessa snorted. "As if he cared."

"At the end of life?" Gloria shot her a look. "You start to care a lot."

"Not enough to get it off his chest," Vanessa said.

"Nope. And he could have, because I was at his house every single day." Gloria sniffed softly, keeping her focus on the road in front of her. "I brought him groceries, I cooked him meals. I tidied up and handled everything for the store, right up to its final closure. No, we were never the best of friends, but we were solid, you know? Dad and I were solid. He recognized everything that I'd done for him and, wow, I just really can't believe he kept this from me."

Vanessa nodded, watching the highway go by as she leaned her head against the warm glass of the window. "I can't believe he didn't ever drop any sort of hint."

"Nothing. Never mentioned her name."

"It was always that way," Vanessa said. "Growing up, Mom was a taboo subject. For all of us. Don't ask questions about her, don't bring her up. We learned quickly to follow that rule."

"And it never changed. You left thirty years ago, and it never changed, Nessie. To the day he died, he didn't want to talk about her. I mean, nothing more than the occasional, 'After your mother died,' or referring to himself as a widower, which was rare. But nothing about her. And certainly nothing that would ever hint that the car accident story wasn't true."

"And that she's still alive and nearby enough for him to be bringing her monthly medicine!" Vanessa shook the paper with the list of prescriptions on her lap as if it would magically give them answers.

"At least we have Jason." Gloria lifted a shoulder. "We'll get all of this info to him and, hopefully, it brings us an answer. He'll find her, and fast."

Vanessa nodded, chewing her lip. She glanced down at Gloria's phone resting on the console, which showed they were only six minutes away from the private investigator's office.

"I just feel like there's only one thing we can take away right now," Gloria said.

Vanessa glanced in her direction expectantly.

"It's that Mom is nearby, and she still doesn't want anything to do with us."

"We don't know that yet, Glo," Vanessa said, wanting to believe there had to be an explanation for that decision. "We can't draw any conclusions, especially if she has dementia."

"Don't make excuses for her," Gloria said. "She hasn't had dementia for all these decades. She was just...crazy."

"About acting."

Gloria threw her a look, silent, then turned into the office park. "Here we go."

Outside, it was blazing, the humidity hitting Vanessa like a sauna as soon as she stepped out of the car. "If he's busy, we'll wait," she said while Gloria called him on her cell phone with the device on speaker.

"We're at your office and we have information," she said when he answered, not even bothering with niceties.

"I'll be right out," he said, and a look of appreciation passed between the two sisters.

A few minutes later, he ushered them into his office smiling warmly, gesturing for them to sit down in the two cushioned chairs on the other side of his desk. "What do you have?"

Gloria took over, explaining the call, the pharmacist, the rules, and then slid the list of prescriptions across the desk.

"She has memory issues," she finished. "And our father must have been getting her medications."

"Wow," Jason said on a soft breath. "Are you absolutely certain these weren't for him and he made some kind of arrangement to keep it secret?"

"We're not certain of anything," Vanessa said.

"Except that he didn't need meds for memory problems," Gloria added. "I mean, I suppose he wasn't as sharp as a tack in his final days, but certainly nothing like what these prescriptions are used to treat. He picked them up for Clarinda Smith, who must be living near there."

"Fascinating." He leaned back in his chair, holding up the paper and staring at them with an intent gaze. "So, not only is she alive, she's nearby. And she was on speaking terms with your father, which is certainly unexpected."

"Majorly," Gloria agreed.

Jason tapped his finger on his desk. "I can find her," he said confidently. "I can get around some of the HIPAA rules and comb the area carefully. I should have an address or information for you very shortly. A matter of days, I promise."

"Thank you, Jason." Vanessa swallowed, letting out a soft sigh.

They said goodbye to Jason Chang and left his office, silently getting back in the car, where it felt like they'd spent the better part of the day.

Gloria started the ignition and slumped down into the driver's seat. "Evidently, there's a lot about Dad that we didn't know."

"No kidding." Vanessa leaned back. "But I think Jason will find her and then we have to make a decision."

"To go meet her or not?"

"Of course we'll meet her," Vanessa said. "But will we forgive her?"

Gloria snorted. "Over my dead body," she muttered, throwing the car into reverse. "No pun intended."

"ALZHEIMER'S?" Emily turned to Vanessa, the light breeze blowing her caramel-colored hair around her face as they walked along the beach as the sun set. "Whoa. That's...stunning."

"Yeah. And that's just about all we know." Vanessa inhaled deeply, closing her eyes as she savored the smell of the salt-tinged air and the sound of the gentle waves on the Gulf.

As soon as Vanessa had come home from her day of surprises with Gloria, Emily returned from closing up the store and was instantly able to detect that something crazy had happened.

The two of them decided to go for an evening beach walk, and Vanessa had filled her daughter in on the rollercoaster of events that had unfolded that day.

"I can't decide what's more astonishing..." Emily pushed her hair behind her ears as they padded along the damp sand side by side. "The fact that your mother has been alive this whole time or the fact that your father was *talking* to her before he died."

"Right?" Vanessa groaned. "That's what's freaking Gloria and me out so much."

"I'm so sorry you're dealing with all of this. It must really hurt to know that she spent all those years away from you, and never wanted to come back." Emily swallowed. "But you said in the letters she knew that Bill made up the car accident story, right?"

"Yes, she was well aware of it. It wasn't clear whether

it was Dad's idea or hers or something they came up with together, but she definitely knew that was the story that Glo and I would be told."

"Well, I guess she just stayed committed to that all of these years." Emily shrugged. "Maybe she just wanted to let you and Aunt Glo go on living your lives without throwing a monkey wrench into everything."

"Your positive outlook is encouraging." Vanessa leaned into her daughter. "But consider that wrench thrown. Hard and fast and smacking me across the cheek."

Emily turned, her brows knitting together in a sympathetic expression. "Why did he leave her in the will?"

"Who knows? Maybe so we would find out the truth? I have no idea, but it doesn't really matter. I talked to Barry, Dad's estate attorney, and he said that unless Clarinda has the mental capacity to sell or run the business and fights us for it, it's mine. Which, based on the cocktail of Alzheimer's meds, she doesn't."

"At least the store is safe. So, what's next?"

"We gave everything we have to the PI, so hopefully he can find her. Although, at this point, I don't even really know what our end game is here."

"Do you want to find her? Talk to her?"

Vanessa looked down at the cool, damp sand, watching it squish around her toes with each step. "I do. I want...closure, I guess. Answers. Insight. All the things. But I don't think Gloria wants to do anything but give her a good tongue-lashing and watch her wallow in guilt and shame."

"That's not like her," Emily mused.

"Well, nothing about this is like...anything," Vanessa said.

"You'll know the right thing to do when the moment presents itself," Emily assured her. "It will be organic and natural and depend on her state of mind, I suppose."

"You're right, honey." She wrapped her arm around her daughter's shoulders and gave her a playful side hug as they strode along the shoreline. "Anyway, I have you. And Glo. And the store. And this whole entirely new and completely unexpected chapter of my life in this gorgeous place. There's no need to hurt for what I didn't have. I never thought I'd see you again after you were adopted and look at us now."

Emily's eyes brightened, and she pressed into Vanessa's shoulder. "I'm so glad you found me."

"We found each other, baby. And life is full of surprises, good and bad. I'm just taking them in stride and appreciating all of the good ones."

"Speaking of surprises, good and bad..." Emily pressed her lips together, giving Vanessa a sideways glance. "How have things been with Noah? He's been around a lot with Cricket's flood and everything. I saw you talking at the Grand Opening and I'm sure you've bumped into each other."

"More than bumped into," Vanessa said on a noisy sigh. "I don't think I even got the chance to tell you this yet with all the craziness of the store opening and the developments about my mother, but I got locked in Cricket's loft with him."

Emily choked on a laugh, but weirdly didn't seem that shocked. "Oh, I heard from the locker herself. How did you fall for that, anyway?"

Vanessa rolled her eyes. "That woman! She told me to go up there and give her an opinion on some flooring sample options. But when I got into the loft, there were no samples, just Noah, sitting at her kitchen table with his laptop, white as a ghost when he saw me. I instantly tried to leave, of course, but the door was somehow locked from the outside. It was weird."

"So weird." Emily cleared her throat. "But how was it with Noah? Do you feel like you guys are..." Emily lifted a shoulder. "Reconciling at all?"

"I don't know if I'd use that word, but it was better than when he first got here, that's for sure. Awkward, of course."

"Of course."

"But it was...nice."

Nice. What a dumb, flat, and totally wrong way to describe her time with Noah.

Vanessa took a deep breath, letting her bare feet get covered with frothy waves while she thought about the time she spent up in Cricket's loft with Noah. The yearbook, the memories, the note... It all set off a whirlwind of emotions in her heart that were so confusing it was impossible to put them into words.

Emily looked at her expectantly, smart enough to know there had to be more than "nice."

"Once we got past the initial awkwardness and feeling like he hates my guts—"

"He doesn't," Emily inserted.

"Debatable," Vanessa teased. "But tensions really eased up, which was a relief. We ended up flipping through an old yearbook from our high school days together that Cricket had *conveniently* left out on display."

Emily snorted. "I kind of love her just for the effort she puts into it."

Vanessa laughed. "So true. Anyway, as we meandered down memory lane, I could feel the very, very outermost layer of his walls come down. It was like, for a tiny piece of time, we remembered what we always were: best friends. We laughed and reminisced and recalled some of our millions of inside jokes and memories together. It was as if, for a few minutes, we were really able to look back fondly on those good times and fall back into that special, close connection we'd always had since we were toddlers."

Emily's eyebrows lifted high as she took in Vanessa's story. "That's amazing! I mean, I know you guys have such a complicated history, but wow. It's great that the connection you once shared is still there. It's incredible."

"I don't know about that." Vanessa lifted a shoulder, exhaling sharply. "The connection I have with Noah is just a blatant reminder of what I could never find—and probably never will find—with anyone else."

Saying those words out loud took even Vanessa by surprise, and she stared out at the Gulf and wondered, as anyone would, if he'd had any remotely similar thoughts.

"Well..." Emily kicked up some sand, giving Vanessa

a hopeful half-smile. "It sounds like things are definitely getting better, rather than worse. And like you said, life is full of surprises. You never know what might happen still."

"I suppose I don't." She turned to Emily and laughed softly, admiring the wise, mature woman who shared so many of her features. "How'd you get so smart?"

"From my Mama," Emily teased, nudging Vanessa playfully. "So, this is totally random, but I assume you've heard about Cricket's prom."

Vanessa chuckled. "I think the entire Florida Panhandle has heard about Cricket's prom."

"And I understand that's your graduating class, right?"

"It would have been, if I had stayed." She pointed a finger at her own chest. "High school dropout and runaway, remember?"

"Well, yeah, but it's still your grade. They're your people."

Vanessa cringed. "That's one way to put it."

"Crazy idea, but I don't know. Maybe you should go?" Emily turned to her, brushing a strand of hair behind her ear and giving a bright smile.

"Hah!" Vanessa glanced skyward. "You're funny, kiddo."

"No, seriously. Maybe it would be fun, and help you integrate back into the community." She shrugged nonchalantly. "Plus, great chance to do some face-to-face marketing for Young at Heart."

"There will be a lot of our target market there, but I

don't know." Vanessa blew a raspberry, sloshing the water around as it splashed up on her ankles. "I feel like I don't belong."

"Maybe that could change," Emily suggested. "You're here now, for the long haul. It could be good."

Vanessa smiled to herself, shaking her head and laughing as she thought about attending a high school prom at age forty-five.

It could do her some good to turn over a new leaf and be a part of the local community and go to cheesy events and pretend she'd walked across the stage in 1997 like everyone else.

But...that was the problem. She would just be pretending.

"You can't erase the past," she said to Emily, her voice coming out sterner and more serious than she had expected. "I didn't graduate. I can't go, Emily. Plus, the memory is painful."

Her mind flashed with images of Noah alone on prom night at home, images of herself in a dingy apartment in L.A. questioning every decision she'd ever made.

Reliving those years and that trauma wouldn't help anyone, and starting over meant starting fresh, not trying to fix something that broke a long, long time ago.

Chapter Sixteen

Emily

Emily was, admittedly, a bit too excited when Noah popped into Young at Heart and asked if she wanted to join him for a quick lunch.

She'd spent the last few weeks trying to come to terms with the fact that her biological father didn't really want to get to know her, that he kept his distance. Because of Vanessa? The past? Not wanting Emily in his life?

She didn't know, but it was a fact of life...until today.

He waltzed right through the front doors of the boutique unannounced and offered to take her to lunch, which just made her giddy. Cricket had said he had a "soft spot" for her, but she still didn't know how, or if, she'd ever understand what that meant.

So, today's spontaneous father-daughter outing gave her a chance to find out, and to bring up the prom again in hopes that Noah might change his mind.

Those hopes were low, though, after last night. Vanessa had seemed slightly open to the idea then quickly shut it down. The chances of either of them attending were looking seriously slim, but Emily had made a promise to Cricket and she intended to keep it.

"You like pizza?" Noah asked, glancing over at Emily from the driver's seat of his Porsche as he pulled out of a parking spot in front of Young at Heart.

"Yeah," Emily said on a laugh. "Almost as much as I like this car." She ran her fingers gently across the shiny wood detailing on the dash, admiring the luxurious smell of leather and high-end features. "This thing is gorgeous."

"Thanks." Noah chuckled awkwardly, shrugging it off. "It's a good car. Bit of an impulse buy after my divorce, if I'm being honest."

Emily was glad to see some openness about her father's personal life. "Hey, no shame in that. It was a great choice. When did you, um, get divorced?" She knew she needed to tread lightly but was eager for any and all information about him.

"Two years ago, but we were separated for two years before that. She was way too into work, like me. Things just didn't work out, we lost each other somewhere along the way. We were both consistently putting our jobs before our marriage, and we knew... Anyway, it ended."

"Oh." Emily chewed her lip and nodded, glancing out the window to see that they were headed east just outside of downtown Rosemary Beach. "I'm sorry to hear that."

"Eh, it is what it is." Noah waved a hand. "That's why I like work and cars. They're...dependable."

"Until a car breaks down or you get fired," Emily shot back, a hint of playfulness in her tone.

"Well, Porsches don't break down, and I'm a partner,

so probably not going to get fired." He gave her a side-eye and a half-smile.

"Pizza, huh?"

"Best in the area, and we're about two minutes away."

"What's it called?"

"Pizza by the Sea."

Emily snorted, raising a brow. "Little obvious, no?"

"No-nonsense, like the pizza," Noah said. "It tells you exactly what you're getting. No questions or uncertainties, just...pizza by the sea."

Emily nodded, leaning back in the smooth leather seat, absorbing every subtle detail about the man who was responsible for half of her genetics.

Pizza by the Sea was, indeed, exactly what its name promised. An adorable storefront in a strip of other businesses and eateries; the funky and fun design of the place was inviting and precious.

"Whoa, the smell." Emily inhaled deeply as they walked through the front door, savoring the delicious tang of red sauce and the sweetness of freshly baked dough that filled the air. "It's heavenly."

"Whatcha like?" Noah asked, pulling out his wallet as they walked up to the counter to order.

Emily thought about insisting she pay for herself, but decided she didn't want to make it awkward, and she was truly grateful for the gesture. "A slice of pepperoni."

Noah's eyes lit up a bit, and a smile brightened his face. "Of course." He turned to the teenage boy behind the cash register. "Two slices of pepperoni, please."

Once they paid and got sodas, they sat at a small two-top table in the back corner. The ceiling was decorated with hanging vineyard lights, and one wall was covered in artwork that was clearly done by local children.

Emily sipped her Diet Coke through a straw, feeling suddenly like she was living in a childhood that she'd never had. "Thanks," she said abruptly, "for taking me to lunch."

Noah nodded, glancing down at his soda cup, then back up. "Look, Emily, I'm sorry I was so standoffish when I first arrived back in town. As you can imagine, this whole thing has been really shocking and overwhelming for me."

Emily smiled, taking another sip. "You don't have to apologize. To even meet my birth father at all is something I never expected in a million years, so I'm happy. You know you're not under any obligation to get to know me, right?"

"I know that," he said quickly. "I want to get to know you. The more I've thought about it, the more I realize that you're most likely going to be the only kid I ever have, and I can't just ignore that. I don't want to, and it would be stupid to try."

Emily swallowed, suddenly feeling very caught off guard and emotional by Noah's authenticity and bluntness.

Cricket frequently described him as having a heart of gold, and Emily was starting to see why. For someone who should be a hardened, workaholic, soulless lawyer, he was very much the opposite.

"So that's why you took me to lunch?" Emily asked.

"Yes. No divorce paperwork, no ulterior motives. I don't know how to be a dad, but I do know that I would..." He took a deep breath, almost as if he'd practiced this little speech. "I would very much like to be a part of your life. If that's okay."

Okay? Emily wanted to burst with joy and leap out of the seat and hug him and possibly dance on the table and shout out to the other Pizza by the Sea patrons.

She opted for a big smile and a thumbs-up. "That's fine by me."

"Good."

"I've got two slices of pepperoni for you guys." The server dropped off their steamy and delicious-looking pizza, a natural and needed pause to the conversation.

As they began to eat, Emily watched her father, her heart swelling with joy and gratitude, especially when she thought about all that she'd been through to get here.

"So, I can ask you questions?" She grinned between bites.

"Ask away." He wiped his mouth with a paper napkin and took a sip of his drink. "I'm not usually an open book, but I'll do my best to be honest with you."

It warmed Emily that he was trying to have a relationship with her. He was putting in effort. Something had changed, and it was really, really good.

"We'll start easy," she teased. "Where did you go to college?"

"University of Miami."

"Miami? Sounds like fun." Emily lifted a shoulder playfully.

"It was, at times. I was busy, though. I double majored in political science and economics, so I studied a lot. Once LSAT studying began around junior year, that was my only focus."

"And where did you go to law school?"

"Georgetown. In Washington, D.C."

She drew back. "Impressive."

"It was great. But I liked Miami a lot, so I decided to take the Florida bar and get a job down there. I like the water and the warm weather, and it was close enough to my mom that I can get to her in, well, not quickly. Miami's a nine-hour drive away, but I can be here fast enough if she needs me."

Emily nodded and plucked some stringy cheese from the top of her slice. "And the ex-wife? How did you meet her?"

"Through colleagues. She was roommates with a girlfriend of one of my associates when I was a fourth-year at the firm. She was climbing to the top of the public relations world fast, and we bonded over our mutual love of late nights at the office."

"Romantic," Emily quipped.

He held up his empty left hand. "Hence the divorce."

Confident in the banter and ease of the conversation, she leaned in. "Okay, can I get a little more personal?"

He glared over the top of his pizza crust. "If you must."

"Do you think you'll ever forgive Vanessa?"

Noah froze mid-bite, obviously stunned by the question.

Emily realized very quickly she'd overstepped. "I'm sorry, you don't have to answer that. I just—"

"No, no. It's okay." He lowered his pizza slice back onto the oversized paper plate and leaned back. "Open book, remember?"

Emily breathed out a small sigh of relief and gave him time to gather his thoughts.

"I guess I'm not sure how to define 'forgive,'" Noah said after a long pause. "There are two sides to this story, and I'm sure you've gotten hers."

"She doesn't exactly paint herself out to be the good guy, trust me."

He looked a tad surprised by that. "Well, anyway, my recollection of the experience is probably pretty different, and I'm just not sure what some sort of formal display of 'forgiveness' would get anyone. Vanessa destroyed me."

Emily winced at the raw emotion in those three words.

"I was a kid, yes," he continued. "But I was also completely in love with her, and willing to do absolutely whatever it took to be with her and help her with...well... you."

Emily put her own slice down, riveted by his candor.

"We had a plan, as I'm sure you've heard. She made a promise, and then just broke it. And I get it, she was young and scared and overwhelmed, but it was like she didn't take me into account at all." He glanced away, lost for a moment.

"I'm sure it's hard—"

"No, no." He shook his head. "It's good to tell you.

Vanessa was so scared of her father and so hurt by his terrible treatment of her. Bill was brutal to her. When he found out about the pregnancy, he essentially told her straight to her face that he never wanted to see her again and stuck to that."

Emily shuddered.

"So, from that perspective, I get it. But you know my mom. She would have taken Nessie in in a heartbeat and things could have been different."

Emily nodded. "I get that."

"It just messed me up, I guess." He scratched the back of his neck, frowning slightly. "She was my best friend, my closest confidante, and she completely broke my trust. It made me feel like I couldn't trust anybody. Couldn't rely on anyone."

"Except for work and cars," Emily said quietly, quoting his words from the drive over.

He smiled, but his eyes looked sad. "Exactly. I was just so wrecked by the whole thing, and, for the record, I wasn't completely on board with the whole adoption thing."

Emily held her breath. She had known that Noah had advocated for Vanessa to keep her and raise her even when it was hard but hearing him say it out loud to her face hit her like a semi-truck.

"I thought we could have made it work," he said, holding her gaze.

"Well..." Emily huffed out a sigh. "I guess I should make sure you know about the amazing woman who raised me. Grandma Gigi was the biggest blessing I've ever had. She was my best friend and closest confidante, too, and she never let me down. She's the only reason I was able to get out of that hellacious marriage."

"Then she has my eternal gratitude."

"Honestly?" Emily continued. "It's incredible getting to know Vanessa, and now you. But I wouldn't change my childhood. That woman made me who I am. I made a dumb choice in husbands, but I don't regret my life or wish it was different." She reached out and put a hand over his. "I recommend you try that. It might help you... forgive."

Noah blinked, his Adam's apple bobbing up and down as he gulped.

"I mean, if Vanessa had come back, with or without me, you never would have gone away to law school. You'd never be in the life you have now, with your unbelievably sick car and your amazing job." She smiled, trying to lighten it up in the face of his obvious emotion. "You wouldn't be sitting here, eating pizza with your twenty-nine-year-old daughter you just met. You wouldn't be who you are, either."

Noah opened his mouth to say something, but shut it quickly, visibly thinking hard. "Yeah that's...that's true. Forgiveness is hard, Emily. Even after all these years. Life has gone on, we've both become such completely different people. And yet, somehow, at the core of both of us, is this massive dark cloud in our past that no matter what I do, I can't seem to escape."

"I understand. And, based on both sides of the story,

you have every right to hold onto that pain and stay away from her forever."

"I don't want to—" he said quickly, then stopped himself. "I don't know what I want to do about it. It seemed that doing nothing and keeping my life separate was my best option, but now I'm not so sure."

Emily studied his expression. "Why not?"

"Because of you. And because being around her again has made me...forget how mad I'm supposed to be." He laughed dryly shaking his head. "I don't know. It's confusing. And I don't like it when things are confusing."

Emily took a sip of soda, letting all he'd said settle on her heart, but mostly feeling overwhelming gratitude for how much he'd taken down his walls with her.

She had a dad. And that, in and of itself, was a massive and unexpected victory.

"So, this prom is coming up," Emily joked, pulling him back to a brighter place.

Sure, her efforts to convince Vanessa turned out to be just a tad bit futile, but Noah's mind could still change. That much was clear.

"Oh, please." He rolled his eyes and shook his head. "Don't even get me started."

"You're not going, I take it."

"To the absolute misery of my mother, no, I am not. And believe me, I hate disappointing her. But these First Class Bash happenings are always a recipe for reliving the worst part of my life. And a prom, of all things? I'll pass."

Emily shrugged, taking the last bite of her crust and

wiping her hands clean on a napkin. "I don't know. You don't think it would be fun at all? Seems like a cool way to, like, get a redo, I guess."

He arched a brow. "You can't redo what's been done for thirty years. I don't need a prom."

"Fair enough." She leaned back, eyeing him. "I'll be there, though."

"You?"

"I told Cricket I'd help out with decorating and running the event and all that."

"Wait a second." He narrowed his gaze. "You're going to be...*chaperoning* the prom?"

Emily laughed, tilting her head back. "Nice twist, huh? Yes, I thought it would be fun watching you oldsters do...the Macarena or whatever you danced to."

"Oh, Cricket Ellison." He let out a sigh and rolled his eyes. "She's a force, isn't she?"

"Hurricane level," Emily agreed. "But I think she just wants you to have fun and be happy."

Well, she wanted a little more than that, but Emily protected Cricket's confidence.

"I know she does." Noah nodded. "And she means well, but I have to prioritize my own life and work and everything over her crazy schemes."

Disappointment thumped in Emily's head, instantly able to acknowledge that she'd basically failed the mission that her grandmother had assigned her, both with Vanessa and Noah.

But she played it off with a smile and focused on the

happy reality of a casual lunch with her dad. "So, how long do you think you're in town for?"

"Until her floors get fixed and the insurance mess gets sorted out." He shrugged. "Could be a few more weeks."

Emily tried not to seem overjoyed. "Well, I know you're busy with work, but I'm always around for pizza and Coke."

He studied her for a long time, giving an authentic smile that reached his blue eyes. "I'm glad to hear that, kiddo. You know, there's an old record shop just outside of town. They've got all kinds of vintage Zeppelin, Def Leppard, great stuff and original copies. All vinyl, too."

"Really?" Emily leaned forward, excited by the prospect.

"Yeah. If you can slip out of work for a couple hours on Saturday, we could go there and check it out."

"That would be awesome!" She brushed her hair out of her eyes. "I'll plan on it."

After they finished up, Noah drove Emily back to Young at Heart, and even though she couldn't successfully convince either one of her parents to attend the prom, she was in an undeniably good mood for the rest of the day.

Chapter Seventeen

Daisy

Today's day shift at the hospital had been particularly long and exhausting, with some emergencies, lots of needy patients, and very few breaks.

Daisy made a conscious effort to leave work at work, and not bring the heaviness and stress of dealing with life, death, and serious illness on a daily basis back to Kyle's apartment.

Which was now her apartment, she kept reminding herself. She'd lived there with him for almost six months now, but it didn't feel like her home at all. She'd been hoping they'd move into a new place together once they were married but had a feeling Kyle would be loath to leave his prime location in a luxury building next to the best golf course in the area.

Just another example of her coming second. Or third. Or tenth.

She marched through the parking lot in her dirty scrubs and shoved her keys into the ignition of the white Mercedes, which, as much as she wanted to hate and resent the car, was still pretty fabulous.

But was that really Kyle's way of making her happy?

With money and lavish gifts? Or worse—was it his way of shutting her up?

The fear and doubt that had been swirling around in her mind since her confrontation with Linda last week was beginning to come to a head, and Daisy knew darn well she couldn't keep her mouth closed for much longer.

Things had been rocky and tense with Kyle ever since, and he wasn't making much of an effort, because he put the blame for that fight square on her shoulders.

Daisy gripped the tan leather of the steering wheel as she made the familiar drive to his place, clinging to the wheel almost as hard as she was clinging to the hope for this to work.

She was engaged. They were getting married. Walking away now would be mortifying and heartbreaking and rip the entire rug out from not only her current life, but the life she'd been planning for the last two years.

Daisy felt a sob sticking in her throat as she turned onto the main road, attempting to calm herself by watching the colors of the setting sun behind the silhouettes of palm trees that lined the streets.

It wasn't working.

Kyle had been so captivating and enchanting. Had she been under a spell these last two years? Had she overlooked every red flag and bad sign he'd thrown her way?

Or was she just completely overthinking and freaking out and getting cold feet, since the wedding was coming up?

After all, her real beef was with Linda, not Kyle,

wasn't it? Daisy didn't know. Ever since he took his mom's side over hers, it felt like she was up against both of them.

It was nearly eight when she pulled in, her heart racing far more than it should be; that's what the stress of the situation at home—his home—had done. She had to talk to him. They had to clear the air.

It's just a conversation, she thought to herself. No rash decisions, no running away, no anything. Just a heart-to-heart with the man she loved and was about to marry...right?

And if that wasn't possible, well, then maybe Daisy really did need to rethink things.

The thought made her nauseous as she walked to the glass and brass elevator, her white sneakers squeaking softly with each step.

Kyle lived on the sixth floor in an apartment building that was decked out to the nines with amenities and luxuries and a state-of-the-art gym and rooftop pool. Daisy had grown to like it, or so she'd thought.

Right now, standing in the marble-floored elevator, the whole place had never felt colder.

She walked down the shiny hallway up to the front door of their apartment, where she used a code to unlock the deadbolt.

"Hey, you're back." Kyle was sitting at the kitchen counter, eyes fixed on the screen of his sleek silver MacBook.

"Hey," Daisy said, willing her voice to be strong and normal sounding. She hung up her work bag on some hooks by the door and set her keys on the shelf underneath them.

She took off her shoes, walked into the kitchen and poured a glass of water, and waited. She waited for a hug, a kiss, a "How was your day?" an "I love you," or "I missed you," or...anything.

Daisy wasn't sure if it was right to put Kyle to the test and analyze his every move but, with how miserable she'd been lately, it was hard not to.

He typed rapidly on the quiet keys of the laptop, then shut it abruptly and looked up at her. "Can you be ready in fifteen?"

Her heart jumped. Had he planned a surprise for her? Had he realized that she was feeling worried and down and wanted to do something to make it better? "Um, sure, yeah. For what?"

"Tristan, Asher, and I are doing a boys' night at the Seagrove. I was hoping you could drive me and maybe pick me up?" He gave an obnoxious grin that used to melt her heart but now made it feel like stone. "Our usual driver is on vacation for whatever reason, and as you know, I do not do Ubers. So I figured, hey, you're not busy."

"I was hoping we could spend some time together." She swallowed, forcing herself to stay as pleasant as possible. "Can you reschedule with the guys?"

"Ah, sorry, no can do." Kyle lifted a shoulder. "Tristan is leaving for the Maldives tomorrow, so it's our last chance to hang for the next ten days."

Daisy resisted the urge to roll her eyes. "Kyle, can we please do something together?"

"Daisy, chill out. I'm going out with the boys not going off to war." He walked over and tapped her nose. "You're so dramatic."

Her mother's voice echoed through her head.

If he truly loves you, Dais, and he is the man for you, then he will put you first. Above his mother, above his friends, above his money. You will be his number one.

Daisy gritted her teeth as she set her water glass on the counter, attempting and failing to calm her coursing emotions. "Why do I have to 'get ready' to drive you and your friends to a bar?"

"Well, I mean, you know..." Kyle gestured up and down at Daisy's lavender scrubs. "I figured you wouldn't want to be wearing your work clothes."

Anger burned her skin. "Why would I not want that?"

"So you look nice, Daisy, geez. What is this, an interrogation?"

"No." She said firmly, crossing her arms over her chest.

He groaned and rolled his eyes. "Fine, wear the nurse clothes. Just be ready to head out in, like..." Kyle glanced at the Rolex on his wrist. "Ten." He turned to walk down the hallway toward the bedroom.

"You're a jerk," she said loudly, with a stern seriousness in her voice that made him freeze in his tracks and turn around.

"Daisy, calm down, please. You can wear whatever

you want. I was just looking out for you. I thought you might be embarrassed to be in—"

"Embarrassed?" She spat the word back on an exasperated laugh. "The only thing I have to be embarrassed about is the fact that I'm dumb enough to marry such a narcissistic, entitled piece of crap."

Kyle's mouth fell open as he walked back into the kitchen. "What's got into you? Are you out of your mind?"

"No, Kyle, I'm not. In fact, I've never felt more in my right mind about anything." She straightened her back, lifted her chin, and willed herself to say the words that had kept her up at night for days and weeks on end. "I don't want to marry you."

He choked out a dry laugh, rolling his eyes as if he simply did not have time to deal with this. "Is it your time of the month or something?"

Rage swelled in Daisy's chest as she stepped forward. "I'm leaving you, Kyle. I don't want to marry you. I don't want to live in your world of country clubs and designer bags. I don't want to stop working and volunteer at the stupid DAR. I don't want to organize fake fundraisers and walk around in five-thousand-dollar dresses pretending I'm happy. I don't want to deal with your psychotic mother who you're obsessed with, and I sure as *hell* don't want to be your well-dressed driver while you drink with your friends. I am out!"

She was breathless at the end of her exclamation, feeling like a giant weight had been lifted from her chest.

Kyle glared at her, his blue eyes looking increasingly

evil and cold. "I would watch your mouth if I were you, Daisy Bennett." He pointed a finger at her. "I'm willing to give you a life that you could never have in a million years without me."

"And I'm telling you to enjoy that life without me, because I want nothing to do with it."

He laughed with utter disbelief, shaking his head as he ran his fingers through his hair. "You're insane, you know that? What woman would walk away from this?"

She wriggled the giant diamond off her left ring finger and slapped it onto the kitchen counter. "One who deserves better."

"Better than everything I can give you? Good luck with that, Daisy," he scoffed.

She just pushed past him and marched through the apartment, pausing at the hall closet to grab a suitcase and her old duffle bag. She dragged it into the main bedroom and into the walk-in closet, yanking open one of the drawers.

"You're serious about this?" He stood over her like a lion watching its prey. "You're actually walking away from the best thing you'll ever have?"

"I'm walking away from money, Kyle." She ground out the words as she whipped every T-shirt she owned into the suitcase, then went to the shorts in the next drawer. Underwear, socks, and a few dresses, and she'd be done. "There's more to life than that."

"You're walking away from us, Daisy." He stood in front of her hanging clothes as if that could stop her.

"What about the wedding? What about Fiji and our Aspen trip in January?"

She reached around him to grab a dress, but he sidestepped so she couldn't.

Frustrated and shaking, she looked up at him. "I hate skiing, and I don't need that dress."

She twirled around, heading to her underwear drawer.

"The wedding is in three months!" Kyle shouted.

"There isn't going to be a wedding." She scooped up as many panties and bras as she could grab, then tossed them on top of the T-shirts and shorts.

"You can't take this back, you know," he growled at her. "Once you leave with all your stuff and you leave the ring, there's no turning back. You're walking away forever."

Daisy zipped the old duffle and leveled her gaze with the man she'd thought would be her forever love.

Sadness mixed with the anger in her heart, and her eyes stung with tears.

Was she sure about this? Was she acting out of emotion or fear or immaturity? Would she regret this decision for the rest of her life?

She'd miss Kyle. She'd miss the life she'd thought they'd have together. Her heart felt as if it was physically cracking in half as she walked out of the closet and back into the oversized bedroom, locked in his gaze.

Daisy shut her eyes, quieting the world around her and listening hard for her own gut...her own truth.

Mom had always told her she was a brilliant decision-maker. She knew how to do the right thing. And when she did the wrong thing...she knew that, too.

"Goodbye, Kyle." Her voice was soft. Calm. Certain.

She closed the suitcase and picked it up with the duffle bag.

He followed her down the hallway toward the front door of the apartment. "You'll regret this."

She grabbed her purse, reaching for her keys. "I'm keeping the Mercedes." Okay, now she was feeling herself.

"Fine," he shot back. "It's the only decent car you'll ever have, might as well enjoy it."

"You suck, Kyle." She swung the door open, turning over her shoulder to add one final note. "Oh, and don't worry. I bet your mommy will drive you tonight."

The door slammed shut behind her and Daisy, fueled by pure adrenaline, hauled her giant suitcase and duffle bag down the hallway, into the elevator and to her parked Mercedes.

She stared at the car for a moment before popping the trunk open. Yup, she still wanted to keep it.

With her belongings loaded into the trunk and her fiancé dumped, there was only one thing to do.

She might have just made fun of Kyle for it, but right now, Daisy Bennett needed her mommy.

"Oh, honey." Gloria opened the door to her condo and knew instantly what had happened. "You left him."

"I did." Daisy sucked in a breath, feeling weirdly calm and at peace. "I wasn't his number one."

"Daisy girl." Her mom wrapped her into a tight, long hug, kissing the top of her head and squeezing her closely. "I know how hard this is. I know."

"Actually..." Daisy pulled back, sniffling but not crying. "I'm okay. I mean, maybe it just hasn't hit me yet or whatever, but I'm all right. It was the right thing, and I'm sure of my decision. There will be a price, I'm sure. Linda will probably come after me for all the deposits—"

"Just let her try," Gloria said, tears filling her kind, blue eyes. "I'm proud of you for knowing what you're worth. I love you."

"Enough to let me move back in?" Daisy asked playfully with a sheepish, teary smile.

"Are you kidding? My home is your home. Come on." Gloria shuffled out to the car and grabbed the duffle bag, eyeing the suitcase. "Is this all your stuff?"

"Not all, but I'll worry about it later. I had a statement to make, and I sure did." She laughed softly. "I ended the engagement, the relationship, and all the plans. All done. All finished."

"Go, you." Gloria slung the bag over her shoulder and rolled the suitcase up the narrow concrete path that led to the front door of her end-unit condo. "Can I make you some tea? And, honey, don't feel like you have to talk about it now. If you want to just wallow and eat ice cream and watch bad movies, that's fine—"

"I'm good, Mom, really," Daisy said, surprising herself as she kicked her shoes off and walked into a living room that was far homier than where she'd been living. "I think I did a lot of my wallowing in advance. Now that it's over, I'm kind of...relieved."

Gloria put a kettle on the stove and wrapped the sides of her cardigan tightly around her waist. "Relief... that's a good sign that you made the right choice."

"I know I did." Daisy lay down on the couch and propped her feet up on the coffee table. "I keep waiting for the heartbreak to hit me, you know? I keep waiting for the dagger in my heart to knock me off my feet and make me want to cry and sob and break down. I used to get so wrecked over fights with Kyle. Arguments. Now, I'm... fine. It's bizarre."

Gloria walked over to join her, carrying a mug of steaming tea that she set on a coaster next to Daisy's feet. "It'll come in waves, honey. Breaking off an engagement is no small deal. It's going to take a lot of time to process and heal."

"I know." Daisy cuddled up to her mother, resting her head on Gloria's always strong shoulder. "Thanks for taking in a refugee."

Gloria snorted and they both laughed. "You know this is your home, Daisy. As long as you need it to be."

"I know. I don't want to live here for too long, though. I really do need independence."

"I know that. And I fully support you in finding it. I'll help however I can. But don't rush, honey. You'll find your own place when the time is right."

Daisy turned to face her mother. "I'm really, really sorry again for how I acted and how I treated you during all the wedding planning stuff. I still feel terrible."

"You are more than forgiven." Gloria took Daisy's cheeks in her palms.

"Thank you. I just was in, like, some sort of daze for so long. I feel like I finally woke up."

"Should we tell Vanessa and Emily? Want them to come over? I have a feeling they'll be overjoyed to hear this news. Worried about you, of course, but you know."

"Wait…" Daisy faked a shocked gasp. "You're telling me that you guys didn't like Kyle? I'm stunned!"

Gloria laughed and rolled her eyes. "I tried, honey, I really did."

"You were right about him. And I'll tell Aunt Vanessa and Emily tomorrow. Right now, let's just be you and me. Like it used to be."

"Okay." Gloria lay back on the couch next to Daisy, and they looked out at the night sky over the Gulf.

"Guess what?"

"Huh?"

"I kept the Mercedes."

Gloria cackled. "That's my girl."

Daisy knew, in that moment, that her future wouldn't look anything like she'd been picturing since the fateful day when she met Kyle Whittington.

It would look better. Filled with things and people and experiences that mattered so much more than money and glamour.

"Are you worried about anything?" Gloria asked after a long break of silence.

"For the first time in months, no. I'm not. I'm just going to work, and hang with you, and go to the beach and heal. That's all that's on my agenda."

"I'm so proud of you, Daisy Elizabeth."

And finally, Daisy was proud of herself, too.

Chapter Eighteen

Gloria

Relief didn't even begin to describe the weight off of Gloria's shoulders now that her daughter was not marrying Kyle Whittington. She nearly floated on the way to work the next morning before sunrise, earlier than any of her employees.

She'd been so happy, she couldn't sleep. In fact, she was a little shocked at how much she'd opposed the union.

But Daisy had to realize it herself, and she certainly had.

This breakup was not going to be easy for anyone, but Daisy was calm and certain and totally at peace. And now, Gloria finally could be, too.

The last thing she'd wanted for her sweet, wonderful daughter was to end up getting her heart broken in some ugly divorce. Divorce was wretched. Even the most amicable of separations, like Gloria had had with Christian, hurt the same as the acrimonious ones, just in a totally different way.

She thought about Christian Bennett as she unlocked the door to the diner, disarmed the alarm system, and headed into her office to prepare for the morning shipment. She wondered about her ex-husband all the time, but it seemed to be even more frequent lately with everything going on with Daisy and finding her mother.

She even thought about shooting Christian a text to ask about their son, since she'd hardly heard from Jeremy in the past couple of weeks, but Gloria resisted. She never really understood how to be friendly with the only man she'd ever loved, the father of her children, the love of her life.

How could they just be simple, polite acquaintances when they were always so much more?

Because of that, they'd become nothing.

She sat down at her desk in the back office, switching her computer on and swiveling in the worn leather desk chair.

She could picture Christian so clearly—his dark hair, nearly jet black. His deep brown eyes that he passed right on to Daisy. His wide, bright smile that could light up an entire baseball stadium...and frequently did.

He'd been freakishly handsome when they'd met, a young kid in his twenties and a rising star in the baseball world. Gloria didn't think she stood a chance with the athlete dreamboat, but for whatever reason, he'd adored her.

Their marriage was not perfect, but they were always close. Faithful, loyal, kind to each other. Christian was a good father when he could be, but the life of a professional athlete was not always an easy one for a young, growing family.

When he got the offer with the Red Sox and had to

move to Boston, Gloria couldn't leave Rosemary Beach. She had her father to think about, and she was all he had. Things had been rocky and distant between them for a while leading up to the Boston news, and, ultimately, they decided to separate.

Now, they hardly spoke, distant enough that she didn't even want to text him about their son. Checking the time, she saw that it was just before six, which meant this morning's shipment of fresh produce would be arriving soon.

She shook off the ache in her heart and focused on her computer screen, pulling up the spreadsheets that logged all of the expenses and inventories of food shipments to the diner.

But as she did, her phone rang, making her think it was a vendor running late or maybe an employee calling in sick or maybe—

Jason Chang

She stared at the name on her screen. "At six in the morning?" Gloria whispered to herself, frowning with confusion as she slid her finger across the screen to answer the call.

"Hello?"

"Gloria, hi. I'm so sorry to call this early, I hope I didn't wake you."

"No, not at all. I'm already at work, actually." She gave a soft laugh. "Restaurant business starts early."

"Of course. Okay, that's good."

Gloria's mind raced with a million questions, knowing full well that the private investigator would not call her at such a weird hour if there wasn't an urgent piece of information to share.

Her heart rate picked up and her palms began to sweat as she held the phone to her ear, waiting.

"Well, I have some news. And I was going to wait until normal business hours to let you know, but it's pretty significant and I figured you'd want to hear this ASAP."

"I certainly do," Gloria said, trying to tamp down the nerves in her voice. "What is it?"

Jason paused for what felt like an eternity. "I found your mother."

Gloria had known this was likely to be the significant development as soon as she saw his call coming in, but somehow that didn't make the impact of his words any less powerful.

"You...found her," she croaked. "Wow. Where is she?"

"She's at a place called Serenity Palms Memory Care Center. It's a nursing home and assisted-living facility for people with Alzheimer's and dementia. It's in a town called Ebro, which is much closer to Rosemary Beach than that pharmacy, which he might have used because it's one of the few not connected to any national databases, like Walgreens or CVS. Anyway, Ebro's about thirty minutes inland from you."

Gloria drew in a shaky breath, steadying herself as she attempted to process the fact that her mother, who she'd believed was dead from the time she was five years old, was living in a nursing home *half an hour away*.

"Okay." Gloria shut her eyes, gut-punched. "Anything else?"

"I confirmed what the pharmacist said, that your father would pick up her prescriptions and bring them to her at this facility once a month. I spoke with the manager of Serenity Palms, and she told me that Bill visited frequently."

Gloria shuddered. How could she have not known?

Jason cleared his throat and continued. "Evidently, her condition is relatively advanced, and she requires a decent amount of care. She's been a resident at Serenity Palms for five and a half years."

For a moment, she couldn't breathe or think or see.

Gathering her wits, she opened a new tab in her web browser, frantically typing "Serenity Palms" into the search bar. She scrolled through a website that depicted older, gray-haired people laughing with nurses and lounging by a pool.

This place wasn't some dingy nursing home; it looked more like a luxury resort.

She clicked on the menu tab for pricing and moved her cursor quickly, scanning the page. At the bottom, Gloria located the list of costs, and her jaw fell slack.

At Serenity Palms, we provide specialized memory care programs for our residents, as well as therapy, support groups, top of the line medical care, and a wide range of recreational activities and amenities on our sprawling, luxury campus. With rates starting at $7,500 per month, you can ensure that your loved one is happy and healthy at Serenity Palms.

"Who..." She stammered, stunned by the number. "Who was paying for this?"

"Your father," Jason said softly, knowing the words would hit hard. "I asked the manager that, too. William Young paid for all of her expenses throughout her entire stay and prepaid for the next three years before he passed."

Gloria swallowed. She had dug through all of his affairs—finances, bills, credit cards, bank accounts. She was fully aware of every single dollar to that man's name, and nowhere had she ever seen a mention of Serenity Palms.

As if reading her mind and the questions racing through it, Jason continued. "I'm assuming he had a secret account, or paid with direct withdrawals, like cash or check. I see this kind of thing a lot. There are ways to leave no traces of payments."

"Oh. Okay." It was all she could manage in the face of this tidal wave of unbelievable information.

"I can give you the phone number of Serenity Palms, and the direct cell for the manager who had the most information."

"Text it to me, please." Gloria grabbed her bag and slung it over her shoulder. "I've got to run."

"Okay. Gloria," he said.

"Yes?" She was already fumbling for keys, thinking of who she could call to come in and oversee the morning shipment in her place.

"Be careful. This is really emotional territory."

She frowned, holding the phone between her

shoulder and her ear. "I will be. Thanks again, Jason. Have a good one."

She hung up the phone then quickly called Manuel, the assistant manager at the diner, knowing he'd be able to come in and handle the morning.

Gloria wasn't sure if she was going to Serenity Palms. She wasn't sure if this was the end of the road on their search for Violet.

All she knew was that she had to get to her sister, and she had to get to her now.

"Can we stop for coffee, please?" Vanessa, who was as beautiful with a natural face as she was with makeup, turned to Gloria from the passenger seat with a frown.

"We're going to see our mother who we thought was dead for forty-five years and you're worried about *coffee*?"

"It's six-thirty." She rubbed her eyes, her caramel-blond hair still in a messy bun from the sleep that Gloria woke her from when she pounded on the front door. "I don't think I can do this without a latte."

"That's fair."

Gloria hadn't been as delicate with waking Vanessa in the early hours of the morning as she maybe could have been. Partially because she was so used to getting up around five to go to the diner, it didn't even feel early to her anymore.

But mostly because this news was so monumental,

and the day ahead of them was so life-altering, the time simply didn't matter.

Gloria pulled into the drive-through of a nearby Starbucks and ordered two large vanilla lattes, giving her sister an apologetic smile as she handed her the hot paper cup, staying parked in the lot while they got situated.

"Thanks." Vanessa took a deep drink of the coffee and stared out the window. "Do you have the GPS ready with the address? I can pull it up if you need—"

"Should we really be doing this?" Gloria let the question tumble from her heart and out of her mouth.

Vanessa turned to face her slowly, her brows knit together in a dramatic expression of shock. "Are you out of your mind? Of course we should be doing this. Our mother, who we've presumed dead for our *entire* lives, is twenty-seven minutes away. Alive and...debatably well. How are you even questioning this?"

"I don't know, Nessie." Gloria leaned back in the driver's seat, holding her latte with both hands, letting the steam rise up to her face. "I don't know if I can face her. I don't know if I want to see her."

Vanessa sighed softly. "Don't you have a million questions?"

"She has dementia. She probably won't even be able to answer them."

"We don't know that."

"She might not know who we are."

"But she might," Vanessa insisted. "We don't know exactly how bad her condition is. There's a wide range when it comes to dementia."

Gloria nodded, knowing her sister was right about that. Clarinda could be anywhere from a little bit forgetful to not knowing her own name. But based on the fact that she'd been living in a memory care facility for the past five years, Gloria couldn't help but assume it was closer to the latter.

"Okay, we'll go," Gloria finally said.

"Good. We have to. I think we'll always regret it if we don't. We'll always wonder. This could be closure for us, Glo."

Closure. Gloria thought about that word, rolling it over in her mind as she shifted the car into reverse and pulled out of the Starbucks parking lot.

Gloria Bennett was not a grudge-holder. She'd welcomed Vanessa back with open arms even after she'd been MIA for thirty years. She'd forgiven Dad for his many shortcomings.

She'd forgiven Daisy with total ease when her daughter realized how bratty she was being about the wedding. She'd even forgiven Christian, not that he'd truly wronged her by following his superstar career.

But this...this felt different. Gloria didn't know if she even had the capacity to forgive what her mother had done, and she wasn't entirely sure she wanted to find out.

"Look, I don't want to have some big, happy reunion and pretend everything is all sweet and good just because she's old and sick," Gloria finally said. "I want her to look at us, to see the incredible grown women that we became in spite of her. I want her to see the years that she missed out on, to hear about the grandchildren she'll never get to know. I want her to understand what she gave up for her stupid, selfish dream. And when the money Dad paid runs out, she can drop dead on the street for all I care."

The words hung in the air between them for a few seconds. Gloria knew she sounded harsh, but that was the truth. That was how she felt.

"I get that," Vanessa said softly.

They stayed quiet for the rest of the drive, passing what had to be the only stoplight in Ebro, turning onto a side road until they eventually reached iron and stone gates with the words Serenity Palms on a small brass plate.

Secret, safe, and incredibly upscale.

A guard asked their names, and they told them they were coming to see their mother, Clarinda Smith. That was all it took to get on the sprawling campus, with two-story tan buildings surrounded by lush greenery and rows of palm trees. Flowering plants neatly lined the curbs, and the windows were trimmed with inviting white shutters.

It looked more like a fancy prep school than a nursing home, and the property was manicured and seriously well maintained.

"Holy cow," Vanessa said under her breath as they pulled up to the visitors parking area in front of the main entrance. "Dad was paying for this?"

"Yeah." Gloria pushed the driver's side door open, stepping out into the humid warmth of sunrise.

Vanessa got out and came around the front of the car, coming face to face with her sister, somehow looking much more together and presentable than she had when they'd started the drive. "Are you ready for this?"

Gloria's instinct was to say, "No," and get in the car and drive home, but mostly because she was scared of what they were about to find.

"Mom's alive," Vanessa said softly. "She's in there. I don't know what I'm hoping to get from this, but I know we need to do this." She held out her hand. "Together."

Gloria nodded, tamping down the prickles of anxiety that spread across her chest, and took her sister's hand.

Together, they walked into the main lobby of Serenity Palms, which felt, again, like an upscale, tropical resort of some kind.

Seating areas sprawled around the marble-floored lobby and a large fountain rained trickling water in the middle of the floor. A couple of young women wearing scrubs walked by chatting, and that was the first sign that this place was anything but a fancy hotel.

"Hello. May I help you ladies?" a woman asked cheerfully from behind the front desk, which was along the right side of the entryway, flanked by potted palm trees.

"Hi." Gloria forced a smile and hustled over, still holding Nessie's hand. "When are visiting hours?"

"Seven to three." The woman grinned. "So if you're here to visit, you're just in time." She pointed at the clock on the wall behind her, which read 7:02.

"Perfect," Gloria replied, although it felt anything but.

"Now, who are you here to see today?" The woman began typing on the computer in front of her.

"Clarinda Smith," Vanessa leaned forward and chimed in, likely sensing that Gloria was nearly frozen with nerves.

The woman behind the desk stared at her with surprise, her eyes widening. "Oh! Really? That's...okay."

"Is something wrong?" Gloria asked, secretly hoping she'd say they couldn't see her, and they'd have to leave and forget about this entirely.

"No, no." The woman shook her head. "It's just that... Clarinda has only ever had one visitor."

Gloria swallowed the lump in her throat. "Right. Well. That was our father. We're here now."

"I'll get you checked in."

The woman got their names and printed out visitor stickers for them to slap on their shirts, like when you went to see someone in the hospital.

The place was quickly feeling less and less like a resort.

Gloria stuck the nametag onto her chest and watched Nessie do the same. She took a slow, deep breath and leveled her gaze with her sister. "You ready?"

"Let's go meet our mother."

Chapter Nineteen

Vanessa

Vanessa felt like she was walking through quicksand as she and Glo made their way around the property. The woman at the front desk had given them instructions to reach Clarinda's unit, 614, but Vanessa had hardly been able to pay attention to her directions.

Her breathing felt shallow as they walked between fresh, clean-looking buildings that surrounded a huge courtyard. Adjacent to the courtyard were tennis and pickleball courts, a large swimming pool, a meandering walking trail, and grills with outdoor dining tables.

"Old folks homes sure ain't what they used to be," Vanessa joked—half-joked—as they located Building Six.

"Yeah, this is..." Gloria took a deep breath. "Something."

They opened the door that led them down a long, air-conditioned hallway with light-red tiled floors and textured walls. The door to each unit was painted a rusty maroon, and many were decorated with pictures or wreaths.

They reached the door labeled 614, and Vanessa turned to Gloria. "You okay?"

Gloria nodded, but her eyes were wide with nerves.

"We got this. Together."

Vanessa lifted her shaking hand to knock gently on the door, holding her breath while they waited for an answer.

The door clicked and slowly opened, revealing a tiny, skinny woman who couldn't be an inch over five feet with a puffy cloud of white hair. "Hello. May I help you gals?"

Vanessa felt her lip quiver as she looked at the woman's eyes. They were blue, the same exact blue as hers and Glo's and Emily's.

"H...hi," Gloria stammered, stepping forward. "Are you Clarinda?"

"To some, yes." The woman nodded.

"We're here to visit you." Vanessa swallowed, her throat dry as a desert. "Can we come in?"

The sisters shared a look of shock as Clarinda stepped aside and gestured for them to enter her little room.

The woman looked and seemed a decade and a half older than early seventies. It was impossible to believe she was the same age as Cricket, but Vanessa guessed that dementia likely aged people quickly. Early onset, in her case.

Her space was simple and neat. A twin-sized bed in one corner, a small kitchenette along the side wall, a small dining table, and a little loveseat in front of a TV. The walls were mostly blank, and nearly everything was a pale shade of pink.

"Do I know you two?" She looked at them, blinking

with confusion as they sat down on the loveseat while Clarinda sat in one of the dining chairs.

Vanessa took a deep breath, reaching for Gloria's hand and squeezing it. "My name is Vanessa Young, and this is Gloria."

They waited in silent anxiety, anticipating the older woman's face lighting up with recognition, or pain, or regret, or just pure shock.

But behind those eerily familiar blue eyes, there was...nothing.

Clarinda smacked her lips. "That's lovely. Are you from the church?"

Vanessa turned to Gloria, and they looked at each other, stunned. She had no idea what to say.

The woman had...no idea who they were.

"Uh, no," Gloria stepped in. "We're Gloria and Vanessa. Do you remember us at all?"

"We've met? I'm sorry, dears, I don't recall. Things do get a bit hazy for me these days." She stood up, her pink nightgown draped around her tiny frame. "I was going to put on some tea. You want some?"

"We're your daughters," Vanessa blurted out, instantly regretting it but completely unable to hold her tongue. "We're the daughters you left behind in 1979 to go and pursue acting on Broadway. When you left Bill Young, our father."

She just stared at them, about as curious as if they'd said they were from...well, the church.

"*William Young*," Gloria added with emphasis, her frustration palpable.

"Oh, I know William." She lit up. "He's the nice man who brings me my pills."

Vanessa turned to Gloria, desperately and silently pleading for her older sister to know what to do next, but Gloria was as white as Clarinda's hair.

"Don't you remember?" Vanessa said softly. "You had two daughters, one was five, and one was an infant. You had a husband. You left them and never came back."

The woman was quiet, her gaze distant. "I used to be a dancer, you know. But I never had any children. No, no. I never married. I used to dance on the big stage. I could sing, too. I wanted to act but wouldn't you know it? Can't remember a line to save my life."

Disappointment and anger burned in Vanessa's gut, but it was met with a different and unexpected emotion.

She looked at her mother, and suddenly saw a pathetically confused, sick woman, who looked and felt much older than she actually was.

A woman who didn't have any comprehension of the wrongs she'd committed in her life or the people she'd hurt or the mistakes she'd made.

She was just...an old woman with dementia.

"Knock-knock." A nurse poked her head through the doorway, wheeling a cart with a computer and a blood pressure monitor. "I'm here to check morning vitals on my favorite superstar."

The woman's energy was joyful and warm, and Vanessa glanced at Gloria with confusion and uncertainty about what to do.

"Oh, Clarinda! I didn't know you had visitors coming

today!" The woman stepped around her vitals machine and held her hand out to greet Vanessa and Gloria, blissfully unaware of the heavy darkness and clouds of the past that filled the little room.

"I'm Sharice. I'm a day nurse here at Serenity. Are you lovely ladies friends of Clarinda?" Sharice was tall and beautiful, with long dark braids and big brown eyes.

"It's nice to meet you," Gloria said, breaking the awkward silence. "I'm Gloria, and this is my sister, Vanessa."

Vanessa smiled and shook the nurse's hand, noticing that Gloria conveniently ignored her question about whether or not they were "friends" of Clarinda's.

"Do you, um..." Vanessa lowered her voice a bit, leaning close to Sharice. "Do you see her every day? You're around a lot?"

"Six days a week." Sharice nodded with pride. "Used to be four, but my hubby and I just started sending the kiddos to private school, so, now it's six." She laughed with a lot of joy for a woman who was working six days a week. "What can you do, huh? But I love coming here and, yes, I do see Miss Clarinda every single day throughout my shift. We chat about old movies, isn't that right?"

"Oh, yes," Clarinda said, her voice sounding far away. "I was on TV, you know. Not movies, but I had a line in... a show." She sighed. "I can't remember the name of it now."

"It's fine, honey." Sharice just laughed to herself as

she unraveled the cord to the blood pressure monitor and slung it over her arm.

"Um, listen, Sharice?" Vanessa placed her hand on the woman's arm. "Would you be able to talk privately to my sister and me outside? Just for a moment."

Sharice's brows knit together with concern. "Sure. Of course." She set her machine back on the rolling cart. "I'll be right back, Clarinda. You go ahead and find something on the TV for us to watch while I chart your vitals."

Clarinda mumbled something that sounded a bit nonsensical, but busied herself with the TV remote as the three other women stepped outside the apartment into the hallway.

"So..." She looked from one to the other. "Who are you two?"

Gloria looked at Vanessa, then spoke. "We're her daughters."

Sharice's face fell and her jaw went slack. "The girls," she whispered softly, her voice barely audible. "You're the girls."

Vanessa shook her head. "What?"

"All this time...I..." Sharice stared at them, her brown eyes wide. "I thought Clarinda was just confused and speaking nonsense when she'd mention her girls, but... here you are."

"Wait a second." Vanessa could hear her heartbeat pounding in her ears. "She's *mentioned* us?"

"She remembers?" Gloria asked on a gasp, her hand clutching her chest.

"Rarely." Sharice swallowed, pressing her lips

together as she glanced back toward the little apartment. "Very, very rarely. Clarinda is in an advanced state of memory loss and confusion, so sometimes it's hard to separate what's real and what isn't when she's talking and telling stories and things. But it makes sense now to see you two here, because she has mentioned 'the girls' when she's in her rare moments of clarity, although she never used your names."

"So she remembers us?" Vanessa asked.

"I wouldn't go that far." Sharice shook her head. "Her moments of lucidity are few and far between. She's mostly confused and doesn't remember much of her past in any detail or accuracy."

Vanessa drew back with the impact of that.

So there were, in fact, rare moments when Clarinda remembered her daughters. The girls she left behind all those years ago.

"What does she say?" Gloria asked, rubbing her hands together anxiously. "When she has a moment of lucidity?"

Sharice lifted her shoulders. "She's told me she used to be married, although she regularly forgets that. She talked about her husband and 'the girls.' She said she had to leave them. And, generally, when she gets to that part of the story, she shuts down. By the time she gathers herself, she's forgotten it all again. I don't know much, but I'm a memory care nurse, so I'm used to it."

Vanessa swore she could feel her heart tug so hard it nearly cracked. She couldn't bear to look at her sister, knowing they were both likely on the brink of tears.

"Haven't you met William?" Gloria asked. "My father brought her meds."

"That was her husband?" she gasped. "He said he was a volunteer with the church, some people who visit our patients and run errands for them."

Vanessa just closed her eyes and could have sworn she felt her sister sway.

She drew in a deep breath. "Thank you, Sharice. This has been a pretty crazy journey for us."

"We thought she was dead," Gloria interjected, her tone jagged.

Sharice drew back, blinking with shock. "What? Why?"

"We were so little..." Glo continued. "She left us, and the story we grew up hearing was that she had a tragic accident and died. And our dad moved us out of state to Florida to start over, and we never heard any more about her. Forty-five years later, we learn she's been alive the entire time."

Sharice was stunned into silence, slowly lifting her hand to cover her mouth in astonishment. "My heavens. I can't imagine. I'm so sorry. I...I really wish I could help you more, but she just doesn't remember."

"But sometimes she does," Vanessa said.

"Rarely," Sharice reminded them. "And when the past does come back to her, it's almost like it's too painful to think about, so her brain just sends her back into confusion and forgetfulness. It's easier. I knew she had some traumas and regrets. I think in a way, her own mind is protecting her from them."

"How often does that happen?" Vanessa asked, desperate for one of those moments right now. "That she's lucid and speaks accurately about that past, and then gets emotional and forgets again?"

Sharice blew out a breath. "It's tough to say. There's no rhyme or reason to this disease, I'm afraid. Maybe a couple times a month? Normally, I feel encouraged when patients start to remember their pasts, but with Clarinda, she gets so sad and tortured over it, I always think it's better for her when she doesn't remember anything."

Vanessa held her breath. She waited for the anger, the rage, the abandonment. She waited to feel spiteful and resentful toward that old woman in that room, the selfish woman who left her family for a dumb dream and let her daughters grow up motherless believing their dad was a widower.

She waited and waited and waited, but the anger didn't come. Through the tornado of emotions in Vanessa's heart and mind, the only thing that really came through strongly was...pity. An aching, bone-deep, full-body bout of pity.

"Thank you, Sharice," Gloria said, shaking the nurse's hand again. "It was good to meet you. My sister and I are going to be heading out now."

Vanessa bit her lip, not sure she was ready to leave but figuring she'd better follow her sister's lead. She thanked Sharice and said goodbye to her, then followed Gloria who, for some reason, was practically sprinting down the hallway.

"Slow down, track star," Vanessa said through heavy

breathing as she speed-walked to catch up to her sister. "What's going on? Why are we leaving already?"

"Because we're done, Vanessa." Gloria turned to her, her eyes cold. "There's nothing left to do here. Nothing left to uncover. Our mother is a sick old Alzheimer's patient who doesn't even remember her despicable and horrifying life choices. She doesn't live with regrets and sorrow and the pain that someone who made those kinds of mistakes should live with. And you heard the nurse. In the rare moments she's lucid and can recall that we even existed, her brain shuts it off." She continued hustling out of the building and through the courtyard.

"What do you mean, 'We're done'?"

"I mean we're done with this." Gloria threw her hands up, visibly upset. "This chase. This search. This whole project. We found her, we met her, she doesn't know who we are. What else is there to do? Personally, I'd really like to just go back to my normal life and, frankly, forget about this."

Vanessa was stunned. "But we'll come back, right?"

"Come back? For what?"

"To see her again. To see if we can catch her in a moment of clarity, a moment where she remembers. She'd know who we are!"

"And then what, Vanessa?" Gloria's face fell as they walked back into the main building, toward the parking lot on the other side of the lobby. "Where does it end?"

"With..." Vanessa nearly choked on her next word, but she had to say it. "Forgiveness."

Gloria made a face of pure disgust. "*What?*"

Vanessa didn't even know how to answer. She didn't know how to explain herself. "Gloria, all I know, in my heart, is that woman is in pain and suffering over what she did. Even if it's only for a few fleeting moments when she remembers."

"She should be suffering," Gloria whispered, her voice breaking. "She left us."

"She may not be around much longer, Glo. She's sick and seems a heck of a lot older than she actually is."

Gloria's lips formed a thin line as she looked away, visibly fighting tears.

"If we can be there when she has a moment of clarity, when she remembers us, we can forgive her. We can free her of her pain and regret and let her finally be at peace."

Gloria stared at Vanessa like she was staring at a ghost. "Are you serious? You want to forgive her? Like, face to face?"

"Yes. And you should, too." Feeling the tension rising between them, Vanessa reached out to put her hand on her sister's arm. "You're the queen of forgiveness."

Gloria didn't laugh.

"Look, I know what it's like to make a mistake. I left my daughter, remember?"

"You put her up for adoption, Nessie. You didn't fake a car crash."

"I know, but my point is, I know what it feels like to live with deep regret. And I can't imagine her confusion and frustration with her disease. Who knows how much it really does torment her when she remembers? It's sad and pitiful and...look at us. We grew. We're strong. We're successful with daughters and businesses and joyful lives."

Gloria bit her lip and fixed her gaze down at the sidewalk.

"I want to come back and see her," Vanessa said. "I want to be here when she has a moment of lucidity, and I want to tell her that she's forgiven. I want her to get to see us and know who we are just one time."

Gloria lifted her gaze slowly, shaking her head. "She doesn't deserve that."

It was so unlike Glo not to be forgiving, but Vanessa had to remember that she took the brunt of Mom's absence. She never left Rosemary Beach because she had to take care of Dad all those years. She lost her marriage over it.

"Glo—"

"I'm not coming back here." She moved past Vanessa into the lobby, walking out the front door and straight to the parked car. "She's been dead to me for forty-five years, and I'm not changing that now. At least you don't have to worry about the fact that Dad put her in the will, she is certainly not taking anything else from us."

EMOTIONALLY DRAINED and exhausted by the morning, Vanessa walked into Young at Heart to make sure everything went smoothly throughout the morning she'd been gone, but she hadn't proven very useful.

The store was running beautifully under Emily, who

was happily training Meredith, a young woman they'd hired as a backup sales clerk. After dumping all the details of the failed reunion onto Emily, Vanessa took her daughter's advice and decided to go for a walk to pick up some lunch for the three of them.

She needed to clear her head and be alone, and Emily and Meredith had things more than under control at the store.

As Vanessa strode down Main Street, she wrestled with her own thoughts and surprising emotions. How bizarre that she was the one who wanted to forgive and Gloria was the one saying no. It was so opposite their personalities.

Vanessa couldn't explain it, she didn't understand why, but she felt it in her heart and soul and bones that she needed to make peace with her mother. Yes, Clarinda was confused and had severe memory loss, but that didn't mean she had to live the rest of her life with flashes of deep torment and regret.

Vanessa knew the value of forgiveness. She knew the weight that it carried, the life-changing freedom it could bring. Forgiveness was everything. Forgiveness was the only way to truly heal. Forgiveness was all—

"Vanessa?" Noah Ellison shielded his eyes from the sun as he walked toward her on the sidewalk.

Speaking of forgiveness, or lack thereof, she thought to herself. "Oh, hey, Noah."

Vanessa barely had a chance to assess her ragged appearance or tear-stained face and, frankly, she didn't care.

"What's going on? Sneaking away from work?" he joked, which made her heart lighten a bit.

"No, actually, um..." She pushed her sunglasses up on the bridge of her nose and lifted a shoulder. "I'm just out for a walk. I'm going to pick up some lunch for Emily and...I needed...a walk."

"Ness? Are you okay?"

Of course, he was Noah, and no matter how much time passed or how much distance grew between them, he could read her every expression. She didn't stand a chance of fooling him into thinking nothing was wrong.

"You know?" She gave a dry laugh. "Not really, actually."

He paused, opening his mouth to say something, then seemingly hesitating.

"I'm sure you're busy and, we're not...yeah, so." She waved a hand as if trying to visibly wipe away this conversation. "I'm fine, don't worry about me. Gotta run."

"Wait." He gently touched her arm.

She turned around. "What?"

Noah gestured in the general direction of the beach, which was a block away. "Come on. Let's go sit by the water."

Vanessa stared at him, blinking with confusion. Was he voluntarily hanging out with her? He wasn't running away?

He guided her between buildings, past a bike rack, and onto the sandy wooden steps that led down to the Gulf.

The waves crashed gently against the shore, sending

white spray through the air. Vanessa felt her skin warmed by the unobstructed sun as she inhaled the salty breeze and let herself relax a little.

"I can tell that something's wrong." Noah sat down on the sand and invited her to sit next to him. "I can see it in your eyes."

"I'm wearing sunglasses," she replied.

"Doesn't matter." Noah turned and faced the water, his profile sharp and handsome.

"But you...you don't want anything to do with me. Why would you go out of your way to help me?"

"Just tell me what's wrong," he said, that note of caring in his voice that nearly took her breath away because she'd missed it so much.

It wasn't until right this minute that she realized just how much.

It was time to stop questioning him and grab the life raft he was offering her sinking ship. She took a deep breath, closed her eyes, and told him everything.

She told him about the letters, the name on the will, how Violet was a nickname and her mother was really called Clarinda, and she didn't die in a car accident when Vanessa was a baby. She told him about Jason Chang, the private investigator, how Gloria got a call from the pharmacy about Bill's meds and they drove there, only to find out the meds weren't for Bill at all.

The story flowed freely from beginning to end, leaving out no detail, and expressing to him how truly confusing and heartbreaking the whole revelation had turned out to be.

Noah, bless his heart, didn't react except to listen intently, taking it in, meeting her gaze with those familiar, sympathetic, understanding eyes. Those eyes that knew her better than anyone on the planet, that got her to her deepest soul.

Vanessa was nearly breathless by the time she finished telling him about their morning at Serenity Palms, about Sharice the kind nurse and Clarinda's alleged moments of clarity, and about how Vanessa felt the need to forgive her, but Gloria was against it.

"Okay." Vanessa tucked her knees into her chest, resting her chin on them as she watched the Gulf waves kiss the shore. "I think that's the entire story. And please, keep all of this between us. I love your mom dearly, but—"

"She'll tell the free world?" He chuckled. "Don't worry."

She smiled. "Thanks."

Noah shook his head as he processed the insane saga of events and discoveries. "Holy cow, Nessie. This is...a lot. For you and Gloria. For...wow." He closed his eyes as if the impact of that story was just hitting him now.

"It was always such a big part of you, the fact that your mother died when you were a baby," he said after a moment of processing. "It was your biggest struggle. I can remember so many nights when you'd wonder about her. We'd put a blanket down in the back of my truck and park at the beach and talk. Remember?"

Vanessa laughed dryly, wiping a tear. "You mean the

Ford pickup where Emily was conceived? How could I possibly forget?"

"You'd think about your mother," he said. "You'd make up stories in your mind about what she must have been like. You'd have done anything to have had her with you all those years, guiding you. You probably..." He paused, inhaling sharply. "You probably wouldn't have left. If you'd had a mom."

Vanessa's throat felt tight. She swallowed and fixed her gaze on the dancing waves of the Gulf, watching the reflection of the sun bouncing on them. "I know. I've thought about that a million times."

"And she was alive. All that time she was...alive." He turned to face her, leveling his gaze. "I can't imagine your pain."

Vanessa nodded, pressing her lips together. "I don't want to think about the what-ifs, but I can't help it. What if she had been here? What if she'd come back? Or never left in the first place? What if she'd reached out when I was in L.A.? But... she never did. She had her story and she stuck to it, all these years. So did my father. And now? She doesn't even know what her story is, and he died without telling us the truth."

"He had to know you'd find out."

She nodded. "And I'm not sure if he thought he was doing us a favor or not, but I'll never know now."

Noah's eyes were a bit misty as he looked at her, his whole body turned to face her, everything about him seeming open and warm and...not distant anymore.

"What are you going to do now?" he asked. "Do you

really want to see her again? It must be so painful, especially with her having no idea who you are."

Vanessa shrugged. "I'd like to catch her in one of those moments the nurse was talking about. When she might know who I am if I tell her."

Noah just shook his head, studying Vanessa. "But why? She left you all those years ago. She broke your family's hearts."

"Because forgiveness is powerful," Vanessa said, looking straight into the eyes of the very man whose forgiveness she desperately wanted. "I don't know why. I didn't go in there expecting to pity her or feel sorry for her or want to give her peace, but...that's what happened. I know what it's like to screw up." She raised her brows, eyeing him. "Big time."

Noah swallowed, glancing away as he clearly saw the parallels with their own past and Vanessa's regrets.

"And I just, I don't know, I felt bad for her. She's only in her seventies, which is kind of young to have such an advanced condition. They said it was early onset, no explanation why. Maybe it was mental, you know? Maybe she was so tortured about what she'd done, letting her two daughters grow up believing she was dead, that her brain just...turned off the memories."

"Wow." Noah closed his eyes.

"I want a moment of peace with her. Just one moment. I want to keep seeing her at Serenity Palms until that happens because forgiveness changes everything."

Noah's lips parted as he took a breath to speak but was visibly at a loss for words.

Vanessa could sense the conflict behind those blue eyes, the reflections of the past, scarred with pain and decades-old wounds, but still...here they were.

And simply talking to him, being next to him, Vanessa felt lighter. She felt clearer. Her burden was lessened just by his presence, just like it always was.

There was no one in the world, to her, like Noah Ellison.

"Nessie, I..." He wiped his face with his hand. "I think that's a beautiful sentiment. And I'm so sorry for what you've been through. No one deserves that. You deserved a real mother."

"It's all right." She leaned closer, losing herself in his gaze that hadn't moved. "Everything is...much more okay than I thought it would be. It hurts, badly, but...I have so much to be grateful for now."

"You've changed a lot." Noah inched closer, close enough for her to faintly smell his shampoo. "So much has changed. But somehow, it feels like..."

"Nothing has."

Noah was still home. Noah was still comfort. Noah was still the safest place in the world for Vanessa.

"Thank you," she whispered. "For...being here for me. For helping me."

He gave a half-smile, his hand reaching out to brush a strand of hair out of her face. "I didn't do anything."

"You didn't have to. You're here. You're you. You're my..."

He kissed her. And everything else went silent.

No questions about Clarinda, no pain about the past, no worries about the future. The world dissipated into perfect, quiet peace as Vanessa melted into the arms of the only man she'd ever loved.

Until he pulled away. Abruptly, his eyes darkened with emotion.

"I can't do this." Noah stood up, wiped the sand off of his jeans and shook his head. "I'm sorry, Vanessa, I just....I can't. I have to go."

Before she could even open her mouth to respond, he was gone, heading back up the stairs to the boardwalk, disappearing.

Vanessa was stunned and breathless, staring at the water as tears filled her eyes for what felt like the twentieth time today. Only these tears were the hardest.

She was still in love with Noah Ellison. Maybe she'd never stopped loving him all these years.

But it didn't matter, because his walls were up. She may have been able to peek through them for a split second, but they weren't coming down. Not now, not ever.

Everything hurt as Vanessa got up and walked out to the water, letting it splash up around her feet as the tears poured down her face.

Chapter Twenty

Emily

Vanessa had been out all morning, but Emily didn't mind running the store on her own. She wasn't nearly as skilled as her mother in the styling department, but she'd picked up a few tips and tricks and was able to help customers find pieces they loved.

Emily had never thought of herself as a fashion guru, but running Young at Heart was opening up a whole new world she never knew she'd love so much.

Her heart broke for her mother, though, who had clearly been enduring a painful rollercoaster of a day. She'd disappeared about an hour ago to pick up lunch and clear her head, and Emily knew that Vanessa should take all the time she needed to process the events at the nursing home that morning.

She'd asked Vanessa over and over what she could do to help her and Aunt Gloria through all of this, and her mom told her the best thing she could do was keep business booming and run Young at Heart as well as she could.

So Emily did.

Plus, she had her plans with Noah in the afternoon to go check out that record store nearby, and Emily had been seriously looking forward to that all morning. It was really beginning to feel like he was her dad, and that in and of itself was an incredible surprise.

"Excuse me, miss?" A tall, slender woman who was likely in her mid-sixties tapped Emily on the shoulder as she was restocking some T-shirts on a display shelf.

"Yes?" Emily turned around with a bright smile. "How can I help you?"

The woman held up a beautiful white midi-length dress with an eyelet design and capped sleeves. "Well, you see, I just love this dress. I have my grandson's high school graduation coming up and I think this is just perfect for the occasion."

"Oh, it's lovely." Emily gently touched the fabric of the sleeve. "You will look stunning in it, and it's a perfect summer graduation dress."

"You see, the trouble is, they're doing the graduation inside this year, in the auditorium you know, to account for the storms. And I just get so gosh darn chilly in those places when they run their air conditioning like it's going out of style."

Emily laughed softly. "I hear ya."

"But I think a jacket would ruin the look of this pretty dress." The woman frowned. "Do you have anything that might go with it? Nothing too heavy, of course, just something to cover my arms because I get so cold in those theaters."

"Hmm..." Emily thought for a moment, glancing around the boutique. This area of the job was certainly new to her, and she didn't want to steer this sweet woman wrong and talk her into buying something that wouldn't look good.

She thought hard to channel her inner Vanessa.

Emily scanned the store, eyeing a caramel-colored leather jacket—no, too punk rock. A black suede blazer—too business-y. Finally, she landed on a butter yellow cardigan with three-quarter-length sleeves and a white floral design.

Perfect.

"How about this cardigan?" Emily walked over to the rack and held it up.

The woman's face lit up with a smile. "I didn't even see that! It's just darling!"

Emily relished the look of joy and excitement on her customer's face. "Awesome! Can I help you with anything else?"

"I'm good for now but I'm going to poke around for some cute shoes." She lifted a shoulder. "Thanks for your help, honey."

Emily grinned. "Anytime. Let me know if you have any questions."

"I have a question."

The distinct and unmistakable voice of Reed Collins's voice caught Emily off guard, and she whipped her head around to see him standing in the front of the store, holding two cups of coffee. "Can you take a five-minute break?"

"Reed." Emily could hardly hide the hint of giddiness in her voice at his surprise visit as she walked over to him. "What are you doing here?"

He held up the cups again. "Isn't it obvious? Coffee break."

Emily looked around, spying Meredith helping a woman find white jeans. The store was relatively quiet. "My mom isn't here, so not a long one. But sure."

It was becoming increasingly obvious that she couldn't say no to him. And, honestly, she didn't want to.

"Let me tell Meredith we'll be in the back office."

After letting the other woman know, she guided Reed down the hallway behind the registers that led into her office.

Emily pulled her office chair out from behind the desk and situated it in front of the only other chair in the corner, gesturing for him to take it.

"To what do I owe this fun surprise?"

He handed her one of the coffees, which smelled like caramel and cream and deliciousness. "For you."

She inhaled deeply and took a sip. "Thank you so much. Why the treat?"

"To thank you," he said. "First off, for being so honest and open." Reed leveled his gaze, his brown eyes as rich as the espresso in her hand. "I know that story about your marriage was not easy to share, especially with someone you hardly know. Like I said, I haven't made a real friend in a while..." He ran a hand through his tousled hair. "It's really nice. I appreciate you being so genuine."

Emily smiled, the crush she had on him making her blush. "Honestly? It felt really good to tell the whole story and sort of just...get it off my chest. I've told people, obviously, but I don't know. It felt different sharing it with you. I'm glad I did."

He smiled back at her. "Well, I found it deeply inspiring. Just the rawness, the emotion, the pain of it all. Everything you said really spoke to me, and I've spent the past couple of weeks tearing down my manuscript and baking in some serious emotion."

"That's great!" Emily took a drink of coffee and leaned forward. "Does Sam Steele finally have a heart?"

"He does indeed. He's broken, and it's affecting him more than he realizes. No matter how he tries to push away the heartache, the failure, the pain of it...he can't, and it affects the entire rest of the plot. Sam doesn't mess up...but he messed up his marriage, and it's cracking him to the core."

Emily lifted a shoulder. "Sounds good. I might have to snag a copy."

"I'll sign it for you." Reed winked.

"Ooh, lucky me."

"But seriously." He angled his head. "Thank you. You saved my book. And me, from getting chewed out by my editor again."

Emily lifted her coffee cup. "Happy to be of service. If my trauma can help you sell books, then I'm all for it," she teased.

Reed laughed, shaking his head at her dry humor.

"So, how much longer do you think you'll be working on this book? What was it called again?"

"*River of Blood.*"

"Right. That *lovely* title," she said playfully.

He chuckled. "Not entirely sure when I'll be done. Maybe another month and a half, two months tops."

"And then..."

"I'm off." He nodded, his eyes flashing a bit as his gaze moved down toward the floor. "I go where my next book is set, but I haven't decided that yet. I immerse myself in the people, the setting, the sense of place. I figure out what kind of crimes would happen in a place like that, and living in my settings full-time really makes them come to life."

Emily tried her best to ignore the tiny pang of disappointment that hit her gut. She'd known Reed was temporary from the day she'd met him. "I totally get that. I'm sure it's why you're R.C. Anderson, bestselling author."

He waved off the compliment, laughing. "Anyway, I'd love to spend some more time with you. You know, while I'm still here."

And because Emily couldn't and didn't want to say no to Reed Collins, she smiled and took a sip of her coffee. "I'd like that."

After some more small talk and easy conversation—like it always was with him—Reed told Emily he'd let her get back to the store, then thanked her again for her help with his divorce storyline.

"Thank you for the coffee." She held up her empty cup as she walked him out to the front of the boutique. "This was really nice."

"You just working the rest of the day?" he asked.

"Actually, my dad is coming by in a couple of hours."

Emily grinned. "We're going to check out a vintage vinyl record shop this afternoon."

"That's awesome, Emily." He waved, glancing over his shoulder as he opened the front door of Young at Heart. "I'll see you around."

"Bye, Reed."

Emily tossed her empty coffee cup into a trash can and smiled to herself as she walked around the store and straightened up the displays.

Noah would be there in less than two hours, and life was good.

"That's weird," Emily whispered to herself as she restocked the fashion necklaces on a tree near the checkout counter.

Noah was over a half an hour late, and he hadn't texted or called.

Emily held out hope, certain that he'd just had an emergency meeting for work pop up, or possibly something with Cricket's loft remodel. Lawyers worked on Saturdays sometimes, right? He wouldn't just ditch her.

She had texted him ten minutes ago, but he hadn't responded. Surely he was just busy, she thought to herself. No reason to get worried yet. It was a casual plan, it wasn't some big, serious event.

She chewed her lip and toyed with the necklaces, spacing them out perfectly on the jewelry display case while Meredith rang up a customer at the register.

Not to mention, Vanessa had been MIA for hours now. But she, unlike Noah, had sent a text saying she was going to meet up with Gloria and deal with some things, so Emily wasn't concerned.

She glanced at the clock...forty minutes late. She'd understand if something had come up, but he couldn't have at least texted her?

Before letting herself go down the path of being hurt and upset, Emily took a deep breath and tried to remind herself that having Noah in her life at all was an unexpected gift. Yes, she'd grown slightly attached and maybe she shouldn't have, but the man she'd sat across from at the pizza place, that was a man who wanted to at least try to be her father.

The chimes on the front door rang and Emily's heart instantly lifted when she heard them.

He was here!

Emily whipped around to face the front door, but was surprised and, admittedly, a little disappointed, to see her mother walking in. "Oh, Vanessa. How are you?"

As soon as Emily walked closer to Vanessa, she saw her mother actually looked worse than when she'd left so many hours ago. Her eyes were rimmed in red, her face pale, her mouth turned down. "What's going on? Did you argue with Aunt Glo? I know you—"

"Let's go talk." She reached for Emily and tugged her toward the back. "Hold down the fort, Meredith?" she called.

"Will do," their lone employee replied.

But Emily resisted the pull from her mother. "Noah

is gonna be here any minute to pick me up to go to the record store, so I can't be—"

"Emily." Vanessa frowned, shutting her eyes slowly as if she didn't want to say what she had to say. "I don't think Noah's coming."

It shouldn't have felt like a punch in the solar plexus, but it did.

"What do you mean?" Emily drew back, glancing toward the front door of the boutique. "We had a plan, he's—"

"Come here."

Emily followed Vanessa back into the office.

"I was with him," Vanessa explained as they sat down in the chairs where she and Reed had been sitting earlier. "I ran into him when I was going to get food. I forgot to bring lunch, I'm sorry."

Emily flicked her fingers. "It's fine. You ran into him?"

"Yes, just by chance. And I was completely heartbroken about my mother, and frustrated and overwhelmed and…" Vanessa ran her hands through her dirty blond hair. "It was a vulnerable moment."

"Of course." Emily pressed her hand to her chest. "I can't imagine."

"We talked. We went down to the beach, and I told him everything. The whole Clarinda saga."

Emily swallowed. "What did he say?"

"Just that it was terrible and painful and he was so sorry it happened to me. We grew up together, you know? He knew how tough it was for me to not have a mom. He was there for...all of it." Vanessa shuddered.

"So, what happened?"

"What happened is..." Vanessa pinched the bridge of her nose, lifting her gaze to meet Emily's. "He's still my... person." Her voice broke. "He's still my safest, most comfortable, softest place to fall. Somehow, after all this time, it's always been him."

Emily felt her heart tug as she watched emotion well up in her mother's eyes. "Oh..."

"And I think..." Vanessa sniffled. "That reminder hit us both pretty hard. We kissed."

"You what?" Emily gasped.

"And then he left." Vanessa let out a sigh, lifted a shoulder. "He took off. Those walls went back up, higher than ever. I'm sorry, Emily. He's not going to let go of the past. He's not going to be close to us." She reached over and placed a hand on Emily's leg. "It's my fault and I'm so sorry. I bet he leaves town ASAP, if he hasn't already."

"No, it's not your fault." Emily stood up, her sadness suddenly shifting to anger and frustration. "How long is he going to nurture this grudge? He needs to forgive you. I'm not saying you two are gonna live happily ever after, but he needs to grow up, darn it!" She pulled her phone out of her back pocket.

"Who are you calling?"

Emily tapped the screen and the call began to ring before she even had time to answer. "Cricket."

"Hello, dearest," Cricket answered the call, her voice sounding sad and heavy.

Emily glanced at Vanessa, and they shared a look, both clearly realizing that Cricket would be devastated by Noah's leaving, too.

"Hey, Cricket," Emily said. "Um, quick question. Do you know where Noah is? We had plans this afternoon, but I haven't heard from him." She decided to leave out the "he kissed Vanessa at the beach" part.

Cricket sighed noisily. "He left, honey." The hurt in her voice was palpable. "He got in his car and drove back to Miami. I think he just got too close. I'm so sorry."

"Too close to...me?" Emily whispered.

"Too close to all of it," Cricket said. "He panicked and ran, just like he always does. He got scared of real emotions and closed off his heart and left."

Emily was at a loss for words. She looked over at Vanessa, who was crying.

"Cricket?" Vanessa said into the speakerphone, wiping a tear as she leaned closer so it would pick up her voice. "It's me, Vanessa. I'm here with Emily."

"Oh, Nessie," Cricket cooed. "Do you know what happened? Why he changed his mind all of a sudden?"

Vanessa bit her lip as a few more tears slid down her cheeks. "Yes, I think I do know. Cricket, I am still in love with him. I didn't realize it until today, but those feelings...they're not gone. They're stronger and more powerful than ever, and the fact that it still feels this way between us after thirty years is...scary. We shared a moment, and...I think he felt it, too. And I think that's why he left. It's all my fault and I know that is a disappointment to both you and Emily."

"Oh. Oh, my heavens, Nessie." Cricket's voice was barely above a whisper.

Emily leaned in. "He and I had spent some time together. We had started to have a relationship, or the early stages of one. I was so excited about it, but I guess he doesn't want to be in my life, either."

"Oh, girls," Cricket said on a soft sigh. "I'm so sorry."

"Can't you talk to him?" Emily pleaded. "Can't you tell him that he should be here and he should forgive my mom and at least try to be a part of our lives?"

"Is that what you want, Nessie? Forgiveness?" Cricket asked gently. "Or something more?"

Emily remembered how dead-set Cricket was on getting Noah and Vanessa back together.

"Of course it's what I want," Vanessa said on a breaking voice. "It's all I want. I want him to know how I live with those regrets. I want him to know that I've spent the past three decades wondering about him, missing him, wishing I'd done things differently. I want him to know that I am so beyond sorry, and I'd do anything on this planet for a fresh start. It breaks my heart that I broke his. It breaks my heart every day."

Emily watched her mother pour her heart out into the speakerphone, admitting her mistakes, owning up to her flaws, and Emily realized how truly and deeply she admired this woman.

She wrapped an arm around Vanessa, and they hugged tightly while Emily held up the phone.

"Oh, Nessie," Cricket said. "I've tried a thousand times to help him see the power of forgiveness, the beauty of letting go. I'm afraid that he's gone, and there's nothing more I can do."

"It's okay, Cricket." Vanessa wiped her eyes. "Thank you."

"I'll let you girls know if I hear from him," she said. "I'm so deeply sorry."

"We are, too," Emily added. "I know how much it meant to you having him here in town. I'm sorry you're hurting."

"Thank you, sweetheart. We'll talk soon. Love you both."

They ended the phone call and Emily slumped back in her chair, feeling a hole in her heart she didn't even know she had.

Surely, she wasn't that attached, right? She hardly knew Noah. But he was her father, and that was special.

She looked at her mother, who took a deep breath and wiped her eyes with a tissue. "I love you, Mom," Emily said, unsure if she'd ever said it before.

Maybe she'd called her "Mom" once in a while. Maybe she'd casually said she loved her. But this? She had to know this.

Vanessa's eyes widened, and a tearful smile came across her face. "I love you, too, sweet daughter of mine."

Chapter Twenty-one

Cricket

"Did you hear that?" She glared at Noah, waving the phone in his face after hearing Vanessa and Emily crying on the other end of the call. "Did you hear Vanessa just now?"

Sure, she had told the tiniest of white lies about Noah going back to Miami, but if Vanessa and Emily had known he was right there in Cricket's loft, they wouldn't have been so honest. Vanessa wouldn't have broken down and shared her realest and deepest emotions.

And, conveniently, Cricket had put the phone on speaker and let Noah listen to the whole thing. *Whoops.*

He stood in the kitchen of her floorless loft, looking like he'd seen a ghost. "I heard her," he said softly, his voice raspy and strained. "I heard her."

"Noah." Cricket walked over to her son, setting the phone down and placing her hands on his shoulders. "What happened? What was the 'moment' that you shared?"

He looked up at her, and she could so clearly see him as the boy who'd cried on her couch over Vanessa Young. Those blue eyes filled with emotion, made cold by years of isolation.

But he was still her Noah. And, clearly, that past was not buried.

"We kissed at the beach. She shared something with me—something personal—and I kissed her."

Cricket resisted the urge to ask what the something personal was—she'd get to that later—and guided him to the table, pushing him into a chair and sitting across from him. "So...there's still something there. For you, too, then."

"Of course there's something there," he said with a dry laugh like, *who wouldn't know they still loved each other?* "There will always be something there. She's... she's it for me. She's always been that girl for me. The one who got away times a thousand. The one who hurt me and broke my trust and messed me up for life."

"You heard her on the phone," Cricket said, leaning forward and meeting her son's gaze. "You heard how she feels."

He nodded. "I didn't know...I didn't know she felt like that. I mean, I knew she was sorry and felt bad about it but I didn't realize..."

"That it broke her, too." Cricket swallowed. "And it's been breaking her for thirty years, just like you."

"Only she's been living with regrets." Noah ran a hand through his hair, dragging it down his face. "I don't know what to do, Mom. I really like Emily. I never thought I'd want to get involved, but...shoot. I'm involved. And Vanessa?" He groaned in physical pain. "She's still the love of my freaking life, despite all my best efforts to change that."

Hope sprung in Cricket's chest, so powerfully that she got up out of the seat, walked around the table and stared right into Noah's soul. "Then go get her, Noah. Forgive her. End this and start new."

"It's not that simple, Mom. It's—"

"It is that simple. You have a daughter. You have a history. You have an entirely new life ahead of you."

Noah looked up at her, his eyes wide.

Cricket remembered when he was a boy, about eight or nine, and he'd give her that same look—the look of, "Mom I need help. I don't know what to do."

He'd try to deny it, try to act like a grown-up who didn't need his mother, but when things went awry, Noah would go to Cricket for help, knowing he could always count on her to guide him.

And guide him she had. Sure, he was grown and successful now, but he was still her same boy. And he still needed her guidance. He probably always would. Even if he didn't, she'd give it.

"Do you want to forgive her?" Cricket asked, the question barely a whisper as she held her breath, awaiting his answer.

He inhaled sharply, standing up from the table and shutting his laptop. "Yes. I do. I've...I've forgiven her already, I think. I'm just too afraid to admit it."

"What are you afraid of?"

He gave a soft, dry chuckle. "Messy Nessie."

Cricket smiled. "Do you still love her?"

"I..." He shook his head with disbelief. "Yeah, I think I do. I could. I do. But I don't know how to go about it now. She's upset, and Emily is hurt, and...I've dug my heels in too long on this."

Ya think? Cricket thought to herself.

"Well..." Cricket lifted a brow, as if this brilliant thought had just occurred to her. "I do have an idea..."

He gave her the stink eye. "Shocker. The master manipulator has a plan."

"More of a...moment. Are you interested in my advice?"

He sucked in a breath and shuttered his eyes. "Yeah. You're pretty good at getting people to do what you want them to."

"All right. Brace yourself. It's a doozy." She looked down at the pen and paper she'd had on the table for her shopping list. Picking up the pen, she wrote four letters and a question mark.

He stared at them, looked up at her, opened his mouth to speak, then shut it and closed his eyes.

"You get what I'm—"

Noah stopped her with a raised hand. "You, my dear sweet mother, are—"

"I know, I know," she scoffed. "A manipulator's... manipulator or whatever you said. I'm just trying to—"

"You are a genius," he said softly. "And I know exactly how to do this. I've been planning it for...thirty years." He stood, kissed her cheek, and gave her a squeeze. "I love you so much."

"Oh." She gave a satisfied shiver, then pushed him toward the door. "Now, make it happen, Noah Ellison!"

He grabbed his wallet, phone, and keys, leaving her standing in shock and optimism.

Only then did she make her tea, smiling to herself.

"And that, my friends," she whispered to nobody, "is how it is done."

Chapter Twenty-two

Vanessa

The rest of the day was a blur, and Vanessa couldn't actually remember the last time she'd been this drained.

From the visit to Serenity Palms, the halfway fight with Glo, the infamous Noah kiss to his abrupt departure, Vanessa was wiped out.

She'd cried all of her tears, voiced all of her emotions, and was left with an aching heart and very heavy eyes.

"How about some ice cream?" Emily called from the kitchen, her face illuminated by the light of the freezer.

Vanessa absentmindedly flipped through the channels on TV looking for a movie, slumped into the corner of the sectional with a glass of wine on the table next to her.

She'd treated herself to a hot bath, but it didn't lift her spirits as much as she thought it would. Emily, of course, was ever positive, and had spent the rest of the most terrible day reminding Vanessa how amazing the store was and how well Young at Heart was going already.

And it was. And that was a remarkable victory. Vanessa envied Emily's ability to always find the positives, even when they seemed hidden and far away.

"What kind do we have?" Vanessa called behind her toward the kitchen, sounding like a child asking about ice cream flavors.

"Rocky road and...something with salted caramel."

"I'll do the caramel. It pairs well with chardonnay and misery."

Emily laughed softly as she walked back into the living room, carrying two bowls of ice cream, and sat down on the couch next to Vanessa. She took a bite of her ice cream and angled her head. "Wanna talk any more?"

Vanessa shrugged, digging into the sweet caramel-y treat. "There's nothing left to say. We hashed it all out, and now we just move forward. It's not like either of us expected Noah to be in our lives."

"Definitely not."

"And with my mother, I mean, I can just go back to thinking of her as dead."

Emily sighed. "So you're not going to visit the nursing home again?"

"I don't know. I don't want to do anything involving this without Glo. I know I can do whatever I want and go back there if I choose to, but it feels wrong without her. My relationship with her is way more important than a minute with a woman who'll never remember it, not to mention that Gloria's not completely wrong in her feelings. What Clarinda Smith did was unforgiveable, and my dad is not much better." She shot her a look. "Sorry about the muddy gene pool, honey."

Emily waved it off. "Did you and Aunt Gloria talk things out at all?"

Vanessa shook her head. "I haven't had a chance. It wasn't like we had some big fight or anything. We just didn't see eye to eye and it wasn't the reaction I expected from her. It hit both of us really hard."

Emily was quiet, nodding sympathetically as she scooped out a bite of ice cream.

"We'll be fine. I'll figure it all out."

"I know you will." Her daughter scooched in and pointed at the TV. "Now please tell me there is something good and soapy we can binge."

"Pick your poison." Vanessa handed her the remote and took a sip of wine. "I'm game for anything that will momentarily make me forget about life."

As Emily scrolled through the channels, she landed on a marathon run of *Gilmore Girls*. "Oh, my gosh, this is perfect."

"*Gilmore Girls*? I've never seen it."

"It's about a mom who had her baby at sixteen and ran away from her ultra-wealthy family when she was pregnant. She raised the kid and they're best friends, and now the daughter is sixteen and..."

Vanessa's heart sank, and Emily sensed it immediately.

"And adoption would have been a perfectly valid and wonderful option." She grinned.

Vanessa smiled, so grateful for this young woman it actually hurt. "Throw it on."

She settled into the couch and the magical world of Stars Hollow, Connecticut, where Lorelai and Rory drank entirely too much coffee and bantered so fast her head spun. The show was charming beyond words, and Vanessa relished the fact that she had her very own daughter to watch it with.

"I guess the only good news is that I talked to Barry, the attorney, again and he said that because of Clarinda's condition, the will with her name on it is null and void – she's unfit to handle the inheritance. So Young at Heart is officially ours for good."

"Well..." Emily lifted a shoulder. "Silver lining, at least."

Suddenly, the doorbell rang, and the two of them looked at each other with confusion.

"Who's here so late?" Emily asked.

"Glo, maybe?" Vanessa stood, shaking off how mesmerized she'd been by the TV show. "But it's late for a person who gets up at five." On her way to the door, she tightened the belt of her fuzzy robe around her waist and peeked out the spy hole.

And nearly melted.

In fact, her hand was shaking when she opened the door.

"Noah?"

He stood in her doorway, his eyes dancing as he met her gaze. "Hey, Ness." Always, always his greeting.

"What are you..." She pulled at the belt again. "I thought you went back to Miami. What are you doing here?"

"Can you come with me?"

She frowned, confusion swirling in her mind. "Come with you where? It's midnight."

"I know." He reached out his hand to take hers. "Just...trust me."

And trust him she did.

Vanessa turned around to see Emily standing in the living room, a huge smile on her face as she shooed Vanessa away and mouthed the word, "Go!" God bless that girl.

Vanessa decided to leave her robe hanging on the hook and just go on this bizarre errand in her sweatpants and oversized Lakers T-shirt. She slipped her feet into sneakers, grabbed her purse, and followed Noah into the driveway.

"You've got to tell me what's going on," she said. "You left. And—"

"I didn't leave." He turned around, his gaze pinning her. "Just come with me, okay?"

She took in a deep breath, her eyes landing on the truck parked in the driveway. That was certainly not Noah's Porsche 911.

"Is that..." She got closer, squinting to see the vehicle in the dim porch lights. "A pickup truck?"

"Not any pickup truck, but a magical Ford F-150, slightly newer than my old red beauty." He opened the passenger door. "Hop in."

Vanessa laughed with confusion and utter disbelief as she climbed into the front seat of the truck. Not the original where they'd made so many memories, but close.

The truck they took late-night drives in, talking about everything. The truck that Noah picked her up in when she was at an awful house party and wanted to come home. The truck that Emily was conceived in.

Wait. What in the world was going on?

"Are you going to explain why you just kidnapped me in a rental truck?" she asked, turning to face Noah as he got behind the wheel.

He smiled. "I'm going to explain everything, including how dang hard it is to rent one of these things. I had to go to Pensacola."

"What? Why?"

"You'll see."

They drove for a few minutes, and finally, he pulled onto a street she recognized like the back of her hand.

Sand Dollar Drive. It was the street where Vanessa grew up, and Noah too. They were neighbors, and Cricket instantly took a liking to Vanessa and Gloria and pitied the widowed Bill.

Vanessa and Noah had become inseparable on this very street, riding bikes, playing ball for him and hopscotch for her—he hated that. The street where it had all started so many years ago.

He slowed the car to a crawl as he approached the house where Vanessa grew up—the front porch they sat on together when she showed him the positive pregnancy test and wept.

Noah stopped the car in front of the house. "This is where we met. Sadly, I don't actually remember meeting you, because we were both about a year old. You didn't have a mother, and my mother didn't have a daughter, and she spotted you in a carrier the day your dad moved you guys into this house."

Vanessa felt tears sting as she looked at the tiny, beachy bungalow that couldn't have been more then twelve hundred square feet. It was well kept, all these years later, with floral landscaping and big palm trees out front.

The porch was the same, and she could practically see her sixteen-year-old self sitting there with a positive pregnancy test in her hand.

"I do remember growing up with you, though." Noah jutted his chin to the cul-de-sac at the end of the street. "I remember when you fell off your razor scooter and scraped your knee right there."

Vanessa laughed and sniffed, looking at him. "You brought me a Band-Aid. And you kissed it, which I always thought was kind of gross."

"It made it better, didn't it?" he teased.

Vanessa had no idea what this random, midnight adventure was with the man who'd stormed away after they'd kissed earlier, but she knew she had to just trust him, lean into it, and go along for this ride, whatever it was.

"We were kids together here." He turned to her. "Best friends. The best friend I ever had."

"I remember it so well." She leaned against the truck's window. "So vividly."

Noah shifted the truck into Drive and left their childhood neighborhood, heading toward downtown Rosemary Beach.

Vanessa figured it was time to stop asking questions and couldn't deny the hope that was springing in her heart.

Noah pulled the truck to a stop in front of Big John's Hotdogs. "So, now this is a hotdog joint, but do you remember what it used to be?"

Vanessa smiled. "Of course I do. Seaside Scoops. The best ice cream shop on the planet. I still can't believe they sold it."

"This is where we had what I would consider our first date," Noah explained. "It wasn't official or labeled or anything like that, but I remember one summer afternoon coming here with you. We must have been thirteen or fourteen. I was watching you eat your pineapple swirl, and I remember thinking, 'This is more than friendship. Also, who puts pineapple on ice cream?'"

She laughed. "I remember that." And she did. So, so clearly.

Vanessa looked at the hotdog shop, perfectly able to visualize the teal and pink exterior of Seaside Scoops. The outdoor tables shaded under plastic umbrellas.

"This was before Rosemary Beach was Rosemary Beach. It was still just sleepy, plain, undiscovered Inlet Beach."

"I loved it," he said. "Let's keep going."

Their midnight journey continued with a trip to Gulfstream Cinema, where they'd had their first kiss, then the high school where he carried her books every day and held her hand on the way to class. He took her to the biking trail where he told her he loved her, the summer before sophomore year, and past the old public pool where they used to make out behind a concrete wall.

With each stop on their trip down memory lane, Vanessa grew softer and more emotional, and Noah's impenetrable walls seemed to magically disappear.

She still didn't understand why he was doing all of this, but like he said, he'd explain everything.

"This brings us to our last stop," Noah said, parking the car.

They were at the beach. The beach access that used to be their go-to in those childhood and teenage years. They'd park their bikes, grab a towel, and spend all day on the sand.

"This is the final destination?" Vanessa asked.

Noah nodded, getting out of the car and walking around the front of it to open her door. "Come with me."

She walked next to him through the dark and empty parking lot, lit only by the dim streetlights and the moon. They stepped onto the wooden boardwalk and began to walk toward the stairs that led down to the sand.

What Vanessa saw next stopped her completely in her tracks at the top of the stairs.

PROM? was spelled out in giant, lit-up marquee letters, surrounded by flowers and petals on the beach.

She gasped and laughed and nearly floated down the stairs, completely unable to believe what she was seeing. "Noah...are you...is this..." she stammered, at a loss for words. "Are you serious?"

He held her hand and guided her down to the adorably cheesy, perfectly high school display on the sand. "I never got to ask you to prom, Nessie Young." His gaze met hers, the gentle breeze blowing his hair around his forehead as he inched closer. "And this is how I always wanted to do it. I used to plan it and imagine it. I wanted it to be the best prom-posal ever."

She inhaled a shuddering breath, her jaw slack with astonishment. "Well. It is."

"Also painfully cringy, but I had to honor my teenage self." He turned and wrapped her in his arms. "Vanessa."

She smiled, giddy despite the hellacious day behind her. "Noah."

"Will you go to the prom with me?" His eyes danced in the moonlight, the wide smile on his face lighting them up. "Please be my date for the silly First Class Prom that my mother probably only orchestrated so this very thing would happen."

Vanessa laughed heartily, tilting her head back. "Yes! Of course I will. Oh, Noah...what does this mean? What does all of this mean?"

Noah took a deep breath. "It means I forgive you, Ness. It means I've been holding on to anger and pain for way too long, and I've been letting you live with such deep regrets. I want to let it all go. I want to be a father to Emily and get close to her, not keep myself far away. I've missed you. I've spent so many years missing you, I'd really rather not waste another second keeping my guard up. I want a fresh start with you, because...you're it for me. You always have been."

Warm tears—joyful ones, this time—sprang from Vanessa's eyes and slid down her cheeks as she fell into

Noah's embrace, which somehow always felt like home. "I'm so happy to hear you say this, Noah. I never thought you'd forgive me."

He touched her chin, tilting her head up to meet his gaze. "Well, I do. And I'm sorry for being so cold and walking away from you today. I had to just...I had to figure this all out. But I did. You bring color into my life, Vanessa. Let's go to the prom."

Vanessa laughed, holding him close as joy washed over her like the waves of the Gulf.

Vanessa didn't recognize her high school gymnasium, which had been radically updated and beautified over the last thirty years. Plus, it was decorated to the absolute *nines*.

Cricket had left no stone unturned with the First Class Bash, having pulled out every imaginable stop to create a magical, nostalgic night meant for reliving good memories, and rewriting the not-so-good ones.

"This is amazing," Vanessa said, hooking her arm through Noah's as they walked through the open doors of the gym.

Noah wore a gray suit with a thin black tie and looked painfully handsome.

Vanessa glanced down at her "prom" dress, which she and Emily had picked out together the day after Noah's unexpected prom-posal. It was blue satin with some sparkly trim detail. Elegant, and timeless, it could have been 1997 or today. Vanessa felt beautiful in every possible way.

"That's one thing about my mother." He turned to her, smiling. "She does not hold back."

The two of them gave in to the adorable cheesiness of the night—taking pictures in front of the starry backdrop, drinking questionable punch from a table in the back, dancing to all of the biggest hits of the nineties in the middle of the dance floor, greeting old friends who barely blinked that they were together.

To everyone from that class, Noah and Nessie had *always* been together.

As they swayed on the dance floor to Aerosmith's "I Don't Wanna Miss A Thing," Vanessa leaned her head against Noah's chest, and let go. She let go of her regrets, her pain, her mistakes. She let go of the hurt from her mother and the years she'd spent distancing herself.

She was in the arms of Noah Ellison, fully immersed in the rewriting of their pasts into something even more beautiful than she could have ever imagined.

"Ladies and gentlemen...Class of 1997..." Shannon Banks tapped the microphone, standing on the little stage in front of the DJ. "We just want to thank you all for coming out to what has got to be our best First Class Bash ever!"

Cheers and hollers echoed through the school gym, and Vanessa and Noah smiled at each other. Word had gotten out that this year's party would be epic, and classmates had come from near and far away, the whole vibe like a high school reunion.

Shannon beamed and continued talking into the mic. "We especially want to thank the amazing Cricket Ellison, a pillar of this wonderful little community who made this whole event possible."

Vanessa had to laugh as she and Noah turned to see Cricket standing on the side of the dance floor, blowing a kiss toward the stage.

"And, in the spirit of fun and prom night..." Shannon grinned. "It's now time to announce our king and queen."

Noah leaned close to Vanessa's ear. "She's going to announce herself? Yikes," he whispered.

Vanessa chuckled.

"And the winners are...drumroll please..." She held up a piece of paper. "Noah Ellison and Vanessa Young."

Oh, good *heavens*.

"You're kidding me." Vanessa laughed, shaking her head as she and Noah walked onto the stage. "I didn't even graduate," she whispered to him.

He laughed, wrapped his arm around her, and bowed as the crowd cheered and Shannon gave them plastic crowns.

Vanessa glanced at Cricket, who was smiling slyly and nodding with approval.

The worst. The woman was the literal worst, but Vanessa loved every bone in her string-pulling body. Of course this had been her doing.

She leaned close to Noah as they smiled and waved. "Your mom put our names in as the winners, didn't she?"

"No," he said, giving her a playful smile. "I did."

"What?" She hooted. "The apple doesn't fall far, eh?"

The night continued on and Vanessa actually found herself enjoying catching up with people she hadn't talked to in decades.

She had always been so scared of judgment, so worried about what the locals had always said about her. But it was so much worse in her head. Old friends were welcoming and kind and mature.

Life really could change.

Emily was situated at a table with Cricket, helping restock the refreshments and serve punch.

Taking a break from socializing, Vanessa headed over, but as she did, she caught sight of the side door opening and Gloria walked in wearing a simple but elegant black maxi.

"Glo!" She pivoted and hustled toward her sister. "You're here."

"Hey, you." Gloria gave her sister a hug and they walked together to the table where Cricket and Emily were. "I know it's not my graduating class, but I'm crashing because I have FOMO."

"Fear of missing out," Cricket explained as though they might not know.

"I'm glad you're here." Vanessa took her sister's arm and gently pulled her away from the busy snack and punch table. "Look, I just wanted to say—"

"I'm sorry," Glo said quickly, shutting her eyes. "I shouldn't have been so dismissive the other day when we were at the nursing home. It's not like me to cling to anger and resentment, it's just, with her...it feels different."

"I understand. I really do. And I would never want you to have anything to do with her if it's only going to make you sad."

Gloria shook her head. "You were right, Nessie. It's hard for me, because I can remember her a little bit. I spent all those years taking care of Dad, and...it's hard."

"I know." Vanessa squeezed her hand. "I know."

"But I'll go with you to see her as much as you want. You shouldn't be in this alone— any of it."

Vanessa didn't know what she wanted to do, but she didn't have to decide right now. She gave Gloria a tight hug. "Come on, let's dance."

Gloria rolled her eyes and reluctantly followed Vanessa onto the dance floor, where they met up with Noah and let themselves feel like teenagers again.

Chapter Twenty-three

Emily

"I can't believe how well it all came together," Emily said to Cricket, having to shout a bit over the speakers blasting the Spice Girls. "It's even more awesome than I imagined."

"It really did turn out to be a great event, didn't it?" Cricket sighed with satisfaction, wrapping an arm around Emily's shoulders as they stood side by side behind the snack table and watched the scene in front of them.

Vanessa was dancing with Gloria and Noah, beaming brighter than the sun.

Emily could still hardly believe her eyes as she watched her birth parents interact and dance together, smiling at each other like a couple of teenagers on a first date.

Was this a real possibility? Could Emily finally have...a biological *family*?

"How did you do it?" she asked Cricket, shaking her head as she kept her gaze fixed on her wildly happy parents. "How did you make this happen?"

Cricket lifted a shoulder, pushing her pink glasses up the bridge of her nose. "I planned this prom with a lot of optimism, but the rest was them. I didn't have my hand in it much at all."

"Really?"

"Well, Noah was in my loft when you two called and Vanessa opened up about how she still loved him. And the phone was on speaker."

Emily's jaw fell slack as she cracked up laughing. "You are truly one of a kind, Grandma. I can call you that, right?"

"I'd cry if you didn't. But I owe a lot to you, my dear."

"No you don't. I couldn't convince either of them to consider coming to this event. It's a miracle they're here, and believe me, I had nothing to do with it."

"Not true," she insisted. "You planted the seeds. Sometimes, that's all it takes—just the tiniest little sliver of hope...to turn into something magical."

Just as Emily turned her head, she saw Reed Collins walking into the gym and head toward her.

What was he doing here? And why did she have butterflies?

"Excuse me for a second," she said to Cricket, walking over to Reed. "Hey, stranger. Researching tacky but precious small-town traditions?"

"I heard you were going to be here," he said, raising his brows with a kind smile.

He had? She wasn't sure how, but she liked that he'd dressed for the occasion, wearing a button-down, khaki slacks, and a tie. And she wasn't sure why, but she was happy to see him.

"So?" she asked on a laugh.

"I wanted to dance with you." His gaze was intense and captivating as he reached a hand out for hers. "Is that a possibility?"

"But...why..." Emily felt her heart rate pick up at his touch.

"Because I can't stop thinking about you." He led her onto the dance floor just as the music shifted to a slow ballad.

Of course.

She placed her hands on his broad shoulders, taking in their considerable height difference and the smell of his aftershave.

She wanted to ask questions, like, What does this mean? What about the fact that he was leaving? Shouldn't she be scared of men and avoid them like the plague after what happened to her?

But Emily didn't say a word. She smiled at him and danced, feeling his hands gently holding her waist as he drew closer to her.

"Excuse me, could I steal her for a second?" Noah raised a brow, nudging Reed.

Emily was surprised and hopeful as she smiled at Reed and he respectfully stepped away.

"Of course." Reed nodded at Noah and gave Emily a playful smile. "I'll see you soon, Em."

Her heart nearly skipped a beat. "Okay."

Noah held out his hand in a cheesy gesture. "How about a dance with your old man?"

She laughed, placing one hand on his shoulder, the other in his empty palm, in a totally different way than she'd been dancing with Reed. "You're not old, but yes, I would love to."

Emily had always ached for a father. On her wedding day when she married Doug, she vividly remembered gazing out at the dance floor, imagining what it would have been like to share the father-daughter dance with a dad who loved her.

She shifted her gaze to Noah, still skeptical about his intentions and commitment level. Did he really want to be...a dad?

"Look, Emily, I'm so sorry I didn't show up last weekend. When we had plans to go to the record store." He shook his head, glancing downward. "I never should have stood you up like that. I feel terrible."

Relief rippled through her. "It's okay. Really. I understand that this has been a whirlwind. For all of us." She shrugged. "I think it's important that we give each other grace."

Noah smiled, angling his head as he seemed to marvel at the young woman in front of him. "You're so dang mature, you know that?"

"I try to be."

"Anyway, look, I just really wanted to apologize, Emily. I know you've never had a father, and I know that nothing about this is normal or predictable or in any way easy to navigate, but...I want to be that for you."

She swallowed.

"I want to be the strong, steady man who you can rely on. I want to give you advice and fix your car when it has problems and scare away the boys—er, men—who want to date you." He notched his chin in the direction of Reed.

Emily laughed, her heart tugging as her eyes filled with tears. "Noah, I...I would love that more than anything."

"Good." He nodded. "I don't know about logistics or plans yet, but just know you can count on me, okay? I'm here, in your life. I've missed twenty-nine years, and I'm not missing a second more."

She slipped her hand out of his and threw her arms around him for a hug, and he hugged her back, making her feel more protected than she ever had in her life.

"Hey, you two." Vanessa walked over, shimmying in her sparkly dress to some nineties pop hit. She took Noah's hand in one and Emily's in the other, and the three of them danced in the middle of the gymnasium.

These were her parents. These were the two people who loved each other so much that they'd created her. These were the two beautiful, brilliant, fascinating people who made up the fibers of Emily's DNA.

And here she was, dancing with them.

She looked back and forth between the two of them, melting away in the joy of the moment.

"Hey, fam." Daisy, who Emily hadn't even realized was here, walked over and tapped Emily's shoulder. "Do you have a sec?"

"Of course." Emily left Vanessa and Noah to their slowly rekindling romance and followed her cousin off the dance floor to stand by the snack table.

"Couldn't stay away from yet another posh event, eh, Dais?" she teased.

"I came with my mom but who could miss this?"

They laughed together, getting some punch that just might have been a wee bit spiked.

"Anyway..." Daisy gave a big grin, her brown eyes dancing with obvious excitement. "Guess what?"

"What?" Emily studied her with curiosity.

"You know that adorable little yellow house on Hibiscus Street? The one you showed me a picture of when you saw it on a bike ride?"

"Yes, of course!" How could Emily have forgotten the adorable cozy beach house with butter yellow paint and blue shutters with the For Rent sign out front of its glorious wraparound porch. "What about it?"

"I called the owner, who lives downstairs. He said he only wants quiet professionals who will lease for a year. I guess he's sick of vacationers coming and going, even though that's so lucrative."

"Huh, interesting. I bet he gets a pretty penny."

"It's pretty, but I put in an application," Daisy said quickly, practically squealing with excitement.

Emily gasped. "Holy cow, girl, that's amazing. You're going to love it."

"No, silly!" Daisy smacked her cousin's arm playfully. "*We're* going to love it. Co-renters. Roommates. Besties! I could never live there on my own. What do you say? He needs a commitment ASAP and wants us to move in tomorrow or we'll lose it, so I said"—she grimaced—"yes, because I know you will do this with me."

Emily laughed with shock and amazement. Living in that precious house with her darling cousin who'd become her closest friend? It sounded incredible. Plus, Vanessa would inevitably start to want some space to herself, especially with things moving forward with Noah.

Emily had thought about moving out, fantasized about having her own place in Rosemary Beach. And now, here it was.

"I say heck yes, Daisy!" She hugged her, practically dancing to the loud music.

They ran over to Gloria and Cricket to share their exciting new plans, and the four of them all watched as Vanessa and Noah danced together, their gazes so locked in on each other it was like the rest of the world didn't exist.

"It's all coming together, my dear." Cricket draped an arm around Emily's shoulder as they kept their eyes fixed on the dance floor. "It's all coming together."

And it certainly was.

A year ago, Emily was trapped, abused, and terrified. She thought she had no future or hope of a better life.

And now, she had so much. A mom, a grandma, an aunt, a dad, and a cousin. Plus, a business she loved in a town that belonged in movies.

Emily closed her eyes for a brief second, sending up a prayer of gratitude, and as always, reminding God to say hi to Grandma Gigi, her champion, without whom none of this would have ever happened.

Chapter Twenty-four
Gloria

"Well, I have to admit, Dais, I was hoping you'd stay here at the condo a bit longer." She gazed at her daughter, handing her a mug of coffee as they sat out on the patio in the early morning sunlight. "But the idea of you and Emily living together in that cute little house is just perfect. I'm so excited for you guys."

"I'm excited, too." Daisy blew the steam off the top of her coffee. "And don't worry, we'll literally be five minutes away. I mapped it."

"Good." Gloria looked out at the calm water of the Gulf.

"You won't lose me again, Mom." Daisy leaned over and rested her head on Gloria's shoulder. "I promise."

Gloria kissed the top of Daisy's head. "I'm proud of you. So, so proud of you."

"Why?"

"Because you walked away from Kyle when it was not easy. You've shown strength and grace through that decision. And you went ahead and put in that rental application for the house. You knew what you wanted, and you did it." She brushed her fingers through Daisy's thick hair. "You're all grown up."

Daisy chuckled softly, sipping her coffee. "I guess I am."

"You're not my baby anymore." Gloria made a mock pouting face.

"Don't worry." Daisy shrugged. "You still have Jeremy."

Gloria snorted. "Yeah, right. If he ever bothers to talk to me again."

"He'll come around. I think." Daisy chewed her lip, sitting up straight and turning to face her mother. "So, what are you going to do about the whole...Clarinda thing? Do you think you'll ever see her again?"

Gloria let out a soft sigh, rolling the question around in her mind. "I think your Aunt Vanessa is right. I think we should find a way to forgive her. I'm not entirely sure what that will look like yet, but I want to respect my sister's wishes and...I have some resentment I could probably stand to let go of."

"I didn't know you knew the meaning of resentment," Daisy said. "You're the most forgiving person I know."

"I appreciate that, hon. This feels different, somehow. But I'm just going to give it to God for now and take it one day at a time. It's all I can do."

They watched the peaceful waves of the Gulf coming up on the shore for a few minutes, chatting about the diner and Daisy's new house and the prom last night.

"You hungry at all?" Gloria asked. "I can go throw some cinnamon rolls in the oven."

Daisy beamed. "You know I won't say no to cinny rolls."

Gloria laughed at her daughter referring to her favorite breakfast the same way she had when she was five. "Be back in a few."

She walked into her condo through the sliding glass door and headed toward the little corner kitchen, opening the fridge to pull out the pack of Pillsbury Cinnamon Rolls.

Gloria hummed softly to herself as she set up the baking sheet and preheated the oven, trying not to think too hard about Serenity Palms.

As she was laying out the cinnamon rolls, a knock on her front door pulled her out of her deep thoughts.

With the slider closed, Daisy couldn't have heard it, so Gloria wiped her hands on a kitchen towel and went to go see who was at the front door.

Expecting Nessie or Emily or Cricket, she swung it open, and could not believe her eyes.

"Jeremy?" Her gaze moved behind her son. "Christian? What's going on? What are you guys doing here?"

She stared for a moment in complete shock at her twenty-one-year-old boy, who looked stunningly grown.

Jeremy's dark hair fell around his eyes, and his pretty, once-boyish face had a light five o'clock shadow around his jaw.

He looked at his mother, and, without a second of hesitation, she could read his expression.

Guilt. Trouble. Something very, very bad.

Her attention shifted to Christian, who had one hand on Jeremy's shoulder.

Christian's jaw clenched as he met Gloria's gaze, and

she was suddenly paralyzed by the deep and wildly unexpected eye contact with her ex-husband. "Hey, Glo."

She could hardly breathe through her tight throat, but Gloria managed to gather herself enough to step onto the front porch and shut the door behind her. She wanted to figure out what was going on before Daisy turned around and saw her father and brother standing in the doorway.

"What are you guys doing here? Jer?" She begged her son for answers. "Did something happen?"

Jeremy rolled his eyes a little and huffed out a sigh. He looked tall and built, the way a college athlete who trains day and night would look. But the expression on his face implied that he wasn't exactly thriving.

Christian didn't look that much better, to be frank. His hair was more salt than pepper, his close-cropped beard looked a little ragged, and his handsome face looked like he'd lost a lot of sleep lately.

"Okay." Gloria threw her hands up. "One of you is going to speak up and tell me why you're here. Because something tells me this isn't just a surprise visit for fun."

Jeremy swallowed. "Mom, I...I got into a little bit of trouble at school."

Christian scoffed. "Yeah. Right. That's one way to put it."

Gloria tried to remember if she'd ever, in twenty-one years, seen Christian mad at Jeremy. He'd always worshipped their son and, frankly, Jeremy had usually deserved it. He was an exceptional kid.

"What kind of trouble?" Gloria frowned.

"He's about to lose his scholarship, get kicked off the team, and expelled from the school," Christian said, glaring at Jeremy. "That kind of trouble."

"What?" Gloria gasped, drawing back as her hand flew to her mouth with shock. "Are you serious?"

"It's not that big of a deal," Jeremy said. "The school is just overreacting."

"To what?" She narrowed her gaze.

Christian sighed. "Jeremy has spent this last semester partying. He's missed practices and workouts all season, and when he does show up, he's hungover."

"That's not true," Jeremy argued. "It happened once or twice. Come on, Dad."

"His priorities are in the toilet," Christian continued. "And I'm at a loss for what to do, so we came here."

Disappointment rolled through her. Jeremy was always such a good kid. This was a shock.

"Is that true, Jeremy? You've been partying a lot and you might get kicked off the team?"

"And get kicked out of school," Christian added.

"I've been having a little fun." Jeremy threw his hands up defensively, an aggression and anger in his tone that Gloria had not heard before. "I'm twenty-one years old and I'm having some fun. Sue me. I've spent every waking moment of my life since I was, like, three focusing and grinding on baseball, so excuse me if I want to let loose a little when all I've ever been able to do is work."

"I don't know where any of this is coming from." Christian shook his head. "You can make it to the pros, Jer, and you're throwing it all away."

Jeremy groaned. "I'm not throwing anything away. I'm just trying to enjoy college like a normal person."

"Okay, okay." Gloria held her hands up. "I'm glad to finally be hearing the truth about what's going on with you. I've been worried and now I know it was for good reason." She took a deep breath, centering herself as she prepared for yet another monkey wrench.

Gloria blinked, looking back and forth between her ex-husband and her son. "Christian, why did you bring him here?"

"Good question," Jeremy shot back.

"Because you can set him straight, Gloria." Christian let out a soft sigh. "You can fix him. You fix everything. Please. His future is on the line here and I...I didn't know what else to do. I think he should spend the summer here with you."

She inched back as the weight of the world settled onto her shoulders once again.

Gloria had no idea how to solve this problem. She didn't even fully understand what on earth was going on, or what was actually at stake.

But her son was standing on her porch, and whether he could admit it or not, he needed her.

"Well, I happen to have an empty guest room as of today." She opened the door slowly. "Daisy's here, so be ready for that."

Gloria shut the door behind them, mentally preparing herself to sit in a room with her very, very broken family, surrounded by a history of fractures and mistakes.

Christian's words echoed in her head. *"You fix everything."*

She honestly couldn't believe he had such faith in her after all these years apart. She also couldn't believe that he still made her heart jump a bit.

She shared a look with her son, seeing a storm of emotion and a lot more pain than just some "partying" in his golden-brown eyes.

She didn't know if she could fix everything…or anything, for that matter. But she'd do anything for this family, which meant she would never, ever stop trying.

Don't miss the next book in the Young at Heart series,

Golden Sunsets in Rosemary Beach!

NEW SURPRISES and unexpected challenges emerge on the shores of Rosemary Beach as the women continue to navigate uncharted waters together.

Gloria's life takes a sharp turn when she learns that her son, a star college athlete, is entangled in a dire situation. Torn between her duty as a mother and the echoes of a past love, Gloria finds herself facing her ex-husband, who has reappeared with his own agenda.

Meanwhile, Vanessa is savoring her own second chance at love. After overcoming years of pain and regret, Vanessa and Noah have come back together. Can they really let go of thirty years of hurt?

Set against the backdrop of Rosemary Beach's warm, tropical beauty, "Golden Sunsets in Rosemary Beach" is a heartwarming tale of family bonds, friendship, and the enduring strength of sisterhood.

The Young At Heart Series

New Beginnings in Rosemary Beach (Book 1)
Old Friends in Rosemary Beach (Book 2)
Golden Sunsets in Rosemary Beach (Book 3)

And stay tuned...there will be more. Sign up for my newsletter or watch my social media for updates, new covers, release dates, and more!

Looking for more Cecelia Scott books? Don't miss the Sweeney House series, now complete at seven books, and available in digital, paperback, and audio.

The Sweeney House Series

Introduction To The Sweeney House

The Sweeney House is a landmark inn on the shores of Cocoa Beach, built and owned by the same family for decades. After the unexpected passing of their beloved patriarch, Jay, this family must come together like never before. They may have lost their leader, but the Sweeneys are made of strong stuff. Together on the island paradise where they grew up, this family meets every challenge with hope, humor, and heart, bathed in sunshine and the unconditional love they learned from their father.

Cocoa Beach Cottage - book 1
Cocoa Beach Boardwalk – book 2
Cocoa Beach Reunion – book 3
Cocoa Beach Sunrise – book 4
Cocoa Beach Bakery – book 5

The Sweeney House Series

Cocoa Beach Cabana – book 6
Cocoa Beach Bride – book 7

For release dates, preorder alerts, updates and more, sign up for my newsletter! Or go to www.ceceliascott.com and follow me on Facebook!

About the Author

Cecelia Scott is an author of light, bright women's fiction that explores family dynamics, heartfelt romance, and the emotional challenges that women face at all ages and stages of life. Her debut series, Sweeney House, is set on the shores of Cocoa Beach, where she lived for more than twenty years. Her books capture the salt, sand, and spectacular skies of the area and reflect her firm belief that life deserves a happy ending, with enough drama and surprises to keep it interesting. Cece currently resides in north Florida with her husband and beloved kitty. When she's not writing, you'll find her at the beach, usually with a good book.

Made in the USA
Coppell, TX
04 October 2024